HELL
with a
GUN

—◆—

The Legend of
Elton Collins

—◆—

by

MICHAEL SHEPHERD

Cover design © 2013 LimelightBookCovers.com
Book design by © 2014 DeAnna Knippling

This book is a work of fiction. References to real people, events, establishments, organizations, or locales are intended only to provide a sense of authenticity. All other characters, and all incidents and dialogue, are drawn from the author's imagination and are not to be construed as real.

Michael Shepherd
Visit my website at www.michaelshepherdwriter.com

Printed in the United States of America

First Printing: January 2014

DEDICATION

To my father, Bill, who loves a good Western.
I hope this qualifies as such.

CHAPTER 1
July 1858

Elton Collins had spent his eighteenth birthday being tossed around the deck of one of his father's ships far off the coast of Massachusetts. He'd spent his nineteenth birthday in the saddle, picking his way across Texas.

Now, as he stared at the gun held by Pete Culhane, he no longer wondered what he'd be doing on his twentieth birthday.

He wondered if he'd be doing anything at all.

The gun never wavered. It held steady on Elton's chest while he stood, empty-handed.

One way or the other, this would end soon.

He'd walk away.

Or he'd be dead.

Elton preferred walking away. But as Pete eased the hammer back, that didn't seem to matter much anymore.

—

Elton had planned to live his life in Maine, working the family's shipping business, but the world selected another course. One night on a Portland street near their house, Elton arrived outside his home as his brother Andrew was being robbed by two roughnecks.

Elton stepped in, fists flying.

The ensuing fight was brief.

One man would never walk again.

The other took his last breath at approximately the same moment as Elton left the city forever.

A drifter travels like a leaf in a stream, seldom finding an eddy or a pool in which to settle. Elton drifted, first from the coast of Maine, slowly south and west across the Mississippi River and finally to Texas, where riding jobs were plentiful, driving cattle from the grazing lands there to the Missouri railheads. He didn't know much about cattle but he knew how to work, and that put him above the majority of young dreamers who had gone west from home. Some left to find adventure, some to find their own way in the world or to escape their mother's apron strings. But a few days riding drag behind a herd of cattle grazing their way up the trail tended to knock the romance out of the cowboy life. It wasn't uncommon for half the greenhorns on a drive to quietly slip away, leaving the remaining crew both short of manpower and pleasant disposition.

So another snot-nosed kid showing up for work was grudgingly accepted by some, yet largely ignored by other grizzled hands who figured one try at a tough river crossing and the newcomer would go running home for good.

Such was the welcome Elton had received days earlier from Lash Buchanan's crew.

Buchanan's herd of nearly two thousand culls and steers was one of the year's first up the trail. They'd made the first two weeks of the drive without issue, but after they'd passed Dallas the trail boss told Buchanan they'd lost two cowboys to work-sickness. They needed more butts in saddles, they needed them now and, given the short crew and large herd, enthusiasm was more important than experience. The young cowboy Buchanan had met at the livery outside Dallas had been anxious for a riding job, so he sent Elton Collins to meet up with the herd outside of town.

Elton had approached Buchanan's chuck wagon while most of the cowboys were eating their evening meal, and was unsure what to do next.

Blank stares met him as he surveyed the tired, dusty riders. His stomach crawled. Maybe he should have kept his sorrel mare pointing northward and ridden on by Buchanan's herd. Maybe, and he'd thought this more than once since he'd left Maine, he should keep riding all the way back home.

He tried to find a friendly face. But at a place and time like this, friends would be slim pickings.

The voice behind him was the most welcome one he'd heard in weeks. "Boy, git your dumb ass over here!"

Elton looked at the cook, who waved a ladle, motioning him over. "You comin' or not? Personally, I don't much care."

Elton took a few steps toward the cook. Before he made it to the chuck wagon a huge, lantern-jawed cowboy stepped in front of him and jabbed a thick finger in his chest. "You ain't eatin' yet. Not till you're introduced to the boys proper."

He spat a stream of tobacco juice, hitting Elton's boot. "Take a good look at the new pup," the cowboy crowed. "I got a Liberty head in my pocket says this one'll be back on his mother's teat before the week's out. Any takers?" A wavering chuckle started nowhere yet everywhere, rolled through the hands and drifted away toward the cattle.

A bowlegged, unshaven cowboy with two missing fingers on his left hand, maybe half the size of the man who had spoken, hooted, "You know 'em when you see 'em, Pete!" He slapped Pete on the back and walked with him to the coffee pot.

Elton studied the tobacco stain on his boot.

Then a tin plate appeared before him, held out by a sandy-haired, angular man wearing glasses. "Come on, let's get you some grub."

Elton glanced toward Pete, who had turned and was eyeballing him. "Wait," he muttered. "This may not be over yet."

"It is for now," the man said. "Let's eat."

The other hands slowly drifted back to their meals away as Elton made his way to the chuck line. There the cook gave him a plateful of beans, a burned-to-a-crisp steak, and a hunk of cornbread big enough to choke a horse. "Good thing you come when you did," the old cook admonished. "Ten minutes later, next thing you'da ate was breakfast."

The bespectacled man took Elton's elbow and guided him to a large rock a short distance from the fire. Away from the other cowboys. And out of earshot of Pete.

After they leaned against the rock, the man stuck out his hand. "John Partridge."

"Elton Collins."

"Good to have you here, Elton. We're always a few men down. It isn't bad at first, but when the drive wears on and tempers get short, every extra hand is appreciated. You have any experience?"

"Brought a herd up the trail last year."

"One's enough. First thing to know around here—you probably learned it with your crew last year—when it's time to eat, don't be shy. If you miss your chance, before Old Mingus feeds you again you'll be so hungry your ribs will be tickling your backbone."

Elton glanced toward the men at the coffee pot. "There any sort of order as to how we do this? Who goes first? Something I should know before the trouble gets worse?"

John Partridge ran a hand through his long, sandy-colored hair. "You mean Pete."

Elton ground his teeth. "I mean Pete. But he changed when you came around. Why's that?"

Partridge paused as if trying to formulate a response. Finally he sighed and said, "Me and Pete have a history. You get that out here when you work together."

Partridge seemed a trifle embarrassed. "Back at Buchanan's ranch Pete and I were pulling steers out of a thicket for this drive. For some reason I'll never comprehend, Pete got off his horse. We all know you don't ever get off your horse when you're working cattle, but Pete did. Some of these steers don't take kindly to getting plucked out of the thickets. One of them, all of a sudden he came out of the brush like the devil was twisting his tail. Straight toward Pete, and not a thing Pete could do. He knew it and I knew it. He was going to have a horn run through him sure as the sun comes up daily, but I got lucky and dropped a loop over that fool steer before he made it to Pete."

"You saved Pete's life."

Partridge scuffed a toe in the dirt. "Pete would have done the same for me. It's what you do out here."

"Helluva guy you saved."

Partridge said, "Yeah, well, he's an ass and we all know it, but it kind of wears off after a while."

Elton snorted. "Don't know if I can wait that long."

Partridge said, "He did the same to me when I first came on. Can't tell you why exactly, but something in Pete drives him to show the new hands who the lead bull is."

Elton worked on a tough mouthful of steak, then said, "Thing about that, though. When I was putting up hay for a farmer in Arkansas he had a bull, mean as all get-out. You couldn't get within cussing distance and he'd start pawing and snorting. He chased a couple of hired men away. One day the farmer had enough, castrated the bull and hung his balls over the barn door." He glanced at Pete, who was in full bluster, waving his arms and drawing guffaws from his listeners.

"Elton, he's a handful. You be careful."

Elton took off his hat and wiped his brow. "Soon after, the bull ended up on the dinner table."

The drive ground on, in good weather and bad, at ten miles or so a day. Elton had been with the crew for nearly a week when they sighted the Red River.

The hands pushed the herd forward and allowed them to drink in the river's shallows, then slowly moved them away to graze and bed down. They'd cross in the morning.

Nightfall approached. Pete would be waiting at the chuck wagon.

Mere words, Elton's father would have said. No injury can come from another man's words.

Elton knew it was true. They were only words, after all. But Pete's words seemed different. They raked across Elton's mind like barbed wire across bare skin. With every taunt Pete hurled, and every laugh that rose from the gathered hands, Elton could feel something once again growing inside him.

Dark.

Violent.

Deadly.

Waiting to come out.

It had come out once before, when defending his brother.

And he'd been on the move ever since.

Tonight Elton chose distance as his defense. He and a young, dark-skinned Mexican named Obregon stayed with the herd while the other hands rode in to eat.

The sun gently kissed the horizon, then seemed to cling there as if reluctant to leave. Shadows slowly deepened in the pecans and cottonwoods near the river's edge. Elton sat amongst them and watched the grazing herd.

He could go hungry. He'd been hungry before.

He could swallow his pride.

He looked north across the river. If he had to, he could ride away.

Then his father's voice came to him: *A man always finishes what he starts.*

Yessir.

A rider wove through the scattered cattle toward Elton. Obregon. When he was close, he spoke. *"Ya es hora, amigo. Vamos."*

Elton watched Obregon ride away. Two riders who'd already finished eating began to circle the herd.

Other hands had drifted away from the chuck wagon also.

Possibly all of them.

He rolled a smoke as darkness settled around him.

It is time, Obregon had said. But time for what?

Elton pinched off the end of the cigarette, studied the herd one more time, and then slowly rode in.

Pete stood.

Yes.

It was time.

As Elton approached, Pete made a beeline for him. Stopping a couple of paces away, he sneered and said, "I been waiting for you, boy. But you been out courtin' your little Mex, aint ya?" Pete turned to the Mexican rider. "Hey Obregon, you have fun holdin' hands and watchin' the sun set?"

Elton felt a surge of anger jolt him. "Let it go, Pete."

Pete ran his tongue over his teeth. "Oh, now you talk? Took Obregon to make a man out of you?"

Elton glanced at the tough Mexican cowboy. Obregon's eyes crackled with fire.

Pete quickly stepped over to him. "Hey, Mex. You and pretty boy got a thing going?"

Obregon stared at Pete for a moment. His hand rested on the hilt of his sheathed knife.

"Don't," Elton said. "Walk away."

Obregon shrugged, then turned. As he walked away he glanced back at Pete and muttered, "*Pinche cabrón.*"

"You greasy bastard," Pete bellowed. He leaped at Obregon, clutched him by the back of the shirt and yanked him around. "You don't run your mouth to me!" Pete cracked repeated slaps to Obregon's face.

Blood flowed from Obregon's mouth and nose.

He spit, spraying Pete's face.

Pete lifted Obregon off his feet and pinned him against the chuck wagon with his left hand. He rained right-handed blows against the Mexican's stomach and ribs.

None of the hands made a move to stop him.

Except Elton.

He lunged forward and caught Pete's arm before he could throw another punch. "Leave him alone!"

Pete bellowed with rage and released Obregon, who collapsed under the chuck wagon, moaning.

Pete spun, his eyes wide, sweat pouring from his face. "You want this beating, huh?"

Elton stepped back, unbuckled his gun belt and handed it to John Partridge. "I believe I'll give you one instead."

Pete looked at the gun belt, then at Elton. "Boy, I'll take you apart."

Elton glanced at Obregon. "He's hurt bad," he said to the other cowhands. "Don't be afraid of what Pete will do if you help him. Be afraid of what I will do if you don't."

Two men shot worried glances at Pete, then scurried to Obregon's side.

Elton stared Pete down. "You cost us a good cowboy. You'll never do that to another." He motioned Pete forward.

Pete howled and charged, throwing a wild overhand right at Elton's head.

Elton jerked away and the heavy punch grazed his shoulder.

Pete stumbled, and Elton dug a short right to his kidney. Pete staggered and dropped a hand to the ground to catch himself from falling.

As Pete rose, Elton followed with a short hook that hit Pete flush on the jaw, staggering him. Elton grabbed Pete's shirt, steadied him, and then fired an overhand right that exploded the man's nose in a shower of blood.

—

Cursing, Pete dropped to one knee, cupped his hands over his busted nose and drew in a painful breath.

Crushed nose.

Broken jaw.

Christ, what a mess.

He spit out a mouthful of blood and shook his head.

Three Fingers reached for Pete's elbow and tried to pull him up. "You can't lose, Pete. I got ten bucks ridin' on you!"

"I'll give you that much to leave me alone!" Pete hoisted himself up and made another headlong run at Elton.

The kid sidestepped and tripped him as he passed. Pete crashed to the ground, face smashing into the dirt.

Someone is screaming, he numbly thought as he tried to stop the sledgehammers from pounding in his head. Why is someone screaming?

Oh hell, he realized. That someone is me.

Elton wiped his hands on his jeans and waited for Pete to get up. "Had enough, big man?"

Pete staggered to his feet and motioned to Elton. Give me a moment.

The kid looked down at his swollen hands and flexed them. As he did, Pete immediately dove forward. He tackled Elton around the knees and drove him into the ground. The kid groaned as the air was driven from his lungs.

Pete smashed two punches against the side of Elton's head. "Let's see some of your blood for a change!"

Elton squirmed, trying to move Pete off him, but Pete didn't let up. He drove his left forearm up to Elton's throat.

Cut the kid's wind off, Pete thought. He leaned forward, his face inches from Elton's.

Elton bucked upwards and bashed his head against Pete's forehead. The sound was like two rocks hitting.

Pete twisted his head away and felt blood trickle from between his eyes.

The kidneys then. If he could get to the kidneys, the kid would piss blood for a month. Pete clutched Elton's belt and tried to flip him on his side.

As Pete started to pull him over Elton twisted, then drove his shoulder into Pete so he could free his arms. He held Pete's head and head-butted him twice on the bridge of his nose. When Pete yanked his head back Elton pounded three bludgeoning punches to Pete's side.

Pete threw himself off Elton and hitched away on his hands and knees. He huddled near Obregon at the chuck wagon.

Can't breathe.

Broken ribs.

To go with the broken nose.

But the kid was hurt worse.

He better be.

Because, Pete knew, he didn't have much more fight left.

He reached for the chuck wagon tongue. As he pulled himself up, knifelike jabs tore at his side.

Head down, Pete Culhane plodded toward Elton Collins.

Elton gauged Pete's lumbering approach. The big man looked ruined.

But men with much to lose go down hard. Until Pete stopped fighting for good, he wasn't done.

Not nearly done.

When Pete was two steps away, Elton lunged forward. As he did, Pete grasped him in a bear hug.

But the big man's strength was sapped.

Elton beat blow after blow on Pete's injured ribs. Pete's agonized moans punctuated each strike.

Pete dropped his arms, defenseless. As he did, Elton fired a clean uppercut to the man's chin.

Pete dropped like he'd been hit by a club.

The crowd that had been whooping it up since the fight started became perfectly silent, as if they couldn't believe what they'd seen.

Then a full understanding seemed to dawn on them. When one king falls, another ascends. Men hooted their approval and pounded on Elton's back.

He pushed them away and walked over to Obregon. "*¿Estás bien, amigo?*"

Obregon's eyes fluttered. He looked at Elton, bit his lip and winced. "*Más o menos.*"

Elton patted him on the shoulder, then slowly walked back to Partridge and reached for his gunbelt.

"Boy, you sure can hit," Partridge said.

"So can Pete," Elton mumbled. "Not sure how much I had left in me."

"You didn't need any more, by the looks of him."

A low murmur rose from the hands gathered around Pete. A gravelly voice, one Elton didn't recognize, said, "Boy, we ain't done with this yet."

Elton slowly turned.

Pete's pistol was pointed at Elton. "Dead forever is a long time, kid."

Pete eased the hammer back.

Elton nodded.

That was the only move he made.

A subtle nod.

Later, around happy hearths or lonely campfires, men who claimed they were there would swear all Elton Collins did was nod.

Then a single shot shattered the silence.

Elton's bullet hit Pete Culhane above the belt buckle. He slumped to the ground, clutching his gut.

"Jesus, you done it," Pete gasped. A handful of ragged breaths later, Pete lay dead.

The next morning, as the sun rose, few eyes met Elton's. Throughout the day, conversations dried up when he approached.

Men didn't merely avoid him.

They scattered.

Three days later, Elton made his decision. Buchanan hadn't asked him to leave, but he hadn't seemed very sad when Elton rode away.

It was the rule of the West. Gunfighters drifted.

It was time for Elton Collins to drift.

As he roamed the story followed him. Like a seed planted in the fertile minds of those who heard it, it took root and grew with each telling.

First, it was an unarmed Elton Collins who killed Pete Culhane.

Then, it was two men who'd drawn against Elton. Neither man got off a shot.

Then Rusty McManus took hold of the story, and his version of the events changed the course of Elton's life forever.

Rusty McManus was a greenhorn transplant from Kentucky who'd followed his horse's nose to south Texas and hired on for his first cattle drive. The first three nights of the drive Rusty had eaten apart from the rest of the hands, all but ignored by them. The fourth night however, as he once again found himself without a soul to talk to, Rusty could bear it no longer.

What he lacked as a cowhand, Rusty more than made up for as a poetic storyteller. On this evening he told a story about how Elton Collins had taken down big, bad Pete Culhane and four other hands on a cattle drive. To hear Rusty tell it, five men stood facing the boy gunman.

A moment later all five lay in pools of their own blood while Collins walked away without a scratch.

It was a certifiable fact, because Rusty McManus had been there. He'd felt the bullets whip past. He'd seen the blood.

He'd buried the bodies.

The men, captivated by Rusty's story, seemed to forget that he had never been on a cattle drive before. They welcomed him to the crew.

And his story spread like wildfire.

In the years preceding the Civil War this story, told on a whim by a man lonely for company on a two month-long cattle drive, solidified the gun fighting legend of Elton Collins.

Cowhand jobs dried up.

But gunfighting wages were always available.

And a man had to eat.

For two years Elton rode the West.

For two years, he was a gunfighter.

For two years, lesser men died.

And then he saw a pretty young blonde at a café in Wichita. At first it was her face that he noticed, then it was her smile. Still, it wasn't until he heard her laugh that he made up his mind to meet her.

But pretty young blondes didn't fall in love with gunfighters. Ever.

14

Elton sought out a local rancher, Oscar Tremaine, and asked about hiring on as a cowboy.

Tremaine shook his head. "I don't know what kind of cowhand you are, but I know you're a helluva gunfighter. I've had men handy with a gun before, and right or wrong trouble always sniffs them out. I'm not hiring trouble, so I'm not hiring you, Elton Collins."

Elton Collins. While they might not know what made the man, they certainly knew the name.

Elton Collins. Gunfighter.

But names could be changed as often as a woman changed her mind. While growing up in Maine Elton had a good friend, Henry Cole, who had been run over by a carriage while walking to school one day.

Henry Cole. A name no one would fear. A name any boss would be glad to hire.

A name a pretty young woman wouldn't run from.

A name he would be proud to call his own.

That evening while watching his campfire burn low the newly-resurrected Henry Cole thought about how he'd killed Pete Culhane two years before.

True, he'd stepped in to protect Obregon. But to save one man, did another have to die?

The Bible talked about turning the other cheek. The Bible talked about the meek inheriting the earth. The Bible said to seek peace, and pursue it.

But the men in the Bible never faced a man with a gun pointed at them, where a split second separated life and death. And what if, in the end, turning the other cheek meant they'd both be hit? What if the meek ended up huddled together like sheep, afraid of everything and too dim-witted to fight back?

Or should a man draw a line and say 'I will be pushed no further,' and then stand up to all those who disagreed?

And would that same man be willing to accept the consequences of these actions?

Because despite leaving the name Elton Collins behind, Henry Cole had a feeling that had begun to fester and grow inside him as he'd watched Pete Culhane draw his last breath: a man who chose to live by the gun would inevitably die by it.

CHAPTER 2
October 1878

Henry Cole watched the sun glisten off his four-year-old daughter Caroline's golden curls while she ran circles around the yard, chasing an increasingly annoyed flock of chickens. The blue ribbon in her hair streamed behind as her legs churned in the dusty yard. The flapping wings, squawking and ruckus the hens made caused her to laugh more as she mimicked their frantic screeches.

Caroline paused and the hens began to settle down. But Henry knew his youngest child well. It would only be a moment before she would charge at them once more.

He stopped chopping wood, pulled his shirt off and mopped his brow. Indian summer had refused to leave the prairie this year, and the sun continued to blaze into October. Usually by now a heavy frost would have already blanketed the ridge overlooking

Piedmont valley, foreshadowing the winter that would soon rage through the Dakota Territory.

Last year temperatures had dropped so low the snow squeaked in complaint when he walked, and trees along the banks of Elk Creek had hung heavy with frost. The creek itself had frozen nearly solid. They had to melt snow for drinking water and chop holes in a small pool to water the livestock. It was the coldest winter he could remember, and he'd seen some cold ones before on the Kansas and Dakota plains. Not to mention the winters he'd spent in the Union Army. The nights huddled against the cold, with little food and less shelter, he'd have given anything for weather like this.

Therefore, he decided, summer could linger as long as it fancied.

He sat on a nearby stump to watch Caroline on the stalk. She was the spitting image of his oldest daughter, seventeen-year-old Marie. Turn the clock back a dozen years and he could swear it was Marie in the yard.

Turn the clock back.

If that were an option he'd have done it many times over. And now that he'd found a few gray chest hairs sprouting he'd thought about it again, for on more than one occasion his wife Amelia had teased him about the salt scattering through his dark brown hair.

At least I'm not going bald, he'd said to her the first time she'd brought it up.

She'd traced a gentle circle around the crown of his head. Don't fool yourself, she said.

Their dog Rip, who'd been napping near the stump, suddenly spun, stared toward the nearby trail and growled.

"What is it, boy?" Henry gave Rip a few firm pats on the shoulder.

The dog continued to stare.

Henry scanned the edge of the clearing. He studied every tree.

Every clump of brush.

Every shadow.

Finally Rip gave a short bark, lay at Henry's feet, and closed his eyes.

Henry patted Rip again and chuckled. "Felt like the old days for a moment." He slid his left hand up to his ribs, where he touched two bullet scars. His fingers probed the scar on the left side of his neck. Running his hands down the legs of his blue jeans, he felt a bullet scar on each thigh.

You can leave the name and the life behind, he thought. But it always leaves something with you.

He watched Caroline, her chubby legs poking out from beneath her gingham dress. Her cheeks were flushed with excitement as she crept back toward the hens, now contentedly pecking the ground twenty feet away. As Henry placed his axe against the chopping block, the slight ticking sound caught her attention. She looked over at him, wide-eyed, gave him an insistent 'shhh,' and turned back toward the chickens.

She crept closer. Closer. Then with a loud scream, she charged the hens. In an explosion of feathers and squawks they scattered throughout the yard. Caroline was instantly lost in fits of giggles, hands on her knees, as her mother came to the door.

Amelia watched them with a serene smile splashed across her face. Henry didn't need to turn the clock back to see the young girl he'd married many years before. Her eyes twinkled with the same intensity that he'd noticed the first time they'd met. A long blonde braid ran halfway to her waist, and he bet if he searched every hair on her head he wouldn't find a single gray strand.

Her gentle eyes, blue as a robin's egg, were a map of long days, short nights, non-stop work and, when he looked deep into them, also carried a mother's sadness from watching her infant son laid in a grave.

"Henry, are we going to eat a chicken or worry the meat off them?" Amelia asked as she wiped her hands on her apron.

He picked up the axe and motioned it toward her. "Both, I think. Wouldn't you be worried if you knew this was coming?"

"Yes, but it's Caroline that has them the most concerned, not your axe. They're so vexed they probably won't lay eggs for a week."

"I'll make a deal with them. If they don't lay eggs, they'll get invited to a good dinner. As guest of honor. They'll be happy to give us eggs then."

Amelia's eyes danced. "So you've fixed the egg problem. Now you need to fix the 'no chicken in the pot' problem."

Henry scooped up Caroline, who'd come over and was hugging his legs. "Caroline, are you done chasing those hens?"

"No, Daddy, I wanna be outside!"

"You like being outside, do you?"

Her face turned earnest. "I like being with you."

Daughters, Henry thought. Thank the Lord for daughters. He ruffled her hair. "I have to go down to the creek after supper. You probably don't want to go with me, though."

Her eyes lit up. "Can we frow rocks?"

"We probably should."

Caroline chanted, "We're gonna frow rocks, we're gonna frow rocks," as Amelia took her from his arms and walked her into the house.

As Henry reached for the axe and eyed a likely hen, Rip once again spun toward the edge of the clearing.

This time the growl came from deep in his throat.

"Easy, Rip." Henry's right hand hovered near his hip.

A lone rider slowly approached. He was hunched over in his saddle and leaned heavily to the left. The horse plodded toward the corral and stopped near Henry's horses, nickering softly. The man unsteadily began to dismount, and then pitched off the saddle, fell in a heap, and didn't move.

CHAPTER 3

Tiny fingers pried Nathaniel Nix's eyes open. Blue eyes stared at his. Golden curls bounced in front of his face. His head thumped as his mind scrambled to grasp what he was seeing. Rosy cheeks. Golden curls, like Norma's.

But Norma was dead.

He gazed around the room and saw a woman at the stove.

Not Ingrid.

She was gone, too. Three years gone.

Now blue eyes and golden curls again.

"Momma, his eyes is open!" the little girl screeched, poking her fingers near his eyes, opening them wider. She bumped his ribs and bullets of pain tore into him, causing him to gasp.

The woman turned to look. "Caroline, leave him alone." She

shooed the young child toward the front door, and then walked over to Nix and touched his forehead.

"Sir, good to see you awake. Let me get my husband." Her skirt whispered as she walked past him to the door.

Ingrid's skirts used to whisper like that.

The woman moved to the door. From behind she looked like Ingrid, slim waist with a long braid running down her back. Nix concentrated to remember Ingrid's face. Freckles. And light blue, almost gray eyes.

Nix stared at the back of the woman's head, wondering if she had freckles, too. When she turned, he saw a light splash across her cheeks and soft wisps of short blonde hair that curled around her face. He heard the woman call, "Henry, he's awake."

Henry Cole. He'd found him. Spent, his head throbbing, he drifted back to sleep, thinking about a little girl with bouncy curls and a beautiful blonde woman who used to love him.

Until they died.

Henry made a final check of the livestock, while Marie washed the dishes and Amelia made a fresh pot of coffee. When he returned to the house Caroline climbed into Marie's lap as the family clustered around the table, eager to learn about their visitor.

"You've had a go of it, it looks like," Henry said.

Nathaniel Nix winced while reaching across the table for the sugar bowl. Henry watched him squirm in the chair, shifting his weight, trying to find a comfortable way to sit. It looked like he hadn't found it yet.

Nix said, "Wasn't so bad at first. I'd heard you lived somewhere between Rapid City and Deadwood, so once I left the stagecoach station in Rapid City I worked my way toward you. As it turned out," he said, grimacing, "I rode on the north side of Harkins Peak and angled off toward Fort Meade. If I'd dropped a mile south along this valley instead of going to the fort I'd have found you a lot earlier."

"You rode up the valley?" Marie asked. "But you didn't stop by the Schwartz ranch?"

Nix finished the last of his coffee and refilled his cup. "Wish I'd have seen it, Miss Marie. It would have saved me a lot of riding. And some beat up ribs. But before I knew it, I found myself nearly to Sturgis, so I went to the fort and talked to the commander there, who gave me directions."

Henry had never met the Fort Meade commander, and was surprised that he would know where to direct Nix. "He sent you here?"

Nix's laugh sounded rueful. "Not within spitting distance. He seemed very busy, but when I mentioned your name he said he knew where you lived. And then he sent me north to Bear Butte."

Henry shook his head. Hard to confuse the heavily wooded ridge overlooking Piedmont valley with the prairie surrounding Bear Butte, but apparently the commander had succeeded. "In time you got yourself oriented."

"Met a rancher with a nice spread, Dorian Handy, out on the plains. I think that's who the commander sent me to see by mistake. Dorian Handy. Henry Cole. I can see how he confused the two. But Handy turned me around and sent me your way. He told me to follow the ruts that General Custer's wagon train cut into the prairie when it came through."

"Four years ago," Elton said, picturing the train again as if it were yesterday. "Remember it, Marie?"

24

"I do," she excitedly said. "I counted more than one hundred wagons. I thought they'd roll by forever."

"And they were driving a herd of cows and horses a Texas rancher would be proud of. Newspaper said more than a thousand men. Glad they didn't swing by, not sure Amelia could have fed them all."

"Well, not in one sitting," she said, smiling. "Please continue, Mr. Nix."

"I followed the wagon ruts to Elk Creek, like Handy said. That's where I fell. Danged horse was probably about as wore out as I was by that time. We came down the bank to ford the creek and I picked the wrong spot to do it. It looked good enough, right until the bank collapsed. My horse went down and off I came. Some horseman I am."

Henry, who'd hit the ground a few times himself, sympathized. "How are those ribs now?"

"Hit a rock when I landed. They'll hurt a while."

Henry, when he was still Elton Collins, had taken a slug in the side one day in Abilene. He knew what busted ribs felt like.

Nix sipped his coffee and continued. "Worst seems to be my head. It's buzzing like a hive of angry bees. A good thing would be if it knocked some sense into me."

Henry felt concern creep closer. Nathaniel Nix had put in a lot of effort to find him. "But you kept riding."

"Mr. Cole, it was my job to find you. It might have taken a little longer than my employer planned, but I'm here now." He looked at Marie, and then at Caroline. "Sometimes the news I bring is best delivered in private."

Henry shook his head. "Whatever it is, we'll hear it as a family."

Nix said, "It's about your brother. His farm burned to the ground two weeks ago."

Henry felt his heart flip. "Indians?"

Amelia looked at Marie. "Please take Caroline outside."

"Yes, Ma'am," Marie said. "May I come back and listen?"

Amelia's lips tightened. "Not this time."

Marie took her sister's hand. "Come on, Carrie."

Henry watched his daughters slowly move toward the door. His brother Andrew had been the reason he and Amelia moved from Kansas to the Dakotas over a dozen years before. Andrew had told them about the great cattle lands, the abundant water, and the rolling hills throughout the Dakota Territory. If you don't want to raise cattle, Andrew had stressed in a heartfelt letter, it's also a great place to raise a family.

The letter worked. Soon after receiving it Henry, Amelia and Marie had made the three-week wagon trek from Kansas to Andrew's farm on a spread of land north of Sioux Falls. When they'd arrived they realized everything Andrew said about the Dakotas was true. It was prime ranch area.

But Henry Cole already had his fill of cattle. It was a peaceful, quiet home he wanted. It was about distancing himself as far from the memory of Elton Collins as he could, and that meant distancing himself from his brother, too. So after visiting Andrew, his wife and two boys for a time he and Amelia had decided to move on.

Nearly a month later the Cole family had found their home on the edge of the Black Hills.

Now, it appeared, Henry would return to Andrew's. And this time he'd be helping his brother start over.

Nix waited until Marie closed the door. "Not Indians, as far as I know," he said.

The only sound in the small room was the gentle squeak of Henry's rocking chair.

Amelia and Nix glanced at each other, unsure of what to say next.

Back and forth the chair went. Slow. Even.

Seemingly endless.

Then it stopped. Henry said, "What about his family?"

Nix said, "That was not conveyed to me."

Henry said, "If it was something bad, I expect it would have been in the telegram."

Nix said, "The message I deliver is generally the worst of the calamity. In this case..."

"The fire."

Amelia stood, kissed the top of Henry's head, and refilled each cup of coffee.

After Henry sipped his he said, "Mr. Nix, who sent you?"

"I'm a messenger by trade. I travel the West to find people who can't, or don't want to, be found. In this case the Western Union office told me they couldn't locate a man named Henry Cole. But they believed I could."

"May I see the telegram?"

Nix dug his hand in his right pants pocket, then drew his hand out, looking confused. He checked his left pocket and pulled his hand out, empty. "You didn't find the telegram when I arrived in your yard?"

"No," Henry said. "Of course, I wasn't looking for one."

Nix cleared his throat. "Apparently I lost it when I fell at the creek. We can ride to the spot in the morning. I'll show you where."

"No need to. I'm sure you remember what it said."

"After mentioning the fire, it requested that you travel to your brother's farm as soon as you're able."

Henry glanced at Amelia, who offered him a tight, forced smile. Did that mean go to see Andrew, or stay? He waited, and she nodded. Go.

Henry turned to Nix. "I'm not surprised no one could find me. We live up here for a reason, and that's to keep to ourselves. Also, telegraphs are spotty around here. Sometimes they're up, but often the wires get cut or they plain don't work. But if you're riding to Hill City tomorrow and the wire is up, please send news that I'll make it to Andrew as soon as I arrange things here."

Nathaniel Nix stood and offered his hand. "And now it's time for me to move on. My next appointment is in Cheyenne." He winced as he walked around the table.

Amelia stepped toward him and placed a hand on his forearm. "Mr. Nix, you're in no condition to travel yet. Spend a few days here while you recover. When you're ready, you can go with Henry to Hill City and catch your stage for Cheyenne."

Nix fidgeted with the back of his seat. "I'm afraid my presence is an imposition. I must go."

Amelia smiled politely. "Nonsense. You're the first visitor we've had this year."

After her mother called Caroline into the house, Marie fussed around the corral. She was old enough to take care of her sister. She was old enough to put in hay, feed the stock, clean the house and cook. And old enough to…well, old enough to kiss a boy.

But apparently not old enough to stay at the table when the grownups were talking.

They needed you to take Caroline away.

"I know," she said aloud. But it didn't make her feel any better. As she brushed her mare, Junie, she thought about what Mr. Nix had said. Uncle Andrew's farm destroyed. And no mention of his family's whereabouts. Her cousins John and Walter, her aunt Millie. But most of all, her Uncle Andrew.

She closed her eyes and recalled the last time she'd seen him. She'd been a little girl when they arrived at his farm, but she could still picture his log house nestled against a small hill and surrounded by cottonwoods. She remembered walking hand-in-hand with her cousin John, two years older and a head taller than she, as they went to fish in a nearby creek. When they returned to the house, Uncle Andrew fussed over the single fish she'd caught as if it were enough to feed both families.

That night, Uncle Andrew and her father stayed up late and told stories about how they'd sailed on their father's ship when they were boys. Even after her cousins fell asleep and the women had gone to bed, she forced herself to stay awake. She rested her head against her father's leg and listened to stories that brought a mysterious world alive. She sniffed the air now, remembering how Uncle Andrew had described the stale, salty smell of the ocean. She would smell it herself one day.

"How's the old girl?"

Marie started. She'd been so preoccupied with her thoughts she hadn't heard her father approach. "I'm fine, Dad."

Henry burst into laughter. "Glad to hear it, but how's the other old girl doing?"

Marie smiled at him with an 'oh-you-mean-Junie' look, and said, "Her left front seemed sore, but I pried a stone out of her hoof. She bruised her frog."

Henry crawled through the bars and went to the mare they'd had since Marie was a baby. He touched her leg, and then lifted it and inspected the hoof.

He allowed Junie to put her foot down. "I think you're right, Doctor Collins. Nice diagnosis."

Marie blushed. "Thanks, Dad." She fidgeted with Junie a bit longer while watching her father. Finally she said, "You're concerned about Uncle Andrew."

He touched her shoulder. "In the end, family's all we have."

Henry ruffled her hair, which pulled a few loose strands from her braid, and marveled that she'd become so much like Amelia. She didn't wait for a man to do things for her. If something needed to be done, she did it. She was a capable girl, and capable girls were needed out here where a family was only as successful as the amount and quality of work they put in every day.

When she was growing up, he'd treated her like she'd have to depend on herself to survive. She could shoot a rifle nearly as well as he, she handled a pistol well enough, she could do what needed to be done.

Marie cleared her throat. "Dad, I was thinking."

"That's a relief."

She scrunched her nose. "What I mean is, I was thinking about going for a walk tonight."

"Would you like some company?"

Marie jumped slightly. "No, Dad. Alone."

But you won't be alone, Henry thought. He shifted his weight from side to side. "Are you headed up on the ridge?"

Words spewed from her like a roiling spring stream. "The aspens are bright gold and I want to see them this evening before the leaves fall off. I have to see them."

When he hesitated, she touched his arm. "I have to do this."

Henry glanced at the setting sun. "Take the rifle. Be home before dark."

She bounced past him. "Thanks, Dad." As she hurried to the house, her hands smoothed her hair.

CHAPTER 4

The next day brought a heavy frost to the ridge. The wildflowers that had spectacularly bloomed all summer along the valley path now stood like motionless, white-crusted sentinels. Henry knew that when the sun hit them full-force today their watch would be done.

As he rode past them he reached down from the saddle to brush the frost off a bright purple blossom. Then he dipped onto the narrow path between the twin pines that marked the edge of the land he'd cleared and made his way toward the valley and Fort Meade.

"Mr. Cole," Major Tinsdale said, after offering him a drink, "it's not my mission to check up on the neighbors, so to speak, when my men and I ride the valley. We are the Army, after all, and we're here to protect the miners working throughout these

Black Hills." Apparently that didn't sound important enough, for he quickly added, "And to keep the Indians subdued, of course."

Thinking of General Custer's massacre a few years earlier at Little Big Horn, Henry wanted to suggest that the major was a little late in quelling the local tribes. For the most part the Sioux were now living near the Nebraska border, two days ride to the south. Henry had been through there once. He considered the Lakota Sioux sufficiently subdued.

Henry pressed the major. "I understand the importance of your mission. But some of your men will surely ride to Rapid City while I'm gone. I am asking you to have them to swing a bit south and check on my wife and daughters."

As the fat, bald major waddled away from the desk and topped off his drink Henry watched Tinsdale's plump hands and finely manicured nails fuss with the bottle. Henry doubted those hands had ever fixed a fence, roped or branded a calf, or pounded a nail. They were administrator's hands. In his time in the Army Henry had met many professional administrators who liked to do their fighting from a desk. Less death that way.

The major turned and faced him. "Mister Cole, your concern for your wife is quite touching." He swayed a bit as he walked to his desk. "Interesting that you've chosen this time, with her well-being in mind, to leave her and your daughters behind."

Henry's hand flinched.

You don't solve problems with guns, you create them. You learned that when you were Elton Collins.

A new wave of guilt replaced his anger. He'd had to break ice from the trough and water bucket this morning. In a few weeks they could be in for another freeze like last winter. And he might not be around to lead his family through it.

But he hadn't chosen the time of his brother's fire and he couldn't wait for good weather to travel. In the Dakotas if you didn't like the weather, wait ten minutes and it'd change, or so the old timers said. He'd seen blizzards in June and October and green grass in January, so even if he did wait, there was no saying there would be a better time. Right or wrong, he would go.

Henry said, "My wife can handle most anything that comes her way. And my oldest girl does a man's work every day. It's the unexpected things I'm concerned about, Major. What I'm asking is for your help with those." He swallowed something that tasted like pride. "Please. Have a patrol swing by, south of Harkins Peak, and check on my family." He picked up Tinsdale's whiskey bottle and held it. "Please."

Major Tinsdale stretched to his tallest, falling six inches short of Henry's height. He stared at the bottle that Henry held. His voice wavered slightly as he spoke. "It so happens I shall be going to the mining camp at Lead in a few days. Weather permitting, of course."

Henry waved the bottle back and forth. "That goes without saying."

Tinsdale watched the bottle slowly move. "And from Lead I will ride to meet the stage at Hill City, where my mother is arriving. This is my first command, and she would like to see it."

Henry tapped the mouth of the bottle with his index finger. "You know how mothers are."

Tinsdale glanced at the whiskey bottle. "Yes. I do."

Henry said, "Let's drink to mothers, then. If you will join me."

Relief blossomed on Major Tinsdale's face. "Drinking because of my mother? That has happened before." He rattled a nervous laugh.

Henry touched the rim of Tinsdale's glass with the bottle mouth, and tipped the bottle forward until the honey-colored liquid hovered at the end of the bottle. "You were saying, Major, about riding to Hill City?"

Tinsdale's glass shivered against the bottle mouth. "Yes," he said. "Hill City."

"Is it a safe assumption that, after meeting your mother, you will ride to my house?"

Tinsdale enthusiastically nodded, his eyes locked on his empty glass.

Henry allowed a tiny drop to escape the bottle. "Though it adds a half-day to your journey."

Tinsdale eagerly licked his lips. "It's the least I can do."

Henry tipped the bottle and didn't stop until Tinsdale's glass was nearly full. "I was thinking the same."

CHAPTER 5

Despite Amelia's protestations Nix continued to bunk in the stable, saying if it was good enough for the horses, it was good enough for him.

Henry stoked the fire, blew out the lamp, and joined Amelia in bed. She wrapped her arms around him and gently kissed him. "The girls and I will certainly miss you."

He stroked her hair. "Figure three days to get to Andrew's place, and then a week or two to help him get something built before snowfall. Honestly, I don't know what I'm going to find when I get there. I have to go, but I hate to leave you with all this."

She sat up and looked at him in the nearly dark room. "Henry Cole, I'm a Western woman." She chuckled. "Maybe I wasn't born one, but after all these years with you I'm one now. You have nothing to worry about."

"You'll do fine, I know." He wasn't quite as certain as his words.

Amelia ran her finger along his jawline. "What else is on your mind, Henry?"

Henry chuckled quietly. "You know me well."

"Twenty years of marriage will do that. It's hard to keep a secret."

Oh, but I have, he thought. Guilt fingered his heart. "Tonight I found myself thinking what it would be like if we lost our place. A tragedy like that, some would say it creates an opportunity to change course. An incentive to do something you wouldn't ordinarily feel the urge to do."

He felt Amelia tighten. "Are you looking for that opportunity? Time to try something new?"

He cupped her cheek in his hand. "This is our home forever. No, I was thinking about Andrew. He loved the sea more than I. Losing his place, I wonder if he'll move Millie and the boys back to Maine. My father always said he'd hold the business until his boys came back."

She aimlessly traced a light circle in his chest hair. "Possibly the thought has crossed your mind, too."

"Not a bit. But Andrew never seemed to have his heart fully into ranching. When we visited him, one evening he mentioned returning to sail with our father. I wonder how he sees this opportunity."

Amelia said, "He may not see it as an opportunity. So as long as Millie and the boys are fine—"

She shook her head. "Of course Millie and the boys are fine. And he will rebuild." She sighed lightly. "If you say three days to get there and three more to get back, plus two weeks more or less to help Andrew and Millie get back on their feet, I expect the girls and I won't see you until the end of the month. Now, surprise me and come home early."

"The garden is in, and the hay is in. There's enough wood split for winter. I think we're good on supplies, aren't we?"

She sighed, a bit deeper than normal. "With one less mouth to feed, certainly."

"I'm leaving you with a lot." He paused. "Too much?"

Amelia playfully shoved him. "You have two women in your house who are quite capable of anything we encounter. You worry too much."

"I sometimes forget that there's another woman here. Now that Marie is…older…I guess she's about outgrown any use for me."

Amelia placed her hand on his chest. "Sometimes I think men don't understand women one tiny bit. You're her father. She still turns to you for advice. She looks to you for approval. You mean so much to her, Henry. Any man she chooses will have to measure up to you, and that's no easy chore. As it always is with fathers and daughters."

"She wants to be careful who she idolizes. Not everyone is who he seems."

Amelia lunged and kissed his cheek. "It's who you are to her that's most important. You're what she needs."

"I'm trying, but she's changing so quickly it's hard to keep up. It seems like last week she and I used to play at the creek. Then all she wanted to do was splash around and chase frogs. Now I'm afraid she has a lot more adult things on her mind."

"A mother knows the look on her daughter's face. There's a boy in her heart."

"Now don't take this wrong, dear, you did the best you could. You gave me two beautiful girls, but if you'd given me sons at least it would be someone else worrying about his daughters' virtue."

Amelia dug her fingers in his ribs and gave him a hard tickle, causing him to squirm away and nearly fall out of bed.

"Okay, okay," he gasped. "Forget I said that. I love my girls."

Amelia giggled. "Oh, if the world could see this. The great Henry Cole, defeated by a tickle."

He seized her wrists in case she tried another sneak attack. "Defeated is such a strong word. Truce? No loser?"

She kissed him hard. "Truce. No loser."

He released her wrists. "I suddenly find myself distracted by your amorous intentions."

"One of my many charms," Amelia demurely said. "But before you get too distracted to think straight, hear me out. I know you think you have to be here every second, but we will make do."

"I imagine you will, like during the war when some headstrong soldier went rushing off with a grand vision to save the Nation." He smiled ruefully. "But tomorrow, I'll see Schwartz and ask him to stop by."

"Though we can make do."

"Though you and the girls can make do. It's less for you than for me. Remember last year, we had snow before November. I may not be back by then."

Amelia's index finger resumed tracing circles on his chest as she said, "It snowed before you were born, and it will keep snowing long after you and I are gone. I don't suppose a little snow while you're in Sioux Falls will change our lives much."

"Then it's settled." He ran his fingers along her hip and lightly brushed her ribcage. Amelia shuddered as his hand continued to climb. "Now, where are those charms of yours?"

—

As Amelia's breathing slowed and she drifted to sleep Henry reconsidered talking to Schwartz, who was their closest neighbor. A young horse in training had thrown Schwartz during the summer and he'd gotten his leg tangled in the stirrup when he fell. Last time Henry had seen him, Schwartz still walked with a hell of a limp. No need to drag an ailing man up on the ridge, especially since Henry had talked to Major Tinsdale.

Let the Army handle it.

Moonlight flickered through the tree branches and painted ever-changing shadows on the walls as Henry silently moved around the house.

He touched the rifle, which stood by the door. A box of cartridges sat in the cupboard.

He pulled a small handgun from the pantry drawer nearest the kitchen and placed it on the table.

He disassembled it, cleaned it, reassembled it, and returned it to the pantry. Then he cleaned the rifle.

He sat at the table.

A small pistol. A rifle.

Amelia. And Marie.

They could do this.

He walked to the fireplace.

He quickly pried up a piece of floorboard, reached under the floor, and lifted out a small burlap sack.

He carried the sack to the table and withdrew two Colt Navy pistols. He ran his finger over the engraved cylinders, their naval battle images now nearly worn off.

He slid his hands over the smooth wooden grips. Along the barrels.

He pulled the hammer back. His finger tightened on the trigger as he gazed down the length of the barrel.

Then he gently eased the hammer forward.

His hands danced over weapons as he cleaned and oiled them. As he replaced the loads.

Only then was he ready to travel. Because, after all, he was still Elton Collins.

And someday, someone might discover that.

CHAPTER 6

A thin film of ice had formed on the water trough overnight, and Henry broke it for the horses to drink. The water pail had also frozen, so he flipped the bucket over and dropped the chunk of ice on the ground. It would be a cold ride to Hill City, for as winter neared the pines covering the ridge pinned the frosty air to the ground. Though the sun was shining, he and Nix would feel little of its warmth.

Henry's breath billowed in the frigid air as he fed the horses. Nix's mount, sassy after a couple of days in the corral, pranced lightly as Henry saddled him and then Sparky. He glanced at the stable but saw no sign of Nix.

In all likelihood it'd be dark when they arrived in Hill City.

The house door opened and Caroline popped out, wrapped in a blanket and wearing an old, worn-out pair of his boots. She struggled to walk, staggering with each step and trying not to trip on the ends of the blanket.

Finally she lunged to him and wrapped her arms around his legs. "Hi, Daddy!"

He scooped her up and pulled the blanket tight. "What are you doing up so early, Miss Caroline?"

"I gotta see you go! But do you have to go?"

He kissed her forehead. "I do, sweetie. What's Mommy making for breakfast?"

"Eggs and biscuits."

Mmmm. And coffee?"

"Yup. For me, too."

He pinched her cheek. "Okay, coffee for you, too. Let's see if Mr. Nix is up, and then get some of that breakfast."

Caroline's face wrinkled. "Yesterday he kept rubbin' his head and saying 'owww.'"

Henry frowned. Maybe Nix wasn't up for a ride after all. Of course, maybe the fresh air would be the trick to clear his headache.

Caroline reached up and pulled his nose. "Why do people say 'owww' when they're hurt?"

"Because we already use the word 'buffalo' for something else."

She gasped and her face lit up. "Next time I get hurt, I'm going to say 'buffalo.'"

"And next time I see a buffalo, I'm going to call it 'ouch.'"

Caroline sighed. "Not 'ouch', Daddy. 'Owww.' You're silly like Mr. Nix."

"Why is Mr. Nix silly?"

"Yesterday he called me Norma."

———

Amelia stood with Marie at the window and watched her husband envelop Caroline in his arms. Last night had been her night for his arms. It was something she had to do for her husband. She wanted his most vivid memory to be of *her*.

She leaned heavily against the sink. She didn't 'need' her husband, but she 'wanted' him home. Need…want. There was a difference. She told herself that again, and hoped the days would speed by.

Amelia glanced out the window and saw that Caroline had taken Henry's hand and was leading him over to Sparky. Henry suddenly threw his head back and laughed, and Caroline joined him, the two of them braying like donkeys.

Marie lingered beside her at the window. Amelia, sensing her distress, gave her a brief hug.

After a moment, Marie leaned away. A slight pout formed at the corners of her mouth. "I don't want him to go."

"I can't imagine you do. From the moment you were born, I couldn't pry you two apart."

Marie's shoulders sagged. "Sometimes I still feel like that little girl. But it's different with us now."

Amelia brushed a stray tendril of hair from Marie's brow. "You know how the garden grows best when it's planted in the sun? Your father wants to make sure you're getting all the sun you need, and he doesn't want to be the shade that keeps you from blossoming into a woman."

"I'm hardly a woman."

Amelia smiled gently. "When you go to town, men look at you. To them you're a woman." Her eyes dropped to the front of Marie's dress. "You have all the makings, anyway."

Marie flushed. "Momma, a bosom doesn't make me a woman."

44

Amelia patted her cheek. "No, it doesn't, but it does change things a bit. When you were a little girl, your father could play with you and wrestle with you and it was fun. But then you started to change. Truthfully now, do you still want your father to be your playmate?"

"Well, not my playmate." Marie giggled. "I mean, I can't see Daddy leading me around on Sparky."

"But you used to rush out like a wild Indian every time he left the house. You were his shadow."

"I miss that sometimes. Just us together. Caroline is his shadow now."

Amelia cradled Marie's face in her hands. "But your father's heart has never left you."

"That's how I feel about him. He's my..." She sighed deeply. "It's hard to put into words."

Amelia held her gaze. "That's the same way I felt about my father. Every time I heard his footsteps on the porch my heart jumped. And for me that feeling about him has never left, even to this day."

Marie took Amelia's hand. "You mean I'll always feel like this?"

Amelia touched her daughter's cheek. "I expect he'll always be your knight in shining armor." She paused. "Even when you find Prince Charming."

CHAPTER 7

The trail winding up the ridge toward Hill City was as cold as Henry had expected. Frost lingered on the tips of the pine needles and hid under bushes and hollows in the landscape where the sun couldn't find it.

A herd of deer scattered ahead of them and then peeled off to the side and doubled back, unwilling to leave the feed in their small, lush meadow. As the climb leveled, Henry reined Sparky and turned to study the land they'd left. While he couldn't see the house, he saw a small column of smoke snaking skyward. That would have to do.

He reluctantly turned away.

When they passed the lightning-split tree that was about halfway between their house and Hill City, Henry turned in the saddle and shrugged. "Ready to eat?"

Nix shrugged back.

Consensus achieved, they dismounted.

Henry fished a small coffee pot out of his saddlebag and pulled out the food Amelia had packed while Nix collected firewood. Within minutes they were heating water for coffee.

After eating, they rode single file for over an hour through thick underbrush and sprawling juniper bushes. When the forest opened up as they worked their way down the ridge toward Hill City, Henry slowed and Nix rode up to join him.

"Nix, you spend much time out here?"

"Yes and no." He chuckled. "Not much of an answer, I guess. What I mean is I came from back East, like most men. Done some mining and a bit of this and that."

Nix paused for a moment and Henry thought he was done, but then he continued. "Mostly I work for people who need to find people. Sometimes I think I spend more time traveling than I do in my house."

"Well, it still seems like a major undertaking to track me down. I appreciate that."

Nix held the reins in his left hand and cupped his head with his right. "Doing my job."

Henry stopped Sparky. "You okay?"

Nix drooped in the saddle. "Every step the horse takes, it's like someone dumped a handful of carpet tacks in my head."

"When we get to Hill City we'll see the doc. He has a whole bag of tricks he's anxious to use. Maybe something in there will help."

Nix lifted his head from his hand. "Far to go?"

"Half hour or so. Not bad."

"Not bad is better than I'd hoped." Nix nudged a heel to his horse's flank, and they headed down the trail.

Not bad, Henry thought, unless you have bees in your head and they're mad at your brain.

They rode down the narrow Hill City main street at sunset and went straight to the livery.

"Shorty," Henry called out.

"Keep yer shirt on, I'm comin'," a voice bellowed from the back.

When Nix winced, Henry put a steady hand on his shoulder. "Sorry about that."

In a moment Shorty Stern ambled out, wiping his hands on his filthy jeans as he walked. Seeing the men, he glanced inquiringly at Henry.

Henry shook his head.

Shorty broke into an easy smile. "Well then, if it ain't my old friend Henry Cole. Been a while since I seen you, boy!"

Shorty looked toward Henry's riding companion. "And who you totin' along?"

"Nathaniel Nix."

Shorty studied Nix. "I ain't real good with names, but faces, now…"

Nix shook his head. "Never seen this one before, friend. Happens a lot though, strangers thinking they know me. You're not the first and you likely won't be the last."

Shorty squinted. "Yeah," he slowly said. "That's it." He turned to Henry. "Where you boys headed?"

Henry said, "He's going south, and I'm catching the train in Pierre, then Sioux Falls."

"You got a brother there, I recollect."

"Lost his place in a fire. I'm on my way to do what I can."

Shorty wrinkled his brow. "Sorry to hear that." He surveyed Nix. "You okay, feller? You look whiter'n a bleached and boiled sheet."

Nix touched the side of his head. "Bit of a thumper."

Shorty whooped. "How I often rise, with thunder twixt my ears and lightnin' in my eyes. Don't suppose it's the same reason, though. Mine comes from tryin' to drink my weight in whiskey. What's the cause of your malady?"

Nix squinted his eyes closed. "Tried to break a rock with my head. The rock won."

Shorty cackled. "Rocks generally do. You leave your horses and swing by Doc's place two doors down. Tell him to give ya what he gives me. It's somethin' that tastes just this side of horsecrap, but it does the trick for me. Could be it'll do the trick for you."

After they'd seen the doctor and he'd given Nix a swig of something that looked like liniment and smelled far worse, Henry and Nix headed to the town's one hotel, the Hanson Inn. The rooms were passable the last time Henry had come through town. It didn't much matter if it'd gotten better or worse, it was either the Hanson or the livery loft. And the Hanson had hot food.

"When's the Cheyenne stage?" Nix asked Einar Hanson, once they'd squared away two rooms.

"Two o'clock arrival, give or take. Pulls out at four or so, depending."

"Like clockwork?"

Hanson leaned forward and measured Nix, who clung to the counter edge with both hands. "Like no clock I've ever seen, but the way I see it you have three choices: board it when it goes, stay here in my hotel and wait for the next one which may or may not run like a clock, or get on your horse and point his nose southwest. Cheyenne's a long ride, even if the weather holds."

Nix ran his right hand along his temple. "Guess I'll go with the stage. Whenever it comes through."

Henry said, "Food any better since the last time I came around?"

Hanson stared him down. "Not that you're in a position to judge since I've eaten your trail cooking before, but ours beats yours any day."

Henry glanced toward the dining room as a tiny woman approached the front counter. "Maybe you should get rid of that has-been, beat-down old cook you're still hanging onto."

"We both agree on that fact. Hard to do though, seeing as I'm married to her."

Wanda Hanson whacked her husband's arm, and then pushed past him to Henry. "Has been? Beat-down?"

Nix tapped Henry on the shoulder. "You have an interesting way with women."

Wanda turned her attention to Nix and smiled. "Henry, who you riding with?" She daintily held out her hand as he made the introductions.

"Well, it's always nice to have a gentleman stop by our establishment. And you too, Mister Henry Cole." With a twinkle in her eye, she turned to the kitchen. Over her shoulder she called out, "Two steaks with all the trimmings coming up."

Hanson was right, it was better than Henry's trail cooking by a damn sight.

Over dinner the men talked about places they'd lived and people they knew. They discovered they'd both worked cattle drives for the Rocking J out of Texas, Henry while he was still Elton Collins and Nix three years ago. Although the stories they told each other were fairly similar, in truth they couldn't have been more different.

Nix had experienced barren, desolate country as he'd pushed a herd from west Texas through Oklahoma without incident. Henry, however, had been paid fighting wages to drive off a band of rustlers who thought it was easier to steal cows than to raise them. After he had shot three from the saddle as they attempted to cut part of the herd, the rest decided that maybe ranching was better than dying.

But mentioning gunfights might get Nix's brain working. As Henry had discovered many times before, one you got a man thinking about gunfights it didn't take long before he began to recollect the great gunfighters. Some remembered the name Elton Collins, and some of those had stated they'd seen Collins in action. If one of them began to study Henry Cole's face too closely and it sparked a hint of recognition, everything he had put in place to hide from his past would come tumbling down. And that was a risk he was unwilling to take.

Instead, Henry let Nix do the talking.

When they finished eating, Henry was ready to turn in and said so.

"I'm feeling a bit better after all," Nix said. "Maybe a beer to finish off the evening? I hear there's a tavern one street back."

One beer led to two, as they often do. After the waitress delivered their replacements Henry said, "All this traveling you do, it's got to be hard on a man and his family."

Nix's brow furrowed. "Got no family." He sipped on the beer. "Not anymore."

Henry silently studied the bubbles chase their way up his beer glass. He'd met many a drifting man through the years who wistfully talked of families made and families lost. Some through sickness, some through Indian raids, some because the families couldn't

51

handle the hardship of a life lived away from the comforts of civilization. He wasn't going to ask in which category Nix fit.

Nix's chair squeaked as he shifted, catching Henry's attention. "I had a wife and a daughter. Ingrid and Norma. Norma was my little girl. Bouncy curls, giggled a lot. Followed me everywhere. Like your little girl."

Elton flinched. Nix had called Caroline Norma. He'd seen before where blows to the head had scrambled folks' brains. Sometimes the injury was temporary.

Sometimes it was permanent.

But as Nix himself had stated, apparently the medicine was helping. Henry noticed some color had returned to his cheeks, and he hadn't touched his temples for at least an hour. For Nathaniel Nix, things were looking up.

Except for the story unfolding as he spoke.

Quietly Henry said, "Tough break to lose a family."

Nix looked distant, distracted. "Lost them both in a week. Norma first. Her throat swole up and she couldn't breathe." He sighed heavily. "One morning we woke up, and she was gone. Ingrid couldn't handle losing her at all. She took to bed right away. We figured it was sadness set in, and we let her be. Didn't know that she had the same thing. Buried her the next week. Side by side graves. A big one and a little one. Ingrid and Norma. Doc told us it was diphtheria."

"Sorry to hear that."

Nix ran his finger down the sweaty beer glass. "I'm fine. It's been three years."

Nix's voice was laced with pain. Henry didn't think three years had healed the scars. Maybe scabbed them over, but they still seemed pretty close to the surface. He tried again. "You're a good man, Nathaniel. You can still have a happy life."

Nix reached for his beer, a dark shadow crossing his face. "Folks keep telling me that, but to date I haven't found evidence of its truth."

Russell pulled his hat a bit lower and observed the two men as they talked. The younger one he largely ignored. But the dark-haired man was good to see in Hill City. And it'd be even better to see him leave. And go away for a spell.

Russell looked over at his riding partner, Earl. "You don't ever know when fortune is going to smile at you. But she's smiling tonight."

"Who's Fortune, and where's she at?" Earl mumbled.

He touched Earl's arm. "Don't look now, but you see that dark-haired feller across the room?"

Earl cocked his head sideways. "If I can't look, how'm I gonna see him?"

"You'll have to trust me. Tonight, Earl old buddy, we hit the jackpot."

In the spring of the year, hitting a jackpot was the last thing Russell thought about. Back then, staying alive had been his primary goal.

A life full of bad breaks seemed ready to catch up with him a couple of towns over, where he and Earl had been working as miners. At a bar one evening a drunken fool with a big mouth had swapped a few punches with Earl. Then he called Earl a lame-brained idiot and pulled a gun. Without hesitation, Russell emptied his six-shooter in the miner's gut.

He and Earl had slipped out of town during the resulting hubbub and made a beeline for the rough and rocky hills a day's ride to the west.

Since he had the worst kind of luck, he was convinced the law wouldn't be far behind. But after days of hard riding, doubling back and constantly watching their back trail, it seemed they weren't being hunted after all. Maybe their luck was about to change for the good.

If that was the case, he decided it was time for them to find a place of their own and mine for themselves instead of breaking their backs for someone else to get rich. While skirting the backside of a ridge they'd followed a stream, looking for any indication of gold. Instead, as they worked their way along the edge of a splintered shale outcropping they noticed an abundance of heavy gray stone, some of it lying exposed. Silver. Not as valuable as gold, but far more plentiful.

Still, miners can only make money if they sell their ore. Russell wasn't about to try his luck in Lead, where the shooting occurred. But Hill City wasn't far off, and he doubted the sheriff there would be interested in a couple of hardscrabble miners.

When their ore was assayed in Hill City it was found to be rich with silver. They quickly filed on the claim, hoping this time they'd hit it big. And so they had. The ore was easy to get out of the ground and it was a miner's dream, for the vein seemed to be widening. There was so much ore, in fact, that he'd hired a local drifter to help.

To keep the inquisitive Hill City townsfolk from gossiping about their strike, he and Earl often hauled their ore to other towns in the area.

Including nearby Sturgis, where on one trip Russell had seen something that seemed too good to be true. Something that he wanted to see again. And he would, as soon as the man in the corner boarded the stage tomorrow.

Russell smiled broadly. "Earlie, I showed you a man on the other side of the ridge a couple a weeks ago. He's the one with the daughter who looked like she was ready for a wealthy miner to teach her about he'in and she'in."

Through whiskey-blurred eyes Earl turned and squinted. "Could be you right about that."

Russell cackled. "That little snippet would like a man such as you. Me, I'd like to give her momma a go. I think she had a hankerin' for a wealthy miner, also. You know one?" He cackled loudly.

Earl gulped the last of his whiskey. "Friend, I know two."

CHAPTER 8

The stage bound for Pierre rolled into Hill City shortly after noon the next day. A short, bowlegged cowboy exited the stage first and headed directly for the bar. Two more men and two women slowly disembarked. As the women made a beeline for the outhouse, Henry assessed that they might be more appropriately dressed for an evening in Paris than a stagecoach ride through the Dakotas. They wore elaborate blue dresses of vastly different shade, one as pale as the afternoon sky on a hot summers' day, the other a dark, cornflower hue that seemed to draw dust and hold it. Each tightly-fitted dress was trimmed with an abundance of pleated ruffles, bows, braids and other things Henry couldn't even begin to name. The women wore their hair piled high in ringlets and pinned into place, topped by small white straw hats with tie-ribbons that matched their dress color.

The hems of their dresses trailed along in the dirt as the women linked arms and strolled by him.

Henry tipped his hat. "Beautiful day, ladies."

They didn't offer so much as a glance his way.

Henry chuckled quietly. "Maybe they'll leave their demeanor in the privy."

Given their outfits, the two men were accompanying the women. They looked equally impressive in black frock coats, vests, matching trousers, and Ascot ties. As they neared Henry they knocked the dust from the bowlers they held, then placed them squarely on their heads.

"Afternoon, gents," Henry said.

The men glanced at the pistol Henry wore, then quickly looked away and hustled after the women.

Henry walked to the horses harnessed to the stage. He scratched around the ears of the one closest to him. "How are you doing, boy?"

The horse nickered in response.

Henry patted the horse's neck. "Well, I haven't completely lost the art of conversation." He offered a hand to the hefty driver as he dismounted the stage to swap horses before the run to Pierre. "You have a full load today?"

The stage driver blew out a big breath. "Full enough with those folks. Been a long ride, and with them gossip birds it's getting longer by the minute." He leaned against the livery wall, slowly rolled a smoke, and then offered the makings to Henry.

After his first draw, the driver said, "Dropping one off, picking none up, unless I'm picking you up. Then it's a wash, I guess." He studied Henry. "'Course, you can always ride up top with me for a while, Elton."

Henry dropped his smoke and studied the driver. "Purnell Boone?"

Boone's face glowed. "The last time I saw you we was boys working like men on your father's ship. I enjoyed that so much, I soon decided to try my fortune elsewhere. Don't even want to guess how long ago that was. Twenty-five years, more or less."

Henry Cole glanced toward the street. When he saw it was empty, he relaxed slightly. "Lots of things have changed since then, Purnell. First thing I have to tell you is this. Folks around here know me as Henry Cole. It's very important that it stays that way. Appreciate it if you call me Henry from now on."

Boone drew hard on his cigarette before speaking. "Something I should know about?"

"Sometimes things needed to be changed, is all. Some folks change jobs. Some folks change wives. I changed my name."

Boone pulled another long drag on his cigarette, then dropped it and stubbed it out. He looked at his friend. "Guess a feller has the right to whoever he wants to be. Now, Elton Collins used to eat like he had two stomachs, I remember that. How about Henry Cole? He know his way around the dinner table?"

Henry clapped Boone on the shoulder. "That's one thing that never changed."

After they had eaten, Henry walked to the Western Union office to send a telegraph letting Andrew know he was traveling to meet him.

The telegraph operator sadly shook his head when Henry walked in. "No need to come any further, mister," he said. "Wire's been down two days. I can talk to Rapid City and Rapid City can talk to me. But I can't go a stop past there."

Henry said, "Not that it's easy to predict, but what's your feel about it coming back up anytime soon?"

The operator shrugged. "Somewhere between three minutes and three weeks is my best guess. Which is based on nothing at all. Sometimes it's down a minute, sometimes it's down a day. Sometimes," the grizzled operator said, pulling on his long, salt-and-pepper beard, "it's down longer. Sorry I can't help you."

So the trip would be a surprise to Andrew. Once Henry left on the stage, he'd keep going until he arrived at his brother's place. Brother's former place, he reminded himself. He walked back to the stage.

As he began to load his belongings he reached to unbuckle his gunbelt, then hesitated. The West was slowly changing and this trip would take him to Sioux Falls, where people relied on the law to uphold justice. It was his experience that the law wouldn't abide by him wandering around with a six-gun on his hip. His initial plan, once the stage rolled in, had been to pack away his Colts.

Now he reconsidered. Before he had a wife and family, the man known as Elton Collins had accepted whatever hand he was dealt. If he died, it was his death alone. Time would pass, the wind would drift dust over his bones, and in a few months there would be no lasting proof that he ever walked the earth.

Then a pretty blonde caught his eye, and over time she'd given him two more pretty blondes. And handguns, the tools of his livelihood before he'd met Amelia, had been traded for a plow against the sod, a hoe against the weeds, and an axe against the trees that crowded the meadow he'd cleared partway up the ridge. He'd put the guns away as easily as he'd discarded his name.

Now he was Henry Cole, a farmer and father, a peace-loving man. A man determined to stay that way.

Because he alone knew the cost his family could pay if he ever became Elton Collins again.

For in the end, he believed, Fate always strove to balance the ledger.

More than once, as Henry watched a lifeless man being dragged away after a gunfight, he thought about how life would have been different if he'd stayed in Maine.

No guns. No death.

But there would have been no Amelia. No Marie. No Caroline. There would have been no life on the ridge overlooking Piedmont valley.

So he'd finally come to uneasy terms with his past, for a man makes his choices and he lives with the outcome, good or bad. Because for all the times he wished he'd never become *that* Elton Collins, he also knew he could not erase the footprints he'd made.

He could simply control their direction in the future.

As Henry Cole.

Father.

Farmer.

Peace-loving man.

All that may be true.

Still, he decided to leave the gunbelt buckled around his hips.

In case Fate came calling today.

Soon the men and women made their way toward the stage. Henry heard them coming before he saw them, a group whose raucous laughter sounded like a gaggle of incoming geese. He calculated the long trip to Pierre and swung beside Boone. "Looks like this is the place for me."

While they waited for the folks to get situated down below, Henry glanced east between the livery and the new jailhouse. He saw the briefest flash of two riders angling up the trail in the direction he and Nix had ridden from the day before. The road to Lead and Deadwood went the opposite way, so the riders weren't bound for the mines.

Maybe they were riding to Sturgis. Or to the growing small town that optimistically called itself Rapid City. Because there wasn't much else in the direction the men rode.

Except one fork of the trail that passed near his house.

Henry rose to get a better look at the men riding into the low brush that skirted the trail. As he stood, Boone shook the reins and the stage lurched off, causing Henry to fall back into the seat.

Boone chuckled. "Elton Collins was a bit steadier. Not sure if I can travel too far with this Henry Cole feller. Hate to have him fall off and land on his wounded pride. There's one good seat down below if this ride's too tough to tame."

Henry let the moment pass. "Caught me gawking, that's all. Let's go."

CHAPTER 9

The stage rolled into Pierre after dark. Boone pulled up to the well-lit, freshly-painted Emerald Hotel in a cloud of dust. "All right folks, this is as far as the stage goes. Train leaves tomorrow, but until then the Emerald has clean rooms and good hot food."

The woman in the dark blue dress grumbled as her husband helped her down. "Are the rooms elegant, driver?"

Boone saw the husband's rolling eyes. "Ma'am, you spent the last night in a stagecoach and you haven't had a bath in days. I suspect these rooms will do."

The woman huffed a bit, but quickly lost her starch. "You're right driver, a bath would feel elegant. And good food?"

"Better than anything you had since Hill City." Meals had been few and far between since they'd left Hanson's, and none of them had been elegant.

Henry watched the rest of the travelers leave the stage, and then rode with Boone to swap out the horses. When they were finished Boone said, "Guess you'll stay here tonight, too."

"Like you said, the train leaves in the morning."

Boone said, "Probably wouldn't hurt a body to get a good meal and some shut-eye. Especially if you're going to hit the ground working when you get there." He looked at Henry. "Maybe a beer, too. Trail dust and all."

Henry clapped him on the back. "You know somewhere a couple of old friends can go to catch up on life?"

"Yessir, I believe I do."

Henry followed Boone one block behind Main Street toward the bawdy Irish Rose Saloon. As they approached, the sound of a tinny, out of tune piano drifted toward them. Now and again, muffled shouts could be heard.

"Hard liquor and soft women," Boone said, pushing his way through the batwing doors. "My kind of place." He shouldered his way past a couple of cowboys at the bar and waved to the bartender at the far end of the bar. "Barkeep," he yelled. "One for me, and one for my long-lost buddy Elton Collins."

Henry Cole's head dropped nearly to his chest. "I wish you hadn't said that," he quietly said. "You might want to step away. Things may get exciting in a moment."

Boone looked at Henry. "Any problem you face, I'll face it with you, Elton."

Henry shook his head. "You don't want to be anywhere near this type of problem."

Boone took two uncertain steps to the side.

When the bartender delivered the drinks he dipped his head and quietly said to Henry, "There's a feller named Orvis over your left shoulder, fancies himself a gunfighter. He's digging his eyes into your back like he's toting a grudge. You might want to turn and face him. But, my advice, turn slow."

Henry turned slowly and assessed the narrow-shouldered, pinch-faced man. He wore a tied-down Colt Walker pistol, butt-forward on his left side. Heavy pistol, carried for a cross-draw.

A cross-draw was slow. A heavy pistol made it slower. *Don't get to the draw*, Henry thought. *Whatever you do, don't let him draw.*

The man ran his left hand through his greasy hair. "Elton Collins showin' up on my doorstep is better than Christmas and birthday, all rolled into one."

Henry's pulse flickered. "You're mistaken, friend. I'm Henry Cole."

Orvis smirked. "Now this here feller who you come in with, he said you're Elton Collins. I'm of a mind to believe him more than you. Which puts you in a world of trouble."

Henry fought to stay calm. "Buy you a beer, Orvis?"

The small man cocked his head and took a small step back. "You know my name?"

Henry said, "You're a gunman. Word gets around."

Orvis's smile appeared to wrestle between pride and confusion. More to himself than to anyone in particular he muttered, "How 'bout that? Elton Collins knows me." Orvis picked at a torn thumbnail for a moment, then his chest seemed to swell. "I been huntin' you since I was a boy. I wore out two horses and I rode my ass clean off trackin' you to the ends of the earth. Now I got you."

"Good thing he walked in though," a voice sounded from the far side of the room. "You ain't left this bar since spring."

Orvis whipped his head toward the sound. He extended his index finger like a gun, pantomimed pulling the trigger, then blew smoke from his fingertip. "You're a dead man, Trent. Right after I plant this feller."

In a soothing voice Henry said, "No need for shooting, son. I'm nothing more than a tumbleweed rolling through town, waiting to see where the wind will take me next."

Orvis reached out to a nervous-looking man who sat at a nearby table. He plucked the man's sweat-stained hat from his head, dropped it on the table, and tilted the man's chin so Henry could get a good look. "See this old drunk here? When you walked in, I heard him say you was Elton Collins. Now, he don't never say nothin' that makes no sense, but seein' as your buddy also named you, well now I got a whole new appreciation for this feller." Orvis slapped the man on the back of his head, then crushed his hat on the table.

The old man lowered his eyes and muttered, "Collins, I seen you do some handgun magic in Bozeman a long time ago. I thought you was dead nowadays, so I got a little excited when you come up for air. 'Course with this damn fool in the vicinity, I shouldn't a said nothin' to no one."

Orvis slapped the old man hard across the face, knocking him from the chair. "Enough of that mouth, you miserable old coot."

Henry Cole reached his left hand out and helped the man up. "Sorry for your troubles, friend."

The old man touched his cheek and glared at Orvis. "No harm done."

"No harm done, he says!" Orvis hooted. "We'll see about that."

Henry turned to Orvis. "Not that it's any of my business, but why are you tracking this Elton Collins fellow you keep mentioning?"

Orvis scowled. "You can call yourself Henry Cole until the moment you die, which won't be long now. We all know who you are, and you know what you done. You're the skunk who shot my father on a cattle drive. Tonight Elton Collins is going to die."

Henry said, "You're Pete Culhane's boy."

Orvis sneered. "Time you paid for what you did."

"You may not know the whole story, son. He drew first. Came down to him or me."

The slight man tried to hitch himself taller. "That don't make it any less wrong. Killin' my daddy, that's a dyin' offense."

"No need for anyone else to die," Henry said. *Especially you, Orvis. Because when you do, I become* me *again.* "Let me buy you that drink and we can both be on our way."

"No chance," Culhane growled through clenched teeth. "You think you're a legend. But I kill one, I become one. Orvis Culhane."

Henry shook his head. "Don't do it, Orvis. You won't end up famous at all. You'll end up dead."

"Wrong!" Culhane's pistol flashed upward.

His shot shattered the mirror behind the bar. Henry's bullet hit the man's second shirt button.

And Orvis Culhane's dreams of glory died with him on a saw-dust-covered barroom floor.

Purnell Boone slowly approached. "I didn't know you was *that* Elton Collins."

A weathered old-timer standing next to Boone muttered, "I heared about a feller name of that. Been a while. I figured you was dead and gone."

The man who'd first alerted the bar to Elton's presence stepped over to him. "Just like I saw you do in Bozeman all them years ago. You remember that one?"

Elton holstered his pistol. "I remember them all."

Like a ricochet his name skipped across the saloon and back.

Elton Collins.

The Elton Collins.

Elton eyed the door for a moment, but he knew leaving was futile. The past doesn't allow itself to be forgotten. Instead, he watched in silence as two men dragged Orvis Culhane's body from the bar.

Soon, a tall, angular man with a handlebar mustache and wearing a star elbowed his way toward Elton. "Sheriff Pat Delahanty," he said, making no effort to shake hands. "You that Elton Collins?"

"Only one I ever met," Elton answered.

Delahanty squinted. "You know what I mean. What I hear, Culhane started it and you finished it. You stick around till tomorrow morning and I'll dig into this a bit more. If I don't come up with anything that smells like dog crap on a sidewalk, you'll be on your way."

The next morning, Collins was waiting when Delahanty arrived to open the Sheriff's office.

"You in a rush?" Delahanty asked.

Collins thought about his brother's farm. "Train leaves at nine."

"Well now, hold on there. You and me can drink some coffee and chat a spell. I ain't talked to a famous shoot-'em-up artist before. Plus the paper editor in this town smells spilled blood better than he smells news. Believe he might want a crack at polishing your star to its former glory."

"For me, getting on that train will be glorious enough."

Delahanty said, "No promises about that. You have the locals yammering, I've got to tell you. On my way over here this morning I saw grandpappies telling grandbabies about you. Elton Collins was dead, buried and all but forgotten, and then last night you popped out of wherever you been hiding. Hell, I ain't heard about you in a coon's age myself. Must be you ride pretty low in the saddle."

"You see what happens when I don't. For years I had my own little corner of the world. I was out of the gun business."

"So you thought," Delahanty said. "In my line of work I've come to the realization that what a man is, he forever will be.

"Apparently so."

Delahanty's head jerked toward the street. He muttered, "Valencia Culhane is walking toward you right now. Orvis was her only child. You get right with Missus Culhane, boy. I got coffee to boil."

Elton watched as the small, dark-haired lady dressed in black slowly approached. In her left hand she held a worn Bible. Each step she took seemed to pain her more than the last. Her stooped appearance cloaked him with sadness. She was a widow and a grieving mother.

Both created by him.

When she was two paces away she stepped onto the boardwalk and turned dark, sad eyes toward him. "Elton Collins?"

"Yes, Ma'am."

Pain flickered across her face. "You killed my son and you killed my husband. You're a coldblooded bastard."

"I'm sorry, Ma'am."

She snorted. "Sorry is just a word to you. You want sorry? I'm the one who's sorry. Old women shouldn't be alone. They should watch their grandchildren play."

He murmured, "Yes, Ma'am."

She motioned him to come closer. "I didn't sleep a wink last night, thinking about how life is hard. And mine's about the hardest a body could get. But when the sun came up I realized it's harder when people hate one another." She tapped the Bible. "This book talks about forgiveness. So right here and now, I forgive you for killing them."

Forgiveness? Elton had never forgiven himself for a single life he'd taken. After each man he'd shot, he'd continually played the scene over in his mind. Men argued, they reached for their guns, the losers were dragged away.

But each man he'd bested had a family, and he'd changed the lives of those families forever. Fathers would never talk to their sons again. Mothers would not see them raise their own families. Children would never again feel a father's embrace.

Valencia Culhane's eyes drew him in. The eyes of a woman who, despite her pain, was willing to absolve him of his deed.

He stepped forward, his head bowed. "Thank you," he whispered.

She whipped a knife out from behind the Bible and slashed it toward his throat. Elton lunged away as the blade whistled past his face, barely missing his cheek. He kicked out one foot and hooked Valencia Culhane's front leg. He pulled back, yanking her down. She squawked as she thudded to the boardwalk. Dust puffed up from the dry boards when she hit.

"You bastard!" she screeched. "You killed my Orvis! I ain't done with you!"

Elton took a dozen quick steps away from her. Forget about finding forgiveness in this world, he fumed. Your best hope is to roll the dice with Saint Peter in the next.

Valencia Culhane pulled herself off the board sidewalk, slapped the dust from her dress and reached down and snatched up her Bible and the knife. She spit in Elton's direction, turned on her heel and limped up the nearly empty street.

—

"Russell, I'm tired a ridin'!" Earl said. "We ain't never gonna find nothin' out here in the boonies!"

Russell glared, for Earl had provided a steady string of complaints since they'd crested the ridge out of Hill City a day earlier. True, they had been riding almost non-stop, crisscrossing the ridge east to west and back again, working their way slowly north, with no sign of the Collins residence.

But he had reason to believe they were close.

Because he'd been told in general terms about the trail. And he'd seen some of the landmarks described to him.

"We're going to keep riding, and we're going to keep looking, damn you," Russell snapped, then saw the hurt in Earl's face.

He reined his horse in, dismounted, and motioned for Earl to do the same. "That girl with the gold hair is going to be your prize. But we have to find her first, and that's going to take some riding. Finding her is like mining. The harder you work, the more you get. Fair enough?"

Earl kicked at a loose stone near his foot. "Sorry, Russell. Jeez o'mighty, you know how I get."

"I know, Earlie. I know how you get."

While Russell made coffee, Earl led their horses to a small patch of dried grass and let them graze. When he returned, he squatted by the fire. "Russell, you think that gold-haired girl is really out here? I ain't never had a girl like her before. I get the used up no-goods."

Russell laughed. "Your class of women is about to improve." He surveyed the slight downslope of the ridge to the east of them. "Time we pushed closer to the valley. We can still go a piece before dark, and then we'll see what we see. I promise you one thing. I'm going to get you that girl, if it's the last thing I do."

CHAPTER 10

The eastbound stage rattled past fourteen-year-old Caleb Forrester as his tired, bony paint gelding plodded along the trail. A stage, Caleb thought, that's what he'd like to ride. Not a knock-kneed crowbait whose best days had ended the better part of a decade ago.

From up ahead, Uncle Zeke yelled out to him. "Boy, what you dreaming about now?"

Caleb pointed through the cloud of dust at the rapidly disappearing stage. "I was thinking that'd be a grand way to get to the mines, don'tcha think? A stage?"

Zeke looked at his brother Otto. "Big man, you ever rid a stage?"

Otto shook his shaggy mane. "Never rid. Drove one a time or two."

"Forgot that. So, I guess you could say you rid."

"Not a paying customer."

Zeke stared at his big brother. "Now, did I say anything about bein' a paying customer? I asked, you ever rid? Your answer, therefore, yes. Conversation, forthwith, done."

Otto clucked his tongue. "Verbal diarrhea, what Pop would call that."

"Who gives a shit?" Zeke burst into laughter. "Like that one? You said diarrhea, I said shit."

"Yeah, you're a hoot. People will pay to hear your jokes. But they'll pay you more to stay quiet."

As they prattled on, Caleb silently trailed. That's what traveling with his two uncles had been like since they'd left home. They'd get a thought going between them, and they would likely forget anyone else was around.

Mostly him.

Caleb figured they must be getting close to Lead. They'd left the farm town of Aberdeen two weeks earlier, full of piss and vinegar, with dreams of hitting it rich as miners. Zeke had big visions. Every night around the campfire he talked about how the Dakota hills had chunks of gold big as a boy's fist laying on top of the ground, waiting for folks to come along and pick them up.

Caleb didn't think it'd be that simple. But what choice did he have? No parents, no family to speak of but his uncles. So when they packed up, he packed up. When they stopped, he stopped. If they found chunks of gold waiting to be picked up, he'd pick them up. If he had to turn a drill while they swung a double jack, well he guessed he would do that too.

He looked to the west through the settling dust. Faintly, he could see a dark line of trees. The Black Hills. A few more days, from what his uncles said, and they'd be in the Land of Gold.

But it sure would have been nice to come rolling up in a stagecoach.

—

Sheriff Courtney Ballew shoved a stack of papers aside, retrieved a bottle of redeye from his desk drawer, and poured a healthy dose into the day's third cup of coffee.

Paperwork. That's what he hated most about this job, the damn paperwork. Vouchers to be signed. Prisoners to be watched. An office to run. And worst, dodgers to be reviewed.

He thumbed through the stack of dodgers he'd been largely ignoring. Each of them described a criminal and the act that they were purported to have committed, along with a reward, if offered, for their capture.

In two years as sheriff, Courtney Ballew had reviewed the many dodgers that floated across his desk. Of the criminals they described, he'd arrested exactly none.

Which hadn't done wonders for his reputation. Especially since he was following in the footsteps of the legendary Donovan McCready, who liked to brag that in his time as sheriff he'd brought over a dozen heinous criminals to justice. "Send me your dodgers, boys," he often crowed from his spot at the end of the Will o' The Wisp saloon, "and I'll bring you back your man, dead or alive."

After McCready had taken a bullet to the back of the head when he'd been caught fooling with a local businessman's wife, Ballew had been the town's next hire. And he saw things a tad differently than McCready. Ballew believed his job was to keep the peace. Keep drunken miners from smashing up the saloons. Keep horses and cattle from being stolen. Keep the mischief to a minimum. In a nutshell, keep his little town safe so the decent people of Hill City could walk the street.

Not to make a name for himself by riding the hills and trails from Sturgis to Rapid City trying to find some criminal who might be half way to Canada by now.

However, the people who'd hired Ballew strongly voiced their opinion on the matter. They'd taken a certain pride in McCready's renown, and now it was high time Ballew did the same. Because, as a local saloonkeeper had reminded Ballew on more than one occasion, 'We hired you to replace one helluva sheriff, and we can damn sure fire you and find a better one. Get you some criminals or we might.'

Ballew got the hint.

Review the dodgers, then find some criminals. Or find other work.

Ballew shuffled through the stack. A non-descript gang who'd hit a bank in Fargo and might have gone anywhere. A gunman who was rumored to have killed his way north from Abilene. Two sisters from Duluth who'd gotten in the habit of marrying and then burying rich husbands.

Three times each.

Two miners who'd killed a man and then fled from Lead.

Lead. Not twenty miles away.

Ballew read their description with increasing interest. One was tall and dark-haired, with a scar on the left side of his face. The other was, as the dodger's writer eloquently put, 'fair-haired and bigger than most.'

The description wasn't much.

But it was a reasonable approximation of a couple of boys who lived north of town.

Ballew pushed the dodger to the side and refilled his coffee cup. He reached for the redeye, thought a minute, and then closed the desk drawer.

Best to conduct this visit with a clear head.

CHAPTER 11

When the train reached Sioux Falls Elton found himself locked into his first challenge of the new day: horse-trading. What the hostler had as far as stock wasn't worth much in Elton's eyes, but the hostler felt differently.

"Naw," he said as he whirled a wad of tobacco in his mouth, "that fine lookin' buckskin you see before you, I don't imagine I can let him go for under forty dollars. And even then, I don't see much profit in it for me."

"Man's got to make a profit," Elton agreed. "Question is how much." He doubted the hostler had more than fifteen dollars invested in the half-blind gelding.

"Tell you what I'll offer," Elton said. "Twenty-five dollars, you throw in the tack, and I won't keep him much longer than a week. When I return I'll sell him back to you for twenty. Five dollars profit for you. Seems fair to me."

The hostler shot a stream of tobacco juice out the stable door. "Horse will be more used by then. Not sure I see the logic in that."

"Tell folks you doubled your money selling a horse to a feller who should have known better. Story only has to be partway true to be of value."

"Could be you got something there. Twenty-five buying from me, then twenty selling back to me?"

"That's a firm offer, friend."

The hostler chuckled. "Since we're such good friends and all, who can I tell folks I beat on this deal?"

"My name's Elton Collins."

The hostler gasped in a harsh breath, nearly choking on the tobacco. "You ain't that gunfighter, are you?"

Elton shrugged.

The hostler spit out the tobacco wad and anxiously wiped his hands on his shirt. "Here's what I'm gonna offer you if you think it's fair, Mister Collins. Now that buckskin, he ain't worth much, but you take him. You take him for as long as you need him and it won't cost you a penny. Long as you bring him back and he's still breathin', I think mebbe we got a deal. You think mebbe we got a deal?"

Elton didn't blink. "I think mebbe we do."

During the three-hour ride to Andrew's house, Elton thought about what he'd see. Fire, Nix had said. The place had burned to the ground. Nothing but rolling hills and scarce trees surrounded Andrew's homestead. Great for raising beef cattle, but poor if a man lost his house and needed to rebuild.

Lumber, especially out on the prairie, was a dear commodity in the Dakota Territory. True, lumber could be brought out from

Sioux Falls by the wagon load, but lumber cost money. And money to Andrew, as to Elton himself, had always been hard to come by.

They could make a dugout maybe, on the bank of a creek. Or a sod house to get them through the winter.

Elton nudged the tired horse with a spur. Whatever Andrew planned, it was his plan. Elton was just here to help.

As he rode over the final rise to his brother's land, he saw the last thing he expected to see.

Andrew's house and stable were intact.

No sign of fire.

No sign of damage.

Nothing.

A solitary figure walked from the house and headed toward the stable.

Andrew.

As Elton approached, Andrew offered him a wave. When Elton dismounted Andrew shook his hand, then gave him a hearty hug. "Good to see you, Henry Cole. Nice horse you have there."

Elton shook his head. "I'm back to Elton Collins again. And your place isn't burned down."

Andrew's brow wrinkled. "You sound disappointed."

"I don't understand," Elton said, after he'd joined Andrew and Millie at the pristine house's small table. "A messenger came to my house a few days ago. He delivered a telegram that said you'd lost your farm, and you wanted me to come out and help."

"As you can see," Andrew said as he swept his arm around the house, "that telegram was incorrect. Supposed to be from me, but it's not. Wonder who sent it."

"And the bigger question is why."

Andrew cleared his throat. "Even bigger question on my mind, Elton. Why, for all those years, you continued to pass yourself off as Henry Cole. Hell, when you were here with the family it was damn near impossible to remember what to call you. I was of half a mind to ignore you altogether on sheer principle."

Elton scratched his chin. "You know why. You've heard the stories as much as anyone has. Out here a man changes his name, maybe he's lucky enough to dodge his past."

Millie quietly said, "Amelia kept calling you Henry, that's what I dwell on the most. Does she know who she married? Does she know she married a gunman?"

Elton chewed on a biscuit before answering. "Never seemed like the right time to discuss."

Millie rose from her chair. It clattered as she shoved it against the table. Her tone was razor sharp. "She's spent twenty years thinking her name is Cole. She may have some hard questions for you, *Elton*." She quickly cleared the table. "Your girls may, too."

Andrew sighed after his wife left. "As you can tell, you changing your name has always bothered her. Mostly because of Amelia. It'd be one thing if you'd told her. But to never let her know… guess I'd want to know what you're hiding from. My money's on guilt."

"Can't shoot a brother when he hits the nail on the head."

Andrew drily said, "Not that you should feel obligated to admit it to me. Probably a few others who you owe an answer to, soon enough. I don't know much, but I know this. A smart man starts with his wife."

Elton walked to the stove and refilled his coffee cup. When he returned and sat he said, "I do believe you're right, brother."

Andrew stood and clapped him on the shoulder. "Been quite a day for you. You regained your name and impressive family lineage, and you found out someone sent you a fake telegram."

"Haven't gotten my mind around why a body would do that."

Millie had re-entered the house and now stood by the door. She said, "Not that I can offer this with any certainty, but it seems like someone wanted you here. Not there."

Elton's heart quickened. The meeting with Orvis Culhane? No, he believed that was a coincidence, nothing more. Then what? Not a thing about this trip had seemed out of place.

Nothing, really, that he'd even noticed.

Except the riders heading up the trail toward his house.

Elton jumped from his chair. As he strode to the door he slipped his gunbelt around his waist.

CHAPTER 12

Once a criminal's face or description makes it to a dodger he isn't normally receptive to a front-door drop-in from the local sheriff. Therefore, after Ballew headed north from Hill City, he chose a trail that led in the general vicinity of Lead. Once he passed Mooney Peak he veered off on an old, barely-visible Indian trail that followed Gold Dust Creek due west.

The trail meandered this way and that through heavy brush as it paralleled the creek bed. What could have been a two-hour trip if he'd stayed on the main road out of Hill City instead took him all morning. Midnight, the all-white stallion he'd raised from a colt, was bathed in sweat by the time Ballew saw the claim and reined in.

He pulled the dodger out of his pocket and read the description again. Not that it helped much, because what he really wanted to do was to hear their story. Find out if they'd been in the Lead mining camp earlier in the year. And maybe, if he asked the right questions or they were dumb as steers, he might learn that one of them had shot a man there. Or he could find that they were as innocent as newborn babies. Or he might learn that his specialty lay in carpentry or farrier work instead of keeping the peace.

Ballew tied Midnight to a tree about fifty paces behind the claim shack and slowly worked his way forward. He saw no smoke from the chimney. Nothing moved in the yard.

He pushed closer.

The corral was empty.

Irritated by the extra riding he'd done sneaking up on an apparently empty claim, Sheriff Courtney Ballew strode up to the tiny shack, pulled the door open, and peered inside.

Empty as well. Congealed grease pooled on the plates and the pan on the table.

Ballew tossed a grubby shirt off the one solid chair in the room and sat down to think this through. No saying these were the men he was looking for.

But in two years, they were the closest thing he had to a lead.

It was time to ride. He'd start by working his way east and south along the ridge that separated Hill City from Piedmont valley. And if a little good old fashioned luck was with him, he'd cut their trail, find them, and bring them in.

Because, after all, that's what the good citizens of Hill City paid him to be.

A sheriff like the late, great Donovan McCready.

CHAPTER 13

While Amelia was in the pantry making bread she could hear Marie push the broom around the front room. Very rapidly, like her daughter had somewhere to go and was in a rush to get there.

Marie soon stepped into the pantry. "I'm going up the ridge." She hesitated for a moment. "If it's okay."

Amelia pushed a loose strand of hair from her brow. It stubbornly fell back and she gave up, too tired to fight. "Be home before dark, dear."

Marie took the rifle and dashed out of the house.

Amelia remembered when she'd felt the first pangs of romance. A tall, quiet cowboy had ambled along the sidewalk in Dodge City, nearly knocking her down as he studied the horizon. His first words, "Excuse me, Ma'am," all flustered and shy, along with his searching, faraway eyes, were enough to make her heart trip.

And now, she was quite certain, Marie was experiencing the same thing. Over the last few weeks she'd noticed Marie fussing more over her hair and clothes, anxiously flitting around the house until her chores were over, and then finding any excuse to hike further up on the ridge.

Once or twice Amelia had thought about bringing it up with her daughter. Instead, she decided she would let Marie court in her own way and in her own time. When she was ready, she'd share it with her mother.

And then would come the hard part. When Marie would have to discuss it with her father.

Russell saw a flicker of movement through the shoulder-high pines dotting the outcropping of rock that overlooked the valley. Deer, he figured, for they'd seen over a dozen already today.

Then another flicker neared the first on the edge of a clearing.

A man.

Approaching a slim, blonde woman.

Russell held up his hand for Earl to stop, then pressed his finger against his lips.

"What is it?" Earl said, loud enough to drive a nearby crow into the air.

"Hush, you dummy!" Russell hissed. He pointed to the rocks. Soon the young man and woman wove their way around the boulders at the base of the outcropping and climbed onto the ledge.

"What they gonn do?" Earl asked.

"Guess if we watch for a spell we'll find out. You like watching?"

Earl blushed. "Not nearly as much as doin."

—

Weeks ago, the first kisses had been uncertain and probing, the kisses of two inexperienced people. Noses got in the way, hands were unsure, lips didn't know when to start and stop. Faces, red and flushed, jerked away, a mixture of shame, confusion and excitement.

But these kisses, delivered by confident, practiced lips, lingered.

Marie closed her eyes, breathless. This...this...this was almost... too good...to bear.

He ran his hand over the front of her dress.

He unbuttoned a button.

And another.

Marie's heart raced as a rising warmth built deep inside her.

She quivered as his hand slid up her thigh.

This time she rose to meet him.

While Caroline napped and Marie walked the ridge, Amelia dropped into the rocking chair and unwrapped a small package that she'd opened many times before.

It was a worn dime novel, titled Hell With A Gun.

She ran her fingers over the lettering.

The cover showed a gunfighter tying off a wound on one arm while preparing to fire his pistol at an unseen enemy.

Once upon a time, she'd have never given a book like this a second thought.

Until that day years ago when they were at Andrew and Millie's house and she'd been wandering near the barn and she'd overheard Andrew call her husband Elton.

Not Henry.

And then Millie had shown her a letter that Andrew had received from his father. While the letter itself made no mention of Andrew's last name, she'd briefly glimpsed the envelope as Millie had slipped the letter back inside.

It was addressed to Andrew Collins.

Not Andrew Cole.

Which would make her husband…Elton Collins.

The renowned gunman.

And, some would say, a murderer.

When she'd seen the dime novel at a mercantile a year or so later she'd almost overlooked it. The last thing she was interested in reading was a book titled Hell With A Gun.

Until she'd seen the subtitle: The Legend of Elton Collins.

She'd spent the thin coin that she kept in her purse as emergency money, took the book home and quickly read it from cover to cover.

The quiet Henry Cole she'd married, was he actually the famed gunman Elton Collins?

It seemed preposterous.

Then, over the years, she'd noticed how his eyes would scan the streets and rooftops as the family rode into town.

She'd seen his right hand hover at his hip, like he was reaching for a pistol, if a stranger approached. And from time to time she saw the look in his eye.

Hard.

Cold.

Ready.

And willing.

One day while sweeping the floor she'd stepped on a board near the fireplace. She'd never noticed anything special about this particular board before, or perhaps had never stepped on it just the right way, but that day it creaked and moved slightly. Not much, but enough.

Enough that she knew something was beneath it.

When curiosity wouldn't stop tantalizing her, she'd removed the board.

She'd found a burlap sack.

Opened it.

And stared at two pistols.

That's when she knew with complete and utter certainty that she wasn't Amelia Cole at all.

She was Amelia Collins.

And her husband was a killer.

Many times over the ensuing years she'd thought about discussing it with him. The times when, as he slept and her fingers found the numerous bullet scars marking his skin, she'd felt like taking his shoulders, shaking him and screaming 'Why did you do this to us?'

In the end she didn't have to ask. She determined that he'd changed his name to protect her and their children. And if he felt it was the right thing to do, she would support his decision. Until he mentioned it, she would call him Henry.

This Elton Collins of sensationalist dime novels? To her he was, as the subtitle said, a story meant to entertain others. A legend. Nothing more.

She gently wrapped the small book once again, placed it on her lap, and let out a sigh. Still no change in the Indian summer. While mornings remained cold, the daytime weather was comfortable enough for her to keep the front door open.

For the past week she'd been preoccupied by the thought of an early snow, and three days ago they'd had a light dusting on the pines. There had been barely enough to make a decent snowman, but she and Marie had scraped some together when they'd gone out to feed the livestock. Their pile of snow was mostly pine needles, and to Caroline's distress it had melted in the warm fall sun.

The rocker's slow movement was like the breeze: gentle, peaceful, seductive. The steady rhythm pulled her toward rest. Tiredness embraced her as she closed her eyes. She reached down to ruffle Rip's neck, but he wasn't beside her. He was probably out chasing rabbits or playing in the creek.

The creek would be nice right now, water babbling over the stones and past towering oaks and pines. Down by the big rock, that's where she should be. Lying in the tall grass, napping, drifting, and feeling the warm sun caress her.

A light breeze puffed in through the front window and flitted the hair from her brow.

CHAPTER 14

Amelia snapped awake. She glanced at the closed front door. It had been open when—

A man's voice from behind her made her jump from the rocker. "I don't think your girl is coming back. Maybe she ran off with that boy she's fooling with."

Amelia whipped her head around and saw two men standing by the door leading into the girls' bedroom.

The man who spoke wore a filthy shirt that might once have been white, with a filthier vest over it, and a half-crushed derby hat. His eyes were flat black, accentuated by high cheekbones, which made his eyes appear to be buried deep within smoldering pits. A dark scar ripped up one side of his gaunt face.

The other man was massive.

He was terrifying.

He was between her and Caroline.

Amelia lunged toward the bedroom, but the scar-faced man stepped toward her and jammed his hand into her chest, stopping her. "Uh-uh, Miz Collins. Only thing you need to go into that bedroom for is to shuck your drawers for me, and you'll do that soon enough."

Her heart galloped as she saw the man sneer.

Time. She needed time. Time to allow for something good to occur. As much time as she could steal from them.

She briskly turned away and went to the stove. "My name is Mrs. Cole, gentlemen. I believe you've made a mistake. Luckily I made stew enough for everyone. Would you care to join us for dinner?"

The scar-faced man snickered. "Gentlemen? You overestimate us, lady. But since you're trying so hard, this here's Earl, and I'm Russell. You're going to get to know me real good in a couple of minutes. And Earl here, he's going to get to know your daughter. If you know what I mean." His harsh laugh assaulted her.

Russell looked around the house, peeking in cupboards and scouting the pantry. "Huh," he said when he finished, "don't see hide nor hair of your husband anywhere. Earl, you see Elton Collins anywhere?"

The big man shrugged. "Last time I saw him was drinking it up at the bar in Hill City a couple of days ago."

"Come to think of it, I saw him there too," said Russell. "Now what on earth do you think would make a man such as him leave his family at the drop of a hat?"

Earl shrugged. "Hard tellin'."

"How about you, Miz Collins? You think a telegram saying his brother's farm burned down might do the trick?"

Amelia's hand flashed to her mouth.

"See," Russell said, leaning against the table, "you don't ever know who's sending the damn things. You just...don't...know." He stared at Amelia. "Do you, Miz Collins?"

Her stomach churned. "My husband is Henry Cole, and he will be back tonight. Now I'm sure you're hungry, so let me feed you and then you can be on your way." She reached for a bowl.

Russell barked a laugh. "I'm hungry all right, but I don't think we're talking about the same thing. And Earl here, he's hungry for the girl with the long hair. 'Course, you'll note when you see her that she may be walking a mite funny, what with that boy cracking her the way he did. I thought wolves howled loud. I'm surprised you didn't hear her yourself."

Amelia snapped, "How dare you say that about my daughter?"

Russell threw up a hand. "I know how you feel, you being a momma and all, but I'm telling you what we saw. Now, I wonder where she learned those woman tricks from?"

He stepped behind her and wrapped his left arm around her waist, and then grasped her right wrist with his free hand. He slid his head beside hers and whispered to her, "Maybe she learned those tricks from you. How about you demonstrate so we can judge you against your girl?" He ran his tongue along her neck. "Best one lives."

She could smell his sweat-crusted filth, could feel his unshaven face scraping hers. His breath reeked.

It was inevitable, what would happen next.

She hoped Caroline would stay asleep.

Russell turned to Earl. "The girl will be here soon. Now scram. I have some work to do. On Miz Collins here."

Earl dutifully nodded and walked out the front door.

—

Marie thought about what she and Ben had done. The kisses, the caresses. Him unbuttoning her dress. And then…then they'd found a small patch of grass on top of the ledge. They'd kissed some more.

He was persistent.

And she didn't say no.

Her mind spun. They were in love, so it was right. They weren't married, so it was wrong. When they'd been together it was wonderful. When they were done they could hardly look at each other.

What had they done?

What had *she* done?

Marie froze at the edge of the clearing. Two unfamiliar horses were tied outside the corral. Visitors were uncommon here away from the valley, and other than Mister Nix she couldn't remember the last time someone had ridden to see them. Certainly no one had ever come without her father present.

Goose bumps popped up on her arms. This didn't feel right. And as her father had often told her, when something doesn't feel right, it probably isn't.

She walked closer to the horses to read their brands. As she did, a stick snapped behind her. She spun around as a large man approached, pointing a pistol at her. "Drop the rifle now and we'll all be happier," he ordered.

She froze. He was huge. He was the biggest man she'd ever seen.

But size didn't matter. She had a rifle. She jerked it to her hip and pointed it toward him.

She pulled the trigger.

Nothing.

She hadn't pulled the hammer back.

The man grasped the barrel and twisted the rifle away. He placed it against the corral fence, stepped between it and Marie, and smiled. "What's your name?"

Mutely, she shook her head, her voice gone, her stomach knotted. *Aim. Pull the hammer back. Then pull the trigger.*

One more chance. Give me one more chance, she thought.

Her gaze flickered to the rifle.

He shook his head. "Can't let you have that, miss. You totin' around a gun, someone might get hurt. Like me. You don't wanna say your name, you don't hafta. So you know, I'm Earl, and you're mine."

The rifle.

Back at Earl.

The rifle. Three quick strides and she'd have it. And this time she'd get it right.

Aim.

Pull the hammer back.

Pull the trigger.

If she couldn't get to the rifle, there was a pistol in the pantry. All she had to do was get to the house before he did. She glanced at the closed door.

The man shook his head. "Your momma's inside with Russell." He reholstered his pistol and moved closer to her. "Maybe she got kinda lonely with your daddy gone."

Earl seized her arm, then pulled her to him. "You know what I mean by kinda lonely?"

As she started to scream, he clamped his hand firmly over her mouth, mashing her lips into her teeth. "Let's not be yellin' now."

He jerked his head toward the house. "Momma's got enough problems of her own."

He ran his hand over Marie's hair. "You're even more prettier than when I seen you in town. Sweet as a little baby."

Marie drove her fist into his groin.

Cursing, he lost his grip. She dove for the rifle, but Earl snagged the end of her braid as she went by, spinning her around.

The ribbon he held onto slipped from her braid, and she was free. "Momma!" she cried, running for the house. "Momma!"

Before Marie reached the front door Earl threw a huge arm around her.

"No!" she yelled. "Let me go!" Marie wildly thrashed against him. Reaching for his head, she found a shock of his hair and yanked.

Earl backhanded her.

Stars exploded in her brain, and her knees buckled. "Momma?" she whimpered.

He moved his arm around her throat and held it tight. "None of that fightin's gonna work. But you wanna go inside so bad, go. That's where I want you anyway." He pushed the door open and shoved Marie in.

As she stumbled into the front room she saw Caroline standing by the table, stock-still, eyes wide.

"Marie," she whimpered.

Marie sprinted to her and scooped her up.

"Carrie, Carrie," she whispered, stroking her hair. "It's all right."

Then Earl caught Marie once again, knocking Caroline from her arms. Caroline hit the floor crying and scampered to the corner, thumb crammed in her mouth, as Earl dragged Marie to the bedroom.

CHAPTER 15

Marie screamed as she saw Russell on her mother. "Get off her!" She lunged toward him, but Earl hooked his arm around her waist and held her as she beat her fists against him.

Russell looked up. "Throw that girl on the bed beside us!" he yelled. "We can ride them side by side."

Earl looked into Marie's eyes and then stammered, "No. I changed my mind. I don't wanna ride her. I just wanna touch her." His fingers found Marie's wildly-flying hair and pulled it taut as she fought against him. "It's okay. I ain't gonna hurt you."

"You big dummy!" Russell howled, climbing off Amelia. "Do I have to tie her down? Is that what it's going to take for you to lay with this girl?" He stood up, grabbed Marie's arm, yanked her away from Earl, and threw her on the bed. Then he slipped behind Earl and shoved him, causing him to topple onto Marie.

"Now either you get your ass to humping or get the hell out of the way so I can."

Howling with fury, Amelia leaped at Earl and bit his hand.

He ripped his hand from her mouth and shoved her off the bed. Amelia cursed as she hit the floor.

Earl tried to roll off Marie, but Amelia jumped onto his back and pounded on his head with her fists.

Russell took Amelia by the hair and tried to pull her off.

Fighting to stay on Earl's back, Amelia dug her fingers into his face.

Into his eyes.

Bellowing, Earl spun and threw himself backward against the wall, crushing Amelia against it. Her bones snapped like tree branches in the wind.

She crumpled to the bed, lifeless.

Russell stared at her for a moment, then shouted, "Look what you did, you idiot!"

Blood seeped through the bodice of her dress and oozed from her shattered skull.

"Jeez o'mighty!" Earl shouted. He struggled to get as far from the dead woman as he could.

Marie recoiled in horror. She dove off the bed and curled up in the corner, arms wrapped around her knees.

She made herself smaller.

Smaller.

But she couldn't get small enough to disappear.

Russell pulled up his pants. Rape was one thing, but murder was worse. He looked at the woman on the bed. She wouldn't tell a soul about either crime.

But the girl could. He pulled his knife from its scabbard and started toward her as she cowered in the corner.

Earl blocked his path. "No. You said she could be mine."

Russell snapped, "Since she saw you murder her momma, I changed my mind."

"It wasn't murder. It was a accident, and that's different." He looked at Marie. "It was a accident." Earl started to cry.

"Call it what you want, you killed the woman. Now I'm going to kill this one. Then the little one."

"But wait," Earl said, wiping his nose on his sleeve. "You promised me I could have a girl one day. And I want this one."

Russell exploded. "That promise doesn't count! We're going to kill her before she tells someone what happened!"

Earl turned to Marie. "If you tell, Russell's gonna kill you. If you don't tell no one, he won't. So you ain't gonna tell, are you?"

Marie whipped her head from side to side. "I won't tell, I promise. Please don't hurt my sister."

"See? She won't tell. So now she's mine. She'll be like another Loretta."

"Damn you, Earl! Why'd you have to mention Loretta?"

Earl smiled. "'Cause this girl looks like her. She's pretty as a angel, like Loretta was." He reached out and stroked Marie's hair.

Russell laughed. "Well, she isn't going to look quite so angelic when I'm done with her." But she wasn't half bad now, he had to admit. And women, especially young ones, were worth something out here.

Twice before he'd swapped females he'd acquired for one thing or another. The first was an Indian squaw he'd won in a card game four or five years ago. He traded her to an old mountain man for a buffalo hide and some beaver pelts. Later on he heard the mountain man had gotten his throat slashed when he'd tried to lay with her.

Which sometimes happened with squaws.

The second time was a girl, barely knee-high to a grasshopper, who they'd found last year wandering around the prairie, crying for her parents. He and Earl had seen their scalped bodies and burned wagon about a half-mile back.

He traded her to a crazy Frenchman for a half-decent mule. No questions asked.

Loretta, though, had been different.

Russell leaned against the doorframe.

Loretta Marsh.

From the moment he'd seen her bathing in the creek so many years ago, her body the color of cream and her golden hair dancing in the breeze, he couldn't imagine a day without her. He was positive she'd known he'd been hiding in the bushes, for she'd slyly looked his way and smiled broadly. She'd boldly stood there in her nakedness, and he'd never seen a more beautiful creature.

The next week he'd met her at a dance and he'd found enough words to talk to her and then she'd danced with him and then they met for coffee and pie and finally one day he met her parents.

He never knew what she saw in him. But it was something.

She must have been something. Because she'd said yes.

Of all the men in the world, she'd said yes to him.

And then she was his.

Until she wasn't.

Loretta Marsh.

And him.

Earl.

And Marie Collins.

Damn it all to hell.

Russell slapped at the doorframe as he walked out. "You cause me enough headaches for three men. We aren't bringing the little one, so don't even ask. She can stay in this house till she rots."

Earl pulled Marie to her feet and gently led her to the door. "Sorry about killin' your momma. Sometimes I have accidents."

Russell yelled, "You aren't courting her! Get her out here now." He stormed out of the house and headed toward the corral.

As she got to the kitchen Marie spotted Caroline, still in the corner, whimpering. "Wait, my sister," she pleaded.

Earl immediately let her go.

Marie hurried to the stove. She ladled Caroline a bowl of stew and put it on the table. She motioned and Caroline walked to her, thumb still jammed in her mouth, unable to take her eyes off Earl.

"It's okay, Carrie baby," Marie cooed, trying her best to sound calm. "Now, you go to bed after you eat."

Caroline nodded slightly, her eyes watery. "Where's Momma?"

Marie cupped her sister's face in her hands. "Momma is…Daddy will be home soon."

Caroline spoke around her thumb. "Daddy home thoon?"

"Yes, baby." Marie bent down to kiss her sister's forehead.

Earl tugged her away. "That's enough. We gotta go, or Russell will be mad."

"Wait! You can't leave my mother in there for Caroline to find!" Caroline began to whimper.

Earl glanced at the bedroom door, then at Marie. "No tricks?"

"No tricks."

Earl dropped her arm. "Stay here," he said and returned to the bedroom.

98

Marie pulled Caroline close to her. The little girl wrapped her arms around Marie's leg.

When he did, Marie noticed the small package on the floor near her mother's chair.

It was something she'd never seen before.

It was a piece of her mother.

She slipped it into her dress pocket. Then she pulled Caroline near the fire, warily watching the front door. "Carrie, you don't go outside for anything, you hear? You wait for Daddy. He'll be here soon." She prayed it would be soon enough.

Caroline buried her face hard against Marie's chest.

Marie stroked her sister's curls.

What if he doesn't get here in time?

Marie forced the thought from her mind. And after he found Caroline he would come find her.

If you're still alive. So do something about it.

She found a small piece of charred wood and ran it over her favorite stone on the hearth.

"Get your ass moving," Russell shouted as the front door banged open.

Marie jumped and nearly knocked Caroline over, causing her to cry again.

"And where is Earl?" Russell yelled, looking around the front room.

"He went out the back door and took my mother outside," Marie whispered, tears choking her voice. "I don't want Caroline to find her."

Russell rolled his eyes. "Dead is dead." He took two long strides and caught her by the hair, and then pulled her out the door with him as Caroline wailed, "Marie!"

CHAPTER 16

Russell was looking for a place to spend the night. The knot in Marie's stomach tightened. She would be alone with these men.

She knew what they wanted.

She'd seen Russell with her mother.

Right before Earl had killed her.

Tears welled in her eyes and everything blurred. Unable to see, she rode directly into a heavy pine bough that swept her off Junie's back. She slammed to the ground and her breath was driven from her lungs. The frightened mare skittered away.

Russell chased Junie down and led her back to Marie. He dismounted his horse, handed her the reins, and then booted her in the behind, knocking her to the ground again. "You fall off that horse again and I'm going to whip you another ass split. You got it?"

Sniffling, she remounted the horse and trailed Russell.

Earl rode closer to her. "You okay?"

She stared at a spot between Junie's ears and continued to ride.

They made camp at the edge of a meadow surrounded by towering pines.

Marie numbly nodded as Russell yelled at her to get off the damn horse. As she dismounted, the vision of her mother's twisted, broken body nearly paralyzed her.

Limp.

Naked.

Dead.

Russell made Marie cook salt pork, beans and fry bread for dinner. When she bent over the fire, he lifted the back of her dress.

He laughed as she spun away. "Fun's just begun, little lady."

Terrified about what would happen next, Marie timidly served the men and then filled her own plate. She doubted she could stomach a bite.

They would attack her once supper was over.

She forced herself to slowly chew each morsel, though the food tasted like sawdust and swallowing was almost impossible. But every second she ate was another second they left her alone.

She choked down forkful after slow forkful, trying to avoid Russell's glowering stares. His black eyes smoldered, and his face looked like a mask as firelight flickered across it.

The devil himself sat five steps away.

Russell laughed, long and harsh. "You keep pushing your chow around the plate if you think it'll help any. Me, personally, I don't think it will."

Marie tore her eyes from him and looked at Earl. He waved, a silly grin plastered on his face.

Three thoughts battled in her brain. She had to get away. She had to get back to Caroline.

They will rape me.

Russell cleared his throat. "Go ahead and finish that last bite, girl," he said. "I'm getting tired of waiting."

She shook her head. "No. You won't touch me."

He jumped to his feet, snatched the plate from her hands, and dumped the food on the ground. "You don't say no to me. You never say no to me." He shoved the plate at her. "Now clean up this mess so we can have some fun."

Her stomach churned as she cleaned the plates. She dawdled over the final one, drawing out the inevitable, for this plate was her final defense, the one thing keeping them from her.

Yet finally it was clean. She placed it with the others.

She expected them to attack her immediately, but instead Earl went behind a bush to relieve himself while Russell moved the horses so they could graze.

Run? Now?

Run!

Marie dashed away from the fire and into the woods like a frightened rabbit. She wove through the trees in the near dark, pushing through spruce branches and dodging boulders as she followed a small stream.

She could get away. She would get away.

She would run forever. She would run herself to death, if that's what it took, before they—

She tripped over a root and sprawled face first onto the ground.

Then Russell was on her. He flipped her over, driving her spine against the point of a rock. He leaned in close and whispered,

"Oh, so you wanted to do it here instead? Why, all you had to do was say so."

Marie hurled herself against him, trying to get free. But his weight bore down on her, driving the rock into her back.

Finally, she couldn't move at all. Like her mother, she would die at the hands of these men. Horrified, she screamed.

"Go ahead, girlie," Russell said, "I kind of like to make women holler."

Marie clamped her mouth shut and violently shook her head.

"Stubborn, are you?" Russell said, "Okay, I'll make you beg for mercy instead."

Then, painfully, he was in her. Each thrust drove the rock into her back. Closing her eyes, she focused on that. A sharp pain in her back. Another pulse of pain.

Another.

Another.

It was the rock digging into her back, and nothing else.

Nothing else...except for the man who was...

No.

The rock.

Nothing else.

Nothing else.

Please don't let it be anything else.

When he stopped, Russell split her lip with a backhand. "You run again, you'll have more than me to worry about. Look at my face!" He grasped her jaw and forced her to stare at him.

He ran his finger along his scar. "You run and I'll do the same to you. Then you can see your mistake in the mirror every day till you die. Got it?"

That night as Marie tried to sleep, pain seared from the raw spot on her back and between her legs.

But the biggest pain was the one crushing her heart, screaming at her, berating her.

You had the chance to escape.

She closed her eyes and saw the moment again. Earl had walked away from the camp, humming something she didn't recognize. Humming like he was happy.

Russell had ambled over to move the horses.

Run!

You had one thing to do, her inner voice intoned. *One thing. Run away. If you'd done that correctly, you wouldn't be laying here now, bleeding on your underclothes.*

But...

You had a rifle in your hands at the house and you forgot to pull the hammer back. You let Earl kill your mother. You left your sister to die. And then you fell down and let yourself get raped.

Yes.

She stifled a sob before it escaped. Before it became a scream.

But maybe...

Could she run now? She squinted through the near-dark. While Earl snored, Russell lay soundlessly on his back, hat pulled low.

Like a rattler staring at her from under a bush, she could feel his eyes on her from under his hat brim. Daring her to try.

She could still smell his foul breath. Could still see his blank, black eyes. Eyes that showed nothing, except for hate.

Hate for her.

Why?

In the end, she reasoned, it didn't matter. She had one job.

Stay alive.

Everything else will follow.

She reached into her dress pocket and ran her fingers over the wrapped package she'd taken from the house. If it was important enough for her mother to keep, it was important enough for Marie to protect, too.

In the dark, quiet evening she wanted to see her mother's treasure.

But if Russell saw it, he'd take it. Then it'd be gone forever.

So she would wait. For an eternity, if that's how long it took, she would wait.

Then one day when this ended, when she was safe, she would look at it.

If this is ever ends, you mean. Because it may not.

Marie tucked the package away and turned on her side, shielding herself from Russell.

She gingerly slid her hand between her legs.

Still bleeding.

The fire burned lower, and she pulled the blanket up around her shoulders. The men couldn't see her, not now.

Thank God. Because she couldn't be strong anymore. Soundlessly, she cried for Caroline, who would die next, alone in their cabin. She cried for her mother, who'd been humiliated, violated, and then killed by these same men.

And the deepest sobs she saved for last. Heart wrenching, body shaking, seemingly endless, for her own shattered soul.

CHAPTER 17

In some ways the ache in Nix's head had improved, for it no longer felt like tacks had been hammered into his brain.

But in other ways it was worse. For while the sharpness of the pain had reduced in intensity it had settled deeper into his skull, like a badger holed up during a blizzard.

Like it meant to stay for a while.

Maybe till the end.

And if it kept up, if the ache kept washing over him in nauseating waves, the end might not be too far off.

Even if he had to arrange it himself.

The wind picked up, tearing through the pines and nearly extinguishing his small fire. Teeth chattering and head drumming, Nix hunched over it, cursing. He hadn't eaten today and, if he hadn't been lucky enough to find a couple of matches in the bottom of his pack, he'd be freezing to boot.

He pulled his coat tighter and tried to find protection against the wind's bitter bite. As the flames writhed against the gusts he thought about his last hot meal and warm bed the previous night at Hanson's. Where he could be right now, if he wasn't such a damn fool.

After he was sure Elton Collins had left Hill City he'd gone back to a lonely shack he'd called home since Ingrid had died, and he'd waited.

Won't be more than three days, he'd been told. You wait, and we'll find you.

Dutifully he'd waited, three days and then another. That was all he could stand in the shanty's walls that had always seemed too confining.

It was a house, but it had never been a home.

A home had a wife and children, maybe a dog. A home had laughter and love. A home you looked forward to returning to each time you were away.

A house, on the other hand, would not miss you. In fact, it would never even know you were gone.

After he left the shanty he found himself back at the Hanson, where after a night's stay he'd weighed his options. Stay in this little bit of a town and wait to see what life would offer next, or ride on to some unknown future?

He rode.

Now he was here. On the backside of nothing.

Thinking about opportunities lost.

And others gained.

CHAPTER 18

Yes, Ma'am," Ben called to his mother. "Be right there." He wrestled to pull on his britches, and then donned his shirt. As he did he glanced out the window. Snow. He studied his father's tracks to the barn. It looked like an inch or two, not a lot, but enough to remind him that winter was nearly here. He thought of Marie and wondered how much snow they had gotten. He would go to the high spot on the ridge today if the snow wasn't too deep. With luck he'd find her there.

His mother called again. "These biscuits are hot, Ben, and Pa's here. Time to eat."

"Yes'm," he yelled. He pulled a comb through his hair, then dashed into the kitchen.

After they were seated, his father took a long sip of coffee and studied him. "Benjamin, eat up. Today we'll go to Sturgis."

Ben blurted, "Why are we going to Sturgis?"

His mother set a plate of biscuits and bacon at the table. "We're low on supplies. And one storm leads to another, as my mother always said."

Ben's heart sank for a moment, and then he brightened. "Pa, I can stay behind and tend the stock."

His father pursed his lips. "You've been tending Skipper a little too much lately for my liking, riding up on the ridge every free moment. You like to ride, so today you'll ride with your mother and me to Sturgis." His father pushed back his plate, slipped his coat from a hook by the door and left to hitch the wagon.

His mother stepped close to him. "She's not going anywhere."

"Her? Who? What?"

She laughed. "Now, you don't think your father and I are total fools, do you? What's the one thing that takes a boy from his mother? Another woman. And you've been going away from your mother for over a month now." She ruffled his hair and gave him a kiss on the top of his head. "You're courting Marie Cole. You picked a pretty one."

Marie shook the snow from her blanket and blinked at the brilliant white sheet that covered the forest. When looking at it from inside her home, a fresh coat of snow looked beautiful. When properly dressed, she enjoyed a brisk winter walk through the woods.

Today, the snow just made her cold and wet. She touched her hair and felt an icy crust. She pulled the blanket tighter, wishing for a coat. And mittens.

And to be home.

And not to be raped ever again.

Earl fired a thunderclap sneeze as he stirred the coals. "Jeez o'mighty it's cold! Ain't it, Russell? Russell?"

"What?"

"Jeez o'mighty, it's cold! Ain't you cold?"

"Yeah, I'm cold. Now why do you think that is?"

Earl's eyes slowly lit. "'Cause I ain't got the fire goin' yet."

"No you don't. And the more you flap your trap, the longer it takes. Right?"

"I'll get it goin' right now." Earl spun around to look at Marie. "Jeez o' mighty, ain't you cold?"

She stared at him and shrugged.

Earl cocked his head and stepped toward her. "Jeez o' mighty, ain't you?"

Russell quickly walked over to her, took her elbow and turned her away from Earl. "Some things get stuck in his brain and he can't make them stop. Answer him or he'll keep asking."

Flustered, Marie blurted, "I'm real cold, Earl." She threw a glance at Russell.

Earl smiled happily. "So am I. But I'll get this fire goin' right now, and we'll be warm. Okay?"

Marie offered him a confused shrug. As she did, Russell leaned close to her. She recoiled.

"Relax, the only thing you're worth to me this morning is to make the coffee and fry some bacon." He rose to walk away, then turned to her. "You take a squat behind that bush, and then fix us some grub."

Russell watched Earl fuss with the coals, but he couldn't raise a flame. He took Marie's arm and pointed her toward the fire. "You have a new job. Keep that fire going at night. You let it die out, I'll cut your throat. Simple as that. Now go. Squat. Then cook."

—

As Marie slipped behind a bush Russell thought about the mess they'd gotten tangled up in. Like cutting the lead steer from a herd of cattle he'd wanted to get Amelia first, and then take the girl when she came back to the house. One at a time, they'd be easier to handle. But he hadn't counted on the woman fighting back, and he damn sure hadn't counted on Earl splitting the mother's head open. In all these years, one thing about Earl though, if there was a way to foul a good thing up, he surely would.

Like getting in the fight at the mining camp, where one man didn't walk away.

Exactly like that.

He stared at the cold coffee pot. It wasn't going to make itself, and the girl was behind the bush. He peered at her, still squatting down. Christ, how long did it take a woman to piss? Grumbling, he stomped over to the fire, pushed Earl out of the way, and angrily worked the coals.

Marie approached the fire. "Hey you," Russell said, "when's your Daddy supposed to come home?"

"I'm not telling you anything." Marie's eyes burned into his.

Russell swung the coffee pot at her, barely missing her chin as she fell back onto the snow. He kicked her in the ribs, causing her to cry out.

Earl stepped toward her, but a glare from Russell stopped him in his tracks.

Russell hovered over Marie and said, "You ready to answer my question now?"

She squirmed away from him.

"When's your Daddy coming home?"

Through gritted teeth she said, "He was supposed to be gone a couple of weeks. Less than a week to go, I think."

Russell whistled. Less than a week. Now that was motivation.

CHAPTER 19

Elton stood at the Sioux Falls train station, anxiously waiting for westbound train to arrive. Someone wanted him away from his home. And right now he was hundreds of miles away, staring at an empty train track.

Two riders heading up the trail might not mean anything. It's not like it was a private trail that went straight to his house. It went hither and yon, forking in a dozen places, and only one of the forks led anywhere near his family.

But someone had sent a telegram, posing as his brother. When Elton had gone to the telegraph office this morning they told him they had no record of a telegram being sent from someone claiming to be Andrew Cole. Or Collins, for that matter.

"Someone sent me a telegram," Elton had said. "Of that I'm sure."

The agent smiled thinly. "Perhaps if you could show me this telegram, sir, I could tell you from where it originated. This may help solve your mystery."

Nix said he was carrying a telegram from Andrew, and Elton had believed him. But he'd never actually seen it.

If Nix had lied about the telegram, what else had he lied about?

Elton checked the train tracks again. Then, resigned, he walked to a restaurant on the corner for some apple pie. He lingered as long as he could over two cups of coffee, standing from time to time to look at the empty train station.

"It'll get here when it does, sir," said his waitress, a short, round woman with a missing front tooth. "Staring won't get it here any faster."

But moving around gave him something to do. He paid her, then walked into the station to check on the train's arrival.

"I know as much about the train now as I did the last time you checked. It' isn't here," the ticket agent said. "You'll know when it's here about the same as I do. In fact, the whole town will know."

Elton found a bench outside the town doctor's office. His eyes continually drifted to his pocket watch. Each minute ticked by as if it didn't want to leave.

"No good staring at it," he finally grumbled. He pocketed the watch.

A well-dressed man with a gray mustache, wearing a black top hat, was seated nearby. He stopped reading his newspaper, folded it, and stared Elton's way.

Elton's mind swam as he studied the face, trying to locate some flicker of remembrance from his past.

Finally the man stood up and walked over. "I hear you were resurrected two days ago. Word of your deed travels fast, Elton Collins. The legendary gunman is thus reborn."

114

"My name is Henry Cole," Elton said as he pulled out his watch and checked it again.

The man reached for Elton's shoulder. "I dare say you don't remember me, gunman, but nonetheless I remember you. I'm Perry Joyce, erstwhile author. While my visage may be a mystery to you, many years ago I made you. And as a consequence, I can say you made me.

"There are some in my field," Joyce said, then dramatically cleared his throat, "who believe the storyteller deserves equal renown, for the skill is not solely in the deed performed, but how the deed is subsequently told. The storyteller is the magician who creates the illusion. And my illusion, Hell With A Gun, was you."

Elton looked long at the man. "You wrote the story about me and the Callahan brothers down on the Brazos."

Joyce's eyes seemed distant. "It was dead summer and hot as the south side of Hades. Can you feel, as I still can, the sun baking the ground around us? The way it assaulted those who dared stray from the shadows? Not a breath of wind. Not a bird flying by, not a dog daring to pant as you strode around the corner to shape your fate."

Elton evenly said, "I was there."

"Of course you were, and you were no more than a fuzzy-cheeked lad who stood his ground against two fearsome gunmen. Yet you, in your indomitable, unconquerable way, dispatched them post-haste. Fastest gun in Texas, that's what I called you. But in the years since, I realized I cast you woefully short. You are the fastest I've ever seen, before or since."

Elton grimaced. "I wish you'd kept that to yourself."

"Come now," Joyce scoffed as he stroked his mustache. "Don't be so modest. I made you famous."

"You made men dead. Without you no one would have known who I was, and I could have lived a life of anonymity. There would have been no victims."

Joyce pivoted on his heel, his arms extended heavenward, and spoke to the horizon. "Anonymity, from the Greek word *anonymia*, meaning without a name. Of course this could no longer be the case when I penned your exploits, for I design castles and monoliths. I create majestic vistas. I construct a playground for the Gods. And, dare I say, it is ultimately me who defines legends. All with the scratch of a pen, good sir. Hence with the gift of my humble prose, I constructed the man who stands before me now." Joyce again touched Elton's shoulder.

Elton jerked away, eyeing the handful of people who had stopped and were now watching them. "And when you created *that* Elton Collins with your 'humble prose,' what do you think happened? Men chose to prove themselves against me."

Joyce clucked his tongue and sadly shook his head. "You'll have to explain the harm in a man seeing an obstacle, measuring it, and accepting a challenge. The greater the obstacle, the greater the reward. It is, after all, the conquering of challenges in life that makes men truly great."

Elton warily glanced at the street, where more people had gathered. "I would like to leave now," he said, edging away from Joyce.

"Nonsense," Joyce crowed. "Let the onlookers celebrate the rebirth of my greatest creation." He faced the crowd. "Ladies and gentlemen, I ask that you lend me your ears and pay witness to a ghost resurrected. His is a name that once rested upon the lips of your fathers. Perchance even you yourself have whispered it in reverence and awe. Please honor, with your applause and kind consideration, the legend immortalized in a factual account of his heroic deeds, penned incidentally by yours truly. He is the man forever known as Hell With A Gun, Elton Collins."

Gasps flickered through the crowd, and the buzzing of voices quickly ratcheted louder.

A brave few stepped forward. Two women timidly reached out to touch his sleeve.

When Elton pulled his arm away they recoiled, blushing.

Joyce faced Elton. "There, you see? Fame is beautiful. Fame is glorious. Fame is wonderful." He theatrically waved his arm past the audience. "Look at those faces, Elton Collins. How many of them would absolutely kill to switch places with you right now?"

Elton's eyes swept the crowd, left to right.

And stopped part way. "I count two."

The men elbowed their way forward, stopping less than ten paces from Elton. The redhead spoke first. "Hey, Rupert! I see somethin' older'n dirt."

"That's nothin', Cory. I see somethin' older'n them fellers in the Bible."

"Well I see somethin' older'n your mama."

"Well, I see somethin' older'n the crust in yer drawers."

Cory pulled on his hat brim. "Now that," he loudly said, "is pretty danged old."

Rupert said, "My pops used to talk about you. He's been dead a long while."

"Pleasure to meet you, boys," Elton said, "but it's time for me to get on that train and go back in my little hidey-hole."

Cory rubbed his chin. "I don't see that happenin'. 'Cause I don't like the look a that gun on your hip, gramps. You're carryin' it as if you think you remember how to use it." He tapped the gun on his right hip. "I know how to use mine. Expertly."

"I wouldn't, Cory," Elton calmly said.

"Wouldn't what?"

"I wouldn't pick today to die."

Murmurs rippled through the crowd.

Cory shook his head. "You don't get to choose, mister."

"But you do."

Something about the man's tone seemed to catch Rupert's attention. "Oh, let him go, Cory. He ain't worth it."

"Listen to your friend." Elton dug his left hand into his pocket and pulled out a handful of coins. "I'll buy you a beer and you can be on our way."

Cory said, "You coward, you looking for a way out of this?"

"I'm looking for a way to save your life."

For Rupert, that did it. "I'm out, mister," he said, looking at Elton. "I'm gonna reach down. But all I'm doin' is takin' off my gun belt."

Elton said, "Go ahead, son. But do it slow."

"Yessir." Rupert's hands eased toward his belt. When it was unbuckled, he gingerly placed it on the bench near him. "We okay?"

"Step a little further from that gun and we'll be great."

Rupert eased into the crowd.

Cory turned to him. "Coward!"

"Wouldn't call it bein' a coward," Rupert said. "I just want to see tomorrow."

"You're yellow as they come! Well, I ain't!" He spun toward Elton and grabbed iron.

Before Cory's gun cleared leather Elton put two holes an inch apart above Cory's left breast pocket.

The crowd that had been raucous now fell utterly silent. Dozens of eyes stared at Elton.

A solo hand clap sounded from amongst the onlookers.

Perry Joyce.

He moved to Elton's elbow. "Magnificent! Brilliant! Exactly as I remembered. You are majestic. You have given me another tale to tell."

Elton reholstered his pistol, grabbed Joyce by the shoulders and threw him to the dirt beside Cory's body. "I could have walked by him and he'd never have known I existed. Men don't come back from being dead. You killed him, Joyce."

Joyce rose, then delicately plucked a handkerchief from his pocket. He wiped the dust from his face and scornfully said, "Don't be absurd. I never handled a gun. I never pulled a trigger. I never put a bullet in him. That was you, gunman."

Elton yanked Joyce off his feet and threw him on top of Cory. "No, you didn't do any of those things, you son of a bitch. But it happened because of something you created."

He stepped on Joyce's top hat. "Nice work, Shakespeare."

CHAPTER 20

Throughout the day Russell kept them moving steadily south-west. As the sun dropped near the horizon, he heard Earl stop behind him. He turned and saw Earl pointing at the trail and talking to Marie. He yanked his horse around.

"What now," Russell said as he slid to a stop in front of them.

"I was tellin' her we was headin' to town," Earl said.

"No, we're not."

"But this is the trail headin' back to town."

"Jesus Christ, you're an idiot! This is also the trail to Cheyenne and Denver. And if that isn't enough, I bet we can ride this trail all the way to Mexico. Now, are we going to Mexico?"

Earl slumped in the saddle. "I don't s'pose."

Russell spat. "Well, we aren't going to town, either."

"But we're headin' *toward* the town."

Russell ground his teeth. "Okay, we're heading *toward* the town. But we aren't going *to* the town. Got it?"

Earl nodded, but without conviction. As usual.

Russell needed to get him to forget about Hill City. "Earlie, I'm trying to get back to the claim quick as we can. I've got a surprise for you." He looked at the girl. "And I have a bigger surprise for her."

Marie sighed. That morning Russell had left her alone. For today that was surprise enough. Instead, the men had seemed far more interested in leaving quickly, and scarcely stopped to clean up the filthy site before they rode out of the hollow.

They'd been in such a rush they hadn't even noticed that she'd tied a handkerchief to the bush when she'd done her business.

Anyone following them would be sure to find the site. And if they found the site and found the cloth and could track at all, they would find her.

If you're lucky. Which you haven't been so far.

While she mulled this over the horses worked their way down a steep, slippery draw. Earl and Russell made it safely, but part way down Junie slipped on the snow and stumbled. She frantically struggled to regain her footing on the slick slope. Limping, but game, Junie finally reached the bottom.

Marie quickly dismounted and stood beside the sweating, shaking mare. "It's okay, girl," she whispered, rubbing Junie's neck. "You're okay."

Earl jumped off his horse and lifted Junie's right front leg. The mare whinnied in pain, her eyes rolling back. Earl shook his head at Marie. "Broke."

Russell said, "You sure?"

"I know broke legs when I feel 'em."

Russell pulled his pistol out.

"No. No! " Marie begged. She stepped between Russell and the horse. "Don't shoot Junie."

"You or the horse," he said. "Your choice."

She hesitated.

Then a gunshot cracked.

Junie crumpled to the ground.

Marie whipped her head toward Earl as he slid his pistol back into the holster.

"Had to do it," he said, sadness cloaking his eyes. "I couldn't let her hurt no more."

Marie dropped to her knees next to the horse and buried her face into the horse's mane. "Junie," she sobbed. "Junie!"

A hand rested on her shoulder. "Sorry," Earl said. "You take some time and say goodbye to your horse." He patted her shoulder. "You take some time."

"This isn't like losing a sister!" Russell yelled. "Which could still happen, if you don't get on your goddamn feet! You'll be walking from now on."

Marie struggled to stand. "What?"

"You heard me. You think you have it bad now. I can make it a whole lot worse."

She stared at him, then she shifted her gaze over his shoulder. She saw movement in the trees.

A rider.

Approaching them.

"Over here!" she yelled. "Help, over here!" She waved her arms over her head and hollered once more. "Help me!"

Russell slid his rifle from its scabbard and stared at the rider as he neared them, then laughed as he replaced it. "You're going to be a bit disappointed by what happens next," he said.

Nathaniel Nix rode to them and stopped. "I did my part," he said, eyeing Marie. "I got the father out of the house."

"You did," Russell said, "although we spent four nights in that damned bar before you two showed up. Earl still may not be dried out from the whiskey he drank. For that, I'm blaming you."

Marie felt dread settle upon her. "You know each other? Mister Nix? You know these beasts?"

Nix dropped his eyes. "I work for them."

"But...the telegraph?"

Russell cackled. "A story I concocted a few weeks ago after I saw your family in Sturgis."

Nix looked at Marie for a moment, then back to Russell. "You never told me why you wanted Henry Cole from the house. You never said she'd be a part of this."

Russell grunted. "Some things are better left unknown. If you weren't riding around out here like you'd lost something, you wouldn't have known this, either." He pointed at Marie. "Probably best to put this out of your mind, Nathaniel. What's left of it."

"But...but..."

"Nathaniel, I told you to stay at your shack and we'd see you there. Where do you think you're going now?"

Nix chewed on his lip. "Something's dragging me back to their place," he said, nodding toward Marie. "Something I can't quite comprehend."

"Well if you get there, you're likely to find a few surprises. Like Miz Collins behind the woodpile. And the little girl at the house. And one angry man when he arrives and sees what happened."

Nix's mouth fell open. "Caroline is there?"

Russell said, "Likely still alive, too."

Tears slid down Marie's cheeks. "My mother...her name isn't Collins. It's Cole. Amelia Cole."

Russell snickered. "Your folks have been lying to you since the day you were born. Wonder how that feels, finding out you aren't who you thought you were. Your name is Collins, not that it's a name I'd carry with any sort of pride."

Nix looked puzzled. "You told me his name was Henry Cole."

Russell sighed. "If I'd told you his name was Elton Collins, would you have gone to see him?"

Nix shrugged. "Just doing my job. Didn't much matter, I guess. But Henry Cole is Elton Collins?"

Russell said, "Story keeps getting better and better, doesn't it?"

Marie stared at Nix. "I don't understand. You helped them kill my mother, and now you're helping them kidnap me. How could you do this to us?"

Nix buried the heels of his hands against his eyes and gave them a good rub. When he looked at her he said, "It was my job. I was supposed to go to your house and tell your parents there was a telegram. Then go back to my house and wait. But I had to see why I did this. Now I guess I know. I'm sorry."

He turned to Russell. "You aren't going to hold it against me if I go to their house to check on the little girl, are you?"

"Your funeral, amigo," Russell said.

Nix wheeled his horse toward the trail he'd been on.

"Wait! You have to help me!" Marie cried, desperate.

"One thing you might want to consider, Nathaniel," Russell called out as Nix moved his horse slowly away. "When her daddy comes back, he might have a concern about you and his daughter. Then there's the issue of the dead wife in the woodpile. I'm not even going to mention how he might feel when he sees what happened to his dog."

Nix reined his horse and turned. "Guess I'll sort all that out if the time comes." He nudged his horse's flank and cantered away.

"I hate you!" Marie yelled. "I hope you die, you bastard!" She dropped to her knees in a patch of snow and sobbed.

Russell watched him go. "Oh, he will," he said. "And a lot sooner than he thinks."

Zeke reined his paint gelding and pointed to a stream near a jumble of boulders. "That old feller said to find us a stream coming out of the rocks. Gold gets washed out right onto the sand." He pointed at a sandbar where the stream bent around a rock wall. "Bet we'll find gold right there."

Otto rubbed his jaw. "I don't see no chunks of gold. You said there was going to be chunks."

"Maybe there is. Maybe there ain't. Maybe we'll have to pan for it after all."

Otto rolled his eyes. "May bees don't fly in October. Only thing gonna be flyin' around here is snow, and it ain't far off. Then our dumb asses will be buried in the drifts till spring. You got a maybe for that?"

Caleb, who'd ridden a ways past his uncles, turned in his saddle. "Maybe that shack up ahead is abandoned. I don't see any smoke coming from the chimney."

Zeke gave a whoop and shot his pistol in the air. "Maybe our luck's about to change. Race you to it!" He spurred his mount and the horse charged along the streambed. It came to a sliding stop beside the ramshackle corral.

"Halloo the house!" Zeke bellowed. His voice skipped around the rocks above them.

Otto stopped beside Zeke. "Don't guess there's anybody here." He turned as Caleb's horse hobbled up to them. "Say hello to your humble abode, boy. Let's shuck these saddles and get our bedrolls inside. We got us some gold to find."

Sheriff Ballew dejectedly stared at the fire while he waited for the coffee water to boil. He may have hated doing paperwork more than anything in the world, but hunting shadows through the underbrush was a close second. He'd cut across a pairs of tracks in the past three days, and those were headed straight for the Cole place. He himself had seen Henry Cole in town a few days earlier, along with another rider.

The tracks he'd cut? Likely Cole and the other rider, heading home.

A cool gust of wind rolled over the pine knoll, catching Ballew's hat and tugging it off his head. It rolled on edge, bounced over some rocks, and ended up in the shallows of a small stream.

Ballew walked to the stream and reached down for the hat. He shook the water from its brim and gingerly placed it on his head.

A dribble of water found its way down his back.

Two more days.

He'd work the hills for two more days.

And then he'd go back to his desk.

Back to shuffling papers.

Back to his redeye.

Back to the specter of Donovan McCready.

CHAPTER 21

Collins, Marie thought over and over as she trudged behind Russell's horse. Her name was Collins. She'd seen the truth in their eyes. Why her folks used the name Cole, she had no idea. They had a good reason, of this she was certain.

But maybe not.

Collins.

Not Cole.

Collins.

Collins.

She was Marie Collins.

And her father's name was Elton.

It sounded as foreign as the French she'd heard a man speak once in town.

Like it didn't belong.

Other thoughts clouded her brain.

At her house she'd had a gun and it was pointed toward Earl.

Why didn't you pull back the hammer?

Why?

You carry a gun to use.

She glanced at the men as they rode. Rifles in scabbards, pistols on their hips. Next time she had a gun, she'd use it. Next time…

She slipped on a rock and fell in the snow, letting out a squeal when she landed.

Russell glared at her as she tried to scramble up. "I guess you know what's coming." He shook out a loop and dropped it around her waist. Now she had to keep up with the horses.

Or she'd be dragged along the rock-strewn terrain.

As she stared at his back while she marched along, Marie could feel her hatred for Russell blossom. He was the most disgusting, vile creature she'd ever met. The things he'd done to her the last two days…she fought to keep from vomiting.

But even with the things he'd forced her to do, nothing hurt more than the way he'd ripped her away from Caroline.

You left your sister to die.

No. He left her to die.

Marie thought about the pot of stew that she'd left hanging over the fire. Enough food for a few days, if Caroline could get to it.

How much bread was left?

Some.

Water. Caroline would need water. They kept a bucket and a pitcher of water in the kitchen. Marie closed her eyes and tried to remember how full the bucket had been.

Was it full enough to keep a little girl alive until someone found her? *And how long will that be?*

She must have slowed, for Russell twitched the rope and yanked her off her feet. Slushy snow soaked her front as she slid along like an otter on ice. "Wait," she yelled. "Let me get up!"

"Your dumb ass shouldn't be down there in the first place," Russell said.

"Stop," Earl yelled. He pushed his horse in front of Russell's, forcing him toward some close-growing pine trees.

With nowhere to go, Russell stopped. "What are you doing, you fool?"

"Nothin," Earl said.

"Nothin'," Russell said. "Well, you better make sure that's the last nothin' you do, you hear?"

Earl looked at Marie, who'd gotten to her feet. "You have to keep walkin'. You can keep walkin', right?"

Her feet ached from the miles she'd already walked that day. Her leather shoes offered little protection from the snow, and her feet were wet. And cold.

And getting colder.

Earl glared at Russell. "You gotta slow down a bit or you're gonna kill her."

Russell spit into the snow. "That's the best idea I heard today." His hand reached for his gun.

"No!" Earl commanded. "You had Loretta, so I get her. But—"

"But what? You have something to say to me?"

"But…nothin'."

"No. You were going to bitch about something. You have a problem we need to discuss right now?"

Earl sighed deeply. "Well, you had Loretta, and she was all yours to do whatever you wanted. And now Marie is supposed to be all mine to do whatever I want, 'cept she ain't all mine 'cause you keep layin' with her. Don't seem quite fair to neither one of us, is all I'm thinkin'."

"Fair? Hoo, let's talk about fair. Apparently I'm saddled with you for all eternity. Me, dragging you along every goddamn step of the way. And it isn't like you're a lot of laughs, getting drunk, starting fights, and being thrown in jail every time I turn around. You can't cook, you don't work worth shit, and you don't have the brains God gave an ox. Yet here I am, taking care of you. And you want to talk about fair."

Earl's breathing hitched with muted sobs. "Sorry," he forced out, when he could finally speak. "Life ain't fair, I guess."

"No, it isn't, and I know that more than most. So it's up to me to make it fair. And poking the princess, well I guess that about evens it up. Let me check one more time. You have a problem with me poking her? Especially since you don't seem to want to?"

Earl shook his head. "I can't poke her. You know why."

"Yeah, I know why," Russell said. "Loretta."

He turned to Marie. "So do you have a problem with me poking you? Because I can always shoot you instead." He patted his pistol.

Marie mumbled, "No."

"Glad we got that settled," Russell said. He reined his horse sideways until he could get by the tree, and then he set off. Faster than before.

While she scurried along the trail, despair gripped Marie.

This wasn't supposed to happen.

Girls weren't supposed to be poked like a heifer.

Girls were supposed to marry the man they loved. And raise a family.

Like your mother did.

She dared to touch the book in her dress pocket.

Yes. Love a family like her mother did.

Be strong. Like her mother.

And then Marie knew that she would not live in fear of these men. Her mother hadn't given up. She had fought for her own life, and when Marie's life was threatened she'd fought for hers, too.

Till her last breath.

So no. Marie would not give them the satisfaction of watching her die. She would not let them see fear in her eyes. No matter what they did, no matter what they forced her to do, she would live.

That night when Russell came to her she shut her mind to him.

Do not think of this.

Do not.

No.

Instead, she was home, tending the garden. She could feel the warmth of the sun on her hair. She could feel it against her face. She could feel the dry earth crumble in her fingers.

She was picking flowers with Caroline. The lightest dust from the petals coated her sister's cheeks and, as Marie blew it away, Caroline batted her eyelashes, giggling.

She was a little girl throwing rocks with her father. Creek water slapped against her legs. As she walked barefooted along the creekbed she could feel tiny stones bite the bottom of her feet.

And finally, at the end, she was a lion, standing alone on a rocky outcropping, fiercely surveying her valley kingdom.

Afraid of nothing.

Master of everything.

After Russell rolled off her and returned to his bed Marie slowly came back to herself, to her muddy bed lined with spruce bows, to her aching body, to her campsite prison. She could feel blood flow to her arms and legs. She could feel where he had been on top of her, could feel where his beard stubble had scratched her forehead.

She could almost taste his stale, crusted sweat smell that lingered on her skin and clothes. But for a moment he hadn't been there. When she needed to block him out he had disappeared. Completely, totally.

She rested her hand on her mother's small package and felt a sense of calm come over her. She knew she wasn't safe, but she found a way to be safe enough. For while they could take her body, she was determined they would never break her will. She would win, she would survive, and they would die.

While the moon hovered overhead, she held the package close to her chest and imagined how.

CHAPTER 22

As darkness draped the clearing in front of him, Nix slowly approached the Collins house.

The cow was bawling. Her calf nuzzled her underside, frantically sucking away. Nix slid from his horse and tossed an armful of hay into the corral. The cow charged to get it while her calf struggled to keep sucking as she walked.

Nix pulled the saddle off his horse and turned him loose in the corral, as well.

He studied the house, but saw no movement. He slowly approached and stepped onto the porch. He heard no sound.

He eased the door open and looked inside. Caroline lay on the floor in the corner, wrapped in a blanket. To his relief, she was alive. As he scooped her up, her eyes fluttered open.

"Hi," she said.

"Are you okay?"

"I'm thirsty."

"I'll get you some water. Are you hungry?"

"I ate all the crackers but I'm still hungry."

"I'll get a fire going, and then I'll make you some food."

She scrunched up her nose. "I'm dirty too."

"A bath will fix that."

Caroline's lip quivered. "Momma's gone. And some men took Marie. Where are they?"

Nix's heart jumped. "They'll be back soon. Now you stay here and I'll get some firewood."

It took him only a moment to find Amelia. He walked behind the woodpile, where he saw a shape. He slowly crept over.

Something—maybe coyotes—had also found her.

He closed his eyes, leaning against the woodpile.

This is what I did?

He walked back into the house, started a fire, and soon felt the comforting warmth push to the corners of the front room. While he cooked Caroline fell asleep in the rocker. He added a bit more wood to the fire, put the coffee water on, and waited for her to wake.

While he did, he thought about the situation.

Amelia dead, Marie with Russell and Earl, Collins nowhere to be found.

A family destroyed.

Well, not totally destroyed.

He glanced at Caroline.

One remained.

CHAPTER 23

Something crept closer. Nix could see it slip through the misty clearing, no more than a whisper as it passed from tree to tree.

A haunt.

A demon.

Coming to get him.

And Norma.

No.

Caroline.

Nix felt around him for his gun, but in the dark he couldn't find it.

How could he not find it? It was his job to protect her, like it was his job to protect Ingrid and Norma.

But they'd died.

And unless he found his gun Caroline would die too.

Like the tide rolling in, the shadow crept nearer. Steadily growing. Soon it was larger than anything he'd ever seen.

It was here.

And he was defenseless.

"You okay, mister?"

Nix jumped awake as Caroline patted his arm. Soaked in sweat, heart thudding, he pushed himself from the rocking chair, shaking his head. The dream that had started soon after he'd hit his head was growing like the shadow.

Darker.

Bigger.

And infinitely more terrifying.

He walked to the window and squinted through the pre-dawn gray. Maybe the shadow was gone.

For this night anyway.

Caroline nudged his leg. "Are you gonna feed me until Momma comes back?"

Could he tell her Momma wasn't coming back?

He looked at her innocent face. No.

He inhaled deeply. "Guess feeding you is my job now. What do you like?"

"Momma makes bacon and stuff. Sometimes we eat eggs." She looked up at him. "Do you like eggs?"

He patted his belly. "I like eggs best of all. Where can we get some?"

Her face glowed like sunrise. "We can look for them in the stable."

"Good idea. You get dressed, and then let's see who can find the most."

Caroline dashed into the bedroom and soon came back with a blanket wrapped around her. "I'm gonna go find eggs!" She slipped into Elton's old boots and struggled to walk out the door. She looked back, waiting for Nix.

Nix thought about Amelia. "Go straight to the stable." Next thing he'd have to do. Find a way to take care of Amelia's body. Maybe bury her in the stone wall a few paces beyond the wood pile.

When he lingered Caroline held out her hand, which he took. "Come on!" she urged. "We gotta go look for eggs!"

At the door Nix tugged her back. "Wait a minute."

She stared up at him, her face showing concern. "What are you looking for?"

His eyes swept the snow-covered ground. Bright sunlight played across the yard, but nothing else seemed to stir.

He studied the trees for shadows.

"Earl, quit your bellyaching," Russell said. "We can't go into town!"

Earl stomped around the horses. "But I'm freezin' my balls off out here, and you keep weavin' us around like you're drunk. Let's take Marie to the town, Russell."

Russell stared at him, fuming. "You damn fool. You killed her momma, you kidnapped her, and now you want to parade her through town where everyone knows us? We do that, all we're going to find is a noose. And this neck isn't ready for stretching."

Earl frowned. "Well, we didn't think this out real good, did we? We seen the girl, we got the girl. And now you keep ridin' around out here in the snow like you don't know what you wanna do with the girl. We're so close to town I can see it, but you don't want to go there neither." His voice softened, pleading. "Jeez o'mighty, why don't we go home instead?"

Russell grimaced. "You saw those tracks we cut a while back."

Earl said, "We cut the same tracks three times. Hard to miss."

"You notice anything different about them? Horse that was stepping kind of funny?"

Earl's brow wrinkled in thought. "Don't guess so."

"Horse that's slew-footed. Hooves bigger than the average horse by nearly half again. Now, you know anyone rides a big old slew-foot?"

"Sheriff Ballew. Put me in jail when I got fish-eyed and smashed a table at the bar."

"Sheriff Courtney Ballew. Riding these hills, crisscross pattern like he was looking for something. Or someone. Maybe us."

Earl's face lit up. "That why you keep jigger-jaggering around?"

Russell said, "If Ballew is out hunting someone, the last thing I want to do is beeline for the claim and give him something to follow." He turned to Marie. "Of course, you'd probably like that, wouldn't you? Ride right up on the sheriff so you could explain your plight, like you tried to do to Nix?"

Marie scowled. "Now, why would I want to get away from you gentlemen? You being so sweet to me and all?"

"Shut it, girl," Russell said. "Or I'll shut that mouth permanent-like."

"Okay, okay you two," Earl said. "It's cold and I'm tired and you don't always gotta fight. But if we keep going we can give Marie a bed. Jeez o'mighty, don't you think that'd be better, givin' Marie a bed?"

Russell nudged Earl's shoulder. "What happened last time you were in bed with a woman? Oh yeah, you killed her. Think if someone found that dead lady and then saw our tracks heading from her house toward our claim, they might deduce it was us?"

Earl sighed. "I guess."

"You guessed right. But if we avoid the town altogether and follow that draw that comes out north of town, we can mix our tracks with the others heading toward Lead and Deadwood. Then ours will be a couple more sets of hoof prints no one can follow."

"Never thought of that," Earl said.

"And that's why I do the thinking for both of us. But let's hold off till dark to come out in the open. Until then why don't you go diddle the girl?"

Earl turned a longing eye to Marie, who was perched on a rock, looking toward the town. "I can't diddle her, you know that. I'm gonna think about her. I always dreamed of having a girl with long gold hair and a skinny waist, and who has a pretty singin' voice when she plays the piano—"

Russell gave him a hearty slap between the shoulder blades. "Well, listen to you! Long hair. Plays the piano. Sings like a bird. Ain't you a hoot!" He looked at the big man. "Earlie, you killed her momma, and she isn't going to forget that. She isn't ever going to fall for you."

"I don't suppose."

"Least I can do, I guess. Let me go ask her if she'll play the piano for you tonight after dinner." Russell howled with laughter as he walked away.

While he scoured around for some dry branches to coax more life from the fire, Russell had to admit that trying to avoid Sheriff Ballew had pushed them far too close to town. So close, any fool with a good set of eyes might see them. Then that fool might wonder why two men had a pretty girl with them. It wasn't like he and Earl were strangers in Hill City. Since their silver strike, word of their luck had spread around town like a persistent case of syphilis. Every time they rode in, people gawked and pointed. So sure as hell, if they were seen skulking around with the girl in tow, some busybody fool would notice that, too.

And that was attention they could do without.

Especially with the sheriff on the hunt.

It was time to leave the ridge and get back to their claim before a big snow fall. Once winter hit and the drifts were waist-high, no one would ride by their place till spring.

By then, one way or another, this would be over.

CHAPTER 24

Elton strode from the stage in the darkness, taking care not to slip in the snow-covered, muddy streets of Hill City as he made for the livery. "Shorty," he called out as he approached. "You have my horse?"

"Some nerve, yellin' this late at night!" Shorty bellowed as he charged from the back room, pulling his britches up. He nearly collided with Elton as he came around the corner. "Looks like you're alone. Can I call you Elton now?"

"Cat's pretty much out of the bag on that anyway."

Shorty said, "So's I hear. Feller like Elton Collins comes back to life, it's bound to get the gums to flappin'."

"I'm afraid that's not all, but what's done is done. Appreciate you keeping my secret."

Shorty shrugged. "Pleasure. And, while I'm hopeful, I don't suppose you come here this late at night to yammer with me."

Elton said, "Now that I'm this close, I don't aim to spend one more night away. Amelia told me to come home early, and home is where I'm going." He started to walk toward his horse, but Shorty stood quickly and held up his hand.

"Been a little extra commotion over the ridge toward your place."

"What do you mean?"

"Well, today when I was pitchin' down some hay from the loft, I looked up the trail and I seen two fellers ridin' this way. Might a seen a body sittin' on a rock, too. Which, come to think of it, wouldn't a made no sense at all, so I likely saw nothin' worth mentionin'."

Elton shrugged. "From time to time folks have cut across the ridge from the valley. That trail is the shortest way over."

"Some folks got a reason to take the trail, but these two birds I seen? Got a claim a bit north, and they haul their ore back here. Had themselves a helluva strike, silver that's pure as a baby's heart. Now why do you think two fellers like that would head off the opp'site direction and go to Sturgis or Rapid City? Then double back like they left somethin' worth comin' back for, yet never go through town?"

Shorty shrugged. "One of them great mysteries of life."

"Well, they're only a couple of miners."

Shorty shook his head like he was trying to shake loose a wasp from his hair. "They ain't the only ones I seen. You know how after a long day, sometimes a beer's what you need? Hell, every day a beer's what I need to get me through this life I call my own."

"Let me guess. You went to get a beer?"

Shorty snorted. "You already know the story?"

"Hard to venture a guess. You haven't told it yet."

"'Cause you ain't give me half a chance with all these questions. Would you be so kind as to let me continue?"

"By all means."

"Thought you'd see it my way. So I go to the bar like I tend to do, and who do I see there?"

Elton shrugged.

Shorty cackled. "So you don't know the story after all, Mister Elton Collins. Then I'll keep tellin' it. So I'm drinkin' my beer, and who do I see but that feller you rid in with a while back. He kinda had my interest since you brung him by, so I got him talkin' a mite. And then I recognized him. Took a bit, but I got him."

"You've seen Nix before?"

Shorty spit a stream of tobacco juice, then wiped his face with his sleeve. "With them miner boys coupla times when they brought their ore in. Appears he works for 'em."

A cold finger ran down Elton's back. "Shorty, I've got to go. But one thing."

Shorty cocked an eyebrow.

"Where does McLaren live? I need him to open up the store tonight."

McLaren jumped out of bed at the sound of pounding on his door. "Hang on, hang on, be right there."

Elton heard the rustle of feet, and then McLaren threw the door open, wrapping an ill-fitting robe around his bulbous girth. "Yes?"

"McLaren, sorry to wake you."

"I'll only be sorry if you wake my wife. Let's step outside, shall we?" McLaren pulled Elton onto the porch. "What's so urgent?"

"I need something from your store before I head home tonight."

A customer was a customer. McLaren stepped inside and slipped his boots on, then quickly closed the door behind him. "Do you mind if I ask what supplies are so important that you have to get them tonight?"

Elton's jaw tightened. "More bullets."

CHAPTER 25

As the sun peeked over the prairie to the east, Ben gave up trying to sleep. Last night, long after he'd gone to bed, his mother had tiptoed into his room, gently woken him and whispered, "Your Pa will let you ride up on the ridge tomorrow. You take Mrs. Cole one of my berry pies, and then maybe you can sit with her daughter."

"How did you convince him?"

She ruffled his hair. "Women's magic."

Ben slipped his clothes on, rushed to the washbasin, and pulled a comb through his hair. He glanced toward his parents' room but heard no sound. He hurriedly stirred the coals in the stove, then added two sticks of wood. He saw the pie his mother had left on the table, wrapped up in a large red cloth.

He quietly pulled on his boots and coat, picked up the pie, and then tiptoed out of the house to do chores.

Today he'd talk to Mister Cole about Marie.

Nix lurched awake, his blanket wadded in his lap. The second night he'd spent in the Collins house had been far worse than the first. This time the shadows had been coming all night. Wave after wave of them, like soldiers assaulting a hill, creeping ever closer to the house.

He closed his eyes. Sometimes they'd seemed so close he could almost touch them.

But he'd never been able to see their faces.

He placed his hand over the pistol in his lap and studied the house. He could see additions they'd made over the years. A table that seemed very new. Fresh curtains in the front windows, an older one dividing the bedrooms. Shelves in the corner. Two small tables flanking the rocker, one that had Amelia's sewing on it, and the other that held a Bible.

Nix stood and stretched, and his fears began to abate. Until today he had always felt he was running away from something—from the memory of Ingrid and Norma—but now he realized that he hadn't been running away from anything at all. In fact, he'd been running *to* something. Today he finally knew what that something was.

His new family.

He eased back into the rocker.

Satisfied, he thought about the life he and Caroline would live on the ridge.

He ran his fingers over the pistol's smooth, cold metal.

As long as the shadows left them alone.

Ben rode up the ridge toward the Cole house, but instead of peeling off to the outcropping where he and Marie normally met he veered right and rode toward a small group of Ponderosa pines. As he neared the Cole's clearing, he saw another rider approach through widely spaced hardwoods beyond the corral.

Ben abruptly reined his horse and stood him behind the head-high pines, hoping he hadn't been seen. He watched the other rider slowly approach the corral, then suddenly dip into the brush, where Ben lost sight of him.

Ben watched behind the corral, watching for some movement. Once or twice he thought he could see something, but through the trees it was hard to tell. Carefully balancing the pie, he slid off the saddle and stepped around the pines to get a better view of the brush behind the corral. He dipped his head and continued to scan where the man had disappeared.

Patience, his father always told him. Be patient.

"All right, young feller, that's enough." Ben spun around to see Mister Cole standing behind a boulder, pistol drawn. Ben placed the pie on the ground, then sheepishly raised his hands at the same time Cole lowered his pistol.

"No need to act like you robbed a stage, son. Piece of advice though, you have to work on your cover. I could see that red cloth you're carrying from all the way across the clearing. Even through these pines," Mister Cole said as he brushed them with his free hand. "Remember, a man shows you what he wants you to see. You saw me going into the brush. I wanted you to lose me there. I figured you'd keep looking at the brush and maybe you'd see my horse tied in the same spot."

He looked closely at the boy. "You have a reason for hiding in the bushes?"

"I...I..." Ben shrugged. "I...I..."

Mister Cole laughed. "Let's start with something a bit easier. Maybe it'll help get those words flowing. Tell me about that pie."

"My mother said to bring it up here, and then maybe I could sit—" He bit off the thought. "My mother thought you'd like a berry pie."

"Your mother is an astute woman, but she's fed me before. Now the other thing you hinted about—the sitting part—maybe you can tell me more."

Ben's stomach felt like it was full of lead. He gulped. "Yes, Mister Cole. I came here, sir, to see you." He nervously fingered the reins in his hands. "About Marie."

Elton studied Ben. He had developed a farmer's broad shoulders and had a tuft of dark brown hair that splashed over his forehead, hanging nearly into his green, gold-flecked eyes. The sleeves of his shirt and coat looked too short, which was normal on a growing boy. Looks like a man, he surmised. He had an idea where this conversation was headed.

He leaned back against the boulder and beckoned Ben to his side. Ben ground-tied his horse and walked over, looking like a scolded puppy.

Elton motioned toward the valley, hidden from his view by a stand of towering pines. "You rode all the way up here to talk to me about Marie?"

"Yes, sir. You see, I…Marie…we…well."

Elton placed a hand on his shoulder. "Go on, son. You're doing fine so far."

"Okay." He breathed deeply. "Marie and I have…" He paused, puffed his cheeks up, then blurted, "We've been courting." His eyes shot wide open.

"I've seen your tracks behind the ledge." When Ben looked shocked, Elton forced a smile. "Hard to believe, but I was young once upon a time."

"We didn't mean to sneak around, but she's so pretty, and her hair looks so golden in the sunlight, and the way she smiles, and her eyes are like—"

Elton tossed up a hand. "I still feel the same way about her mother. Now, between you and me you can court Marie, but we have to break it to Marie's mother, slow and easy." Elton hesitated for a moment. "Son, before this goes any further, there's something I want to tell you. My name's not Cole. It's Collins. Elton Collins."

Ben gulped at the sound of the name. "The gunman?"

"I'd like to think of myself as your neighbor, and nothing more."

Ben nodded, his eyes a bit wider than normal. "Yes sir, Mister Collins."

"Now that we have that out of the way, talking to Marie's mother may be the least of our problems."

"What do you mean, sir?"

"There's a horse in the corral that doesn't belong there. My mare's gone and I don't like that, either. I don't know what we're going to find, so we're going to hold to some cover as we approach the house. You keep your head down, and you do what I do."

Ben's face tightened. "Do I bring the pie?"

"That would please me immensely."

In the daylight they didn't look like faceless shadows anymore.

They looked like men.

Men, he could handle.

Nix cracked the door open.

And pointed his pistol toward the closest one.

CHAPTER 26

A bullet whipped so close to Elton's face he felt it pass. He dove behind a rock as another one buzzed by. "Ben, get down!" he shouted. Another shot ripped through the clearing. He heard a grunt and spun to see Ben on the ground, grasping his arm.

Elton crawled to Ben and helped him behind the boulder. Small pines in front of it provided a bit more cover. Elton looked at the house. At least ten more strides to the front porch, and past the boulder and pines there wasn't so much as a tall blade of grass to hide behind.

Ben groaned. The boy's face was pale. He winced as Elton pulled his coat away and inspected the wound.

"Mr. Collins," Ben mumbled. "I'm hit bad."

Elton slipped Ben's coat back over the wound. "Every time you're shot it's bad, son. This one went through the muscle in your upper arm and missed the bone. Could have been a lot worse."

"Could have been better, too," Ben said. "He could have missed altogether."

Elton shucked his own coat, then tore a strip from his shirt and bound Ben's wound. The boy winced, but made no sound. "You okay, son?"

Ben gritted his teeth. "Yes, sir."

Elton said, "When we get to the house I'll bandage that up better. But that'll have to wait until the shooting stops."

He cursed himself for getting Ben shot. After all, it was he who had suggested Ben come to the house with him. He had expected…well, he wasn't sure what he'd expected. But he sure as hell hadn't expected this.

One man down.

Nix stared at the boulders from the narrow slit made by the partially open door. He massaged his temple.

One to go.

And then the nightmares might end for good.

Elton surveyed the snow-covered yard. The only tracks he could see were ones from the corral to the house.

He was even more convinced they weren't up against an army. Nix's gelding stood in the corral.

One horse.

One man.

One shooter.

Nix.

But why?

Of course, he thought, it didn't matter why. Nix was shooting.

Therefore Nix had to be stopped.

But not with a frontal attack.

Elton placed a hand on Ben's good shoulder. "Son, you've already been brave. You have any more sand in you?"

"Yes, sir."

Elton drew a small map in the nearly melted snow. "Everything I see tells me there's one shooter, but walking through the front door is out of the question. However, if I can get behind the house, I can approach unseen all the way to the back door. You use that red cloth you brought. Between that and my coat, maybe we can fool him a bit. If we're lucky, he'll believe what his eyes tell him. It may be the break I need."

CHAPTER 27

As Ben tied the red cloth onto the tree branch, he had second thoughts. To him it looked exactly like what it was—a cloth tied to a tree. He propped the coat up and spread the arms out a little. He hoped it looked more convincing to the shooter.

Ben prodded his left arm. Pain shot out like a lightning bolt.

Won't do that again, he mused as nausea gripped him. He struggled to stand. Instantly, a shot slammed into the tree beside him. He dropped like a stone.

I guess he's still watching over here, Ben thought. Maybe that'll help Mister Collins get closer.

Elton soundlessly crept toward the back of the house. If Nix had seen him, lead would be flying his way. Instead, the shooting had been from the front of the house. Elton had already gotten

Ben shot once, and he hoped be hadn't bought the boy more trouble.

He slipped around the corner and studied the distance to the back door. Three steps.

Two.

One.

Gently, slowly transferring his weight onto the back door step, he pushed the door.

It silently swung open, and he stepped into the pantry.

He slid past the door frame and eased into the kitchen. His eyes swept the room. No Amelia. No Marie. But Caroline sat in the corner, staring at Nix, who crouched by the front door, looking outside.

This wasn't the time to ask questions. It would end now.

Elton raised his gun.

"Daddy!" Caroline screeched. She flew from the corner toward Elton and threw her arms out. "Daddy!"

Still in a crouch, Nix spun.

Elton reached out to catch Caroline in his left arm while leaning around her to shoot at Nix.

Nix fired twice.

Elton's pistol barked in response.

CHAPTER 28

Nix froze, horrified, as he watched blood seep from Elton Collins and onto the floor. He felt the weight of the pistol in his hand, could still feel the recoil from the shots. His mind told him to run over to Collins, to stop the bleeding, to check for breathing, something, anything to help.

But his legs couldn't bear his weight.

He crashed to the floor. He looked down and saw blood pouring from a wound on the inside of his thigh.

He banged his leg with the pistol grip. No pain.

In fact, there was no feeling at all.

Then he noticed blood bubbling from a bullet wound in the center of his stomach. Rich, dark blood. Bullet to the spine.

The kind of wound that guaranteed he'd never walk again.

And worse.

He coughed, showering his shirt front with blood.

He'd seen enough men die to know that coughing up blood this way pretty much sealed the deal.

His eyes shifted to Caroline, who lay on her father's chest, arms draped around him.

Blood stained the back of her dress.

His mind flickered. Moment by painful moment.

An hour ago, he'd made Caroline breakfast.

Thirty minutes ago, they'd played with her doll.

Her enchanting laughter rang in his ears.

A child's laugh. Full of joy.

Full of trust.

Blissfully unaware.

Ten minutes ago, she'd cowered in the corner as he opened the door to shoot.

A minute ago, she'd squealed in happiness.

For her father.

Seconds later, Nix had ended her life.

First Norma.

Then Ingrid.

Now this.

Nix coughed again and more blood dripped from his mouth and nose.

"I'm sorry, I'm sorry, I'm sorry," he said as his voice faded to a whisper.

His lips silently moved.

And then stopped.

Schwartz heard the volley of shots from the ridge. From time to time over the years he'd heard solitary shots from that direction. A person hunting. But these sounds, rapid-fire, a volley...

He dropped the harness he'd been mending and limped to the house. He burst through the door. "Trudy, where did Ben go?"

She smiled. "I told you last night, remember? Ben has been courting the Cole girl. He went to see her family this morning. He brought Mrs. Cole a pie."

Schwartz muttered a curse. "I'll be back as soon as I can."

CHAPTER 29

Ben jumped as the sound of the shots ripped through the clearing. The echo rolled past him and down the valley.

He had no weapon.

He shouldn't move.

However, if people inside the house were hurt...

He waited until absolute silence settled on him like fog.

Move.

Now.

He hitched himself to his feet and crept toward the cabin.

Stepping on the porch, Ben listened. No sound. He slowly reached out and pushed the door, but it barely moved. He shoved harder and it opened a bit more. He shoved again and heard a quiet thump, like a feed sack falling over. The door opened enough that he could step inside. What he saw made him retch.

On the far side of the room Elton Collins lay on the floor, motionless. Blood ran down the side of his face, matting his hair.

Ben leaned against the doorframe to steady himself. There was something far worse.

The little girl lay on top of her father, her back soaked in blood.

She was dead too.

Ben looked beside the door and saw another man, toppled over, blood pooled around him.

Three people.

All dead.

He heard a low gurgle. He glanced at the girl.

Let it be her.

Please.

He moved closer.

He touched her.

No.

It was Mister Collins who struggled to breathe.

Against the weight of his dead daughter on his chest.

Ben looked at the girl's face. He had to do it. He took her by the shoulders and gently pulled her off her father.

Elton gasped a deeper breath and then his breathing steadied. Ben pushed the man's hair aside and saw blood oozing from a deep furrow along his scalp. It was a mess. But he was alive. A half-inch more and he would be as dead as his daughter.

Ben looked at the girl. Her golden curls. Her baby face, her pudgy hands.

Gone.

He tore his eyes from her and turned to the man in the corner. The man's glassy eyes stared back.

Ben returned to Mister Collins. In addition to the head wound he'd taken a shot through the outside of his thigh. Ben found a rag and wrapped it tightly around the leg.

He forced himself to rise again, then walked into the back room to get a blanket to cover the girl. To his horror he saw blood on the bed. "Ma'am?"

No answer. Shaking, he exited the house and saw a small, dark stain on the corner of the porch. He scouted around in the snow where Mister Collins had walked to the house.

Nothing.

He turned toward the corral and approached the woodpile.

Froze.

Something had been there.

Then was moved.

He followed the drag marks to the stone wall.

Many stones had been piled together in a haphazard attempt to cover something wrapped in a sheet.

But it wasn't covered completely.

A woman's hand extended from the rocks.

The fingers had been gnawed off at the knuckles.

Horrified, Ben backed away. He tripped over a rock, slipped on the snow, and smacked his head against the woodpile as he fell.

CHAPTER 30

As Schwartz approached the Cole homestead he came upon Ben's horse standing near some small pines. He dismounted, tied his horse next to his son's and tried to assess what had happened.

Two sets of footprints led through the snow toward the house. Schwartz slowly moved forward, following them.

He came upon an area where snow had scattered. There was blood in the imprint where someone had fallen. Then tracks that led to some trees and boulders.

Schwartz rapidly scanned the area. No sign of his son.

"Benjamin!" he hollered. "Ben!" Birds that had been clustered around the smashed berry pie exploded into the air and flew to a nearby bush.

"Benjamin!" Again the sound rolled away.

Schwartz saw a red cloth tied to a tree a few paces away. One of his wife's napkins. A coat in the tree. What was this? And where was his son?

One set of prints followed a low dip in the ground toward the back of the house.

Another went directly to the open front door.

Cautiously, Schwartz followed those. When he reached the door he melted against the wall and listened.

No sound.

Not a whisper.

He leaned around the door frame and stepped in. First thing he saw was Henry Cole on the floor with a little girl beside him. He went to the bodies, fearing the worst. Though bloody, Cole was still breathing. He looked around the rest of the room, struggling to take in what he was seeing. A dead man near the front door.

The little girl.

Ben?

"You've got to get up, I'm going to need you," Schwartz implored, gently shaking his son.

Ben stared up at him.

Schwartz walked Ben inside and pulled his coat off, then untied the bandage from the boy's arm.

It didn't look too bad, as gunshot wounds went.

Unless it was your son.

He replaced the bandage, then looked at the dead man in the corner. "Ever seen him before?"

"No sir," Ben answered. "Mister Collins said we'd have trouble."

"Collins? You must be hurt pretty bad, boy. His name is Cole. Henry Cole."

"No, sir. He told me his name was Elton Collins. I guess he didn't want anyone to know that."

Schwartz was stunned. Quiet, unassuming Henry Cole was actually Elton Collins? He thought about the stories he'd heard regarding the famous gunman's exploits. "No wonder he changed his name." To Ben he said, "What happened here?"

Ben said, "After I met Mister Collins he and I walked toward the house, and then bullets started flying. This man shot at us. I didn't duck fast enough."

"Hard to duck a bullet. If a shooter wants to hit you, he's going to hit you."

"But why was he shooting in the first place? Why did he want to kill us? Kill Mister Collins? His family. And now his daughter is dead." Ben shook his head. "I've never seen a dead person before. And the girl…" His body quivered as he spoke.

Schwartz remembered the first dead body he'd ever seen. He stayed quiet and let the boy work through it. *Death is a natural thing*, he thought. *Except when it's like this. And this memory won't ever leave.*

Schwartz touched Ben's wound.

The boy gasped and jerked away. "Bullet wounds hurt."

Schwartz said, "Be glad he missed your collarbone. Now that would have really hurt."

Ben snorted. "Worse than it does now?"

Schwarz nodded. "You sit a while and—"

"There's a woman out back. Buried in the stone wall. I saw her hand. Something chewed her fingers off. Is she—?"

"Yes. She's dead."

Ben rolled his eyes. "I know she's dead. Her fingers are gone. I want to know who it is."

"It's Mrs. Cole. Uh, Collins. Not her daughter."

Ben exhaled deeply. "But if she's not here…Marie, I mean, where is she?"

"That's something I can't decipher, not without looking around some. And right now it's more important to get you and Collins off this ridge. Once we get to the valley you can take him to our house and I'll ride to Sturgis to get the doc."

"But your leg. You can't ride that far."

"Don't you worry about what I can do. If something needs to be done, I'll do it. Then we'll see about finding your girl."

After Ben untied Sparky from a tree behind the corral Schwartz harnessed the gelding, then hitched him to the wagon. Together they moved Collins to the rig. Although Ben had to stop often, he stuck with the job until Collins was loaded in the wagon, wrapped in blankets.

"What about the girl?" Ben asked. "The mother. And—"

"After we get Collins off the ridge I'll come back. The woman and the girl, I'll find a place to bury them. The man…"

The man. He'd killed the girl. From the looks of it, Amelia Collins. And God knew where Marie was. Another day, Schwartz would bring the man's body to Sturgis. Or maybe bury him down on the flat. One thing he knew for sure, he wouldn't bury him up on the ridge. His bones would not remain up here to haunt whatever remnants of the Collins family remained.

They tied their horses to the back of the wagon. Ben rode next to Collins in the back of the wagon as they slowly crept down the ridge. Finally they crossed the creek.

Schwartz looked at Ben. "I know you're hurting, and I'm sure you've started bleeding again." The memory of the house came to him again. "You swap with me now. I'll get Doc Anderson, and you drive this wagon straight home. Your mother will know what to do. Then you get some rest yourself. You've done enough for today."

Ben nodded. Rain began to splash against his face as he took the reins and turned the wagon across the valley toward home.

Sheriff Ballew found the campsite in a hollow behind a stand of pines. He dismounted and checked the remains of the fire. He walked to where the horses had been tied.

"Three," he mumbled to himself. He studied the hoof prints the horses had left, and then poked around under trees, studying the snowy, bough-lined beds, not quite sure what he was looking for, but not quite ready to stop looking.

Yet the time finally came when Ballew figured he'd learned everything he could about the campsite. He went to the rock-lined pit they'd left. In it he built a small fire and began heating some water.

While he waited, he thought about what he'd found.

For not only did he see the tracks from the horses, but also the boot prints of two men.

Plus a smaller set with pointed toes.

And at the edge of the campsite, he'd seen something else.

Something that confused the hell out of him.

He found a woman's handkerchief tied to a bush.

CHAPTER 31

A bed. Soft linen. Many pillows piled around him.

Clicking.

Clicking. His mind searched everything it knew, trying to identify the clicking.

Every second, a click.

Every sec…a clock.

They didn't have a clock in their home.

Elton forced his eyes open and stared at a whitewashed ceiling. His home didn't have a whitewashed ceiling, either.

He tried to sit up, but he was so weak he could hardly lift his head from the pillow. A headache pounded the back of his skull. He reached up and felt heavy bandages.

Another on his leg. He felt around the bandage. Nothing broken, as far as he could tell.

He closed his eyes, exhausted. He'd been so close to getting home to Amelia.

And the girls.

He could still hear Caroline call out, "Daddy!" She ran to him and jumped. As Nix turned to fire, Elton reached out.

He waited to catch her.

He waited.

When he awoke again it was dusk. A lamp in the corner lit the room. Elton heard footsteps approach the bed. A woman hovered over him. He looked at her face.

Trudy Schwartz.

She fidgeted with his blankets. "We wondered when you might join us. Can I get you anything?"

He croaked, "Water?"

She patted his hand. "Of course."

I should have asked her to take away some pillows.

In a moment she was back. She sat on the edge of the bed and held a cup for him. He began to gulp the cold water, but she quickly pulled it away. "A sip at a time, no more. If you can keep that down, I'll bring you some broth. That'll help you get your strength back." She stood up. "Do you want me to bring you another pillow?"

He tried to shake his head no, but this caused a mini-explosion behind his eyes. He ground his head into the bed, but the pain stayed.

She smiled. "Maybe another will be better. I'll be right back."

He listened to the clock ticking as she walked to another room. This time he'd speak, no matter how much it hurt.

Because he kept seeing Caroline leap toward him, but he couldn't remember catching her.

—

The doctor came by again early the next morning. Elton was determined to speak, although it wasn't much more than a whisper. "How am I?"

Doc Anderson said, "You're still breathing, and likely to remain so for many years, so in that way it's not too bad. You were shot in the thigh and you lost some blood, but you've been hit before. You'll heal. With your head you were very lucky, because the bullet grazed you. A lot of blood loss, but little damage. It knocked you unconscious, no more."

Elton slowly formed the words, "The man who shot me?"

"Dead."

"When?"

"You were shot yesterday. Good thing you had young Benjamin with you, or you'd probably still be up on that ridge."

Elton's mind fumbled over this. "Ben?"

"Bless his soul, he was shot himself and still helped his father get you off the ridge. Tough boy." He rose to leave. "You've got the best kind of nursing a man could have. You eat Trudy's cooking and you'll be ten pounds heavier before you know it. You see what it's done to Schwartz."

"Thanks. And Doc," Elton said as Anderson turned to leave, "ask Schwartz to tell Amelia and the girls I'll be home soon."

Doc Anderson's face tightened. "I'll do that."

CHAPTER 32

After dinner, Elton asked to talk to Ben.

The boy pulled a chair to Elton's bed as his parents hovered over his shoulder. "Sir, I'm glad you pulled through. Are pulling through, anyway," Ben quickly added as he glanced at the bedridden man.

"Doc says it was you who saved me."

The boy blushed. "Pa mostly. He heard the shooting, and came up and found us. I couldn't have done it without him." Ben leaned close. In a near-whisper he said, "I told my Pa your real name." His eyes held a question that remained unasked.

"No need for me to hide anymore, Ben. Thank you for helping me." Elton reached out to shake his hand, and Ben took it.

"Trudy, I don't want to be too demanding a guest, but I miss my girls something fierce. Would it be all right for them to visit?"

Ben scrambled from his chair and lurched away from the bed.

The clock's tick hammered in the otherwise silent room.

"What?" Elton asked, scanning their faces. "What?"

Schwartz sat in the chair near the bed. "Elton, I don't know the whole story, though I've been trying to piece it together. That man in your house—"

"Nix," Elton interjected.

"He…when I went up to get you, I saw your wife. She is…" He looked to Trudy, who placed her hand on his shoulder.

Schwartz said, "She's dead."

A low light started deep in Elton's brain, as subtle as approaching daybreak. It flickered gently, then steadily strengthened in intensity, like a log catching fire.

It glowed, brighter and brighter, hotter, pulsing until it raged like a lightning storm behind his eyes.

Amelia. Dead.

It can't be true.

Because if it were true, it meant they would never share another moment together.

It meant his daughters had lost their mother.

It meant…it meant…he shook his head. "It can't be."

Schwartz said, "I'm so sorry."

Like a ball of yarn trickling across the floor, Elton felt himself unravel. Amelia was gone. He closed his eyes and remembered the last time he'd seen her, standing at the door with Marie and Caroline as he rode from the yard.

Marie and Caroline.

"The girls? Are the girls okay?" He pleaded to Schwartz, "please tell me my girls are okay."

Schwartz remained silent.

Elton sunk deeper into the pillows, eyes closed, handfuls of quilt balled in his fists. Almost inaudibly he moaned, "Tell me about my girls."

Schwartz said, "Your youngest was shot by that man."

That's why Caroline had never made it to him. His mind played it over again. He had quietly stepped into the kitchen. Nix crouched, back to him, peering out the door.

He should have shot him then. He should have—

"Daddy!" Caroline screeched, and ran toward him as Nix spun around, pistol pointed toward Elton. "Daddy!" Caroline leaped toward Elton as he and Nix fired. He felt a burning slug slam him in the leg, and then Caroline…Caroline…

"Marie?" He gasped, struggling to swallow. He lay there, shaking, afraid of the answer yet needing to know.

Schwartz scratched his head. "This is where it gets tricky. We haven't found hide nor hair of her."

Trudy clucked her tongue and shook her head disapprovingly.

Schwartz quickly added, "We haven't found her yet." He pointed at his son. "The last time Ben saw her was nearly a week ago. That night we had a big snow. It kept him off the ridge."

Elton's mind struggled to process what he was hearing. Amelia dead. Caroline dead. And Marie was missing.

Missing. But maybe still alive.

Elton released the quilt, forced his hands down on the bed and pushed himself up. As he attempted to swing his legs over the side, Trudy stopped him.

"You need rest more than anything. I know Marie is missing, but you're in no shape to find her."

Elton's head spun wildly as waves of dizziness overcame him.

He lay down and motioned for Ben to come closer. "Were there any other places you and Marie spent time? Places she may have gone?"

"We liked the rocks the best. We could see the whole valley from there. We'd look out over it, and dream about having our own place out there. That's what I was going to talk to you about when this all happened."

Schwartz placed a hand on Ben's shoulder. "My son and I have ridden around to see if we could find any clues. We haven't found much that makes sense. A rifle leaning against the corral railing. A hair ribbon that Ben said Marie had been wearing. Some footprints. Could be something, could be nothing."

Elton said, "Marie used to take my rifle sometimes." He looked at Ben. "I was never entirely sure what she was hunting."

Ben blushed mightily. "We both did some hunting, but mostly we'd end up looking over the prairie and dreaming."

Elton remembered the dreams he and Amelia had shared.

A farm.

A family.

A life together.

Forever.

Everything gone. Except…maybe…

"The last day you saw Marie, did you notice anything else? Think hard. Sometimes little things bring big results."

Ben sat on the edge of his chair, eyes closed.

The clock ticked.

Schwartz's chair complained as the big man shifted.

Trudy said, "It's okay if you don't remember. After all, it's been—"

Ben's eyes shot open. "We saw hoof prints. When we were walking back from the rocks we saw hoof prints."

Schwartz said, "I looked around a bit today. Where the snow melted I saw some tracks." He shrugged. "It rained after you were shot and now half of the ridge is muddy slop. And hoof prints could just be hoof prints. They may not have anything to do with Marie."

Elton had to admit that might be true. But if that was all he had, that was what he would start with. He tried to swing his legs over the edge of the bed again but Trudy pushed him down. "You're in no condition to do anything tonight. Doctor Anderson will be back to see you tomorrow."

Elton sank into the bed. He felt exhausted beyond belief. Right now he couldn't imagine saddling a horse or riding, not to mention scouring the ridge trying to find his missing daughter.

When the Schwartz family went to bed he lay in the nearly silent house, the clock his sole companion.

Punishment? Was this his punishment for all the lives he'd taken?

He forced his eyes shut and remembered each man he'd killed.

This is how their families felt.

Now I know.

Unable to sleep, Elton's mind drifted to his family.

Of the three rays of sunshine in his life, two had been extinguished.

And the remaining one barely flickered.

CHAPTER 33

Schwartz awoke to the sound of wood being placed into the stove. He peered around the curtain as Elton put another stick in. He swayed as he moved around the front room. But he was standing. Schwartz pulled his pants on and limped out to join him.

Elton saw him as he came around the curtain. "Figured you'd want the fire going."

"Figured you wouldn't be in bed long."

"Got a girl to find. Won't find her on my back." He looked out the window. "Snowed a bit last night. Enough to see tracks heading toward the ridge. Looks like your boy beat me to it."

Schwartz coughed lightly. "Heard the door close before the sun came up. I let Trudy sleep through it. Figured it would be easier for her that way. Tell me about your daughter."

Elton tapped the piece of split ash in his hand. "She's a good girl, Schwartz. Lots of questions, not a lot of answers yet, but that's to be expected. Seventeen years old, you're not quite sure what's ahead of you in life. I want to give her the chance to find out."

Schwartz leaned against the wall and stared out the window at his son's tracks. They looked determined. He turned to face Elton. "Sorry about your wife and little one. It's a tragedy you can't foresee."

Elton slowly massaged his temples. "We lost a boy a few years back. Amelia used to say every father needs a daughter, every mother needs a son, and our son only lived a couple of days. She took it hard. He was there, then he wasn't there. Amelia had a couple of long years after that. But then Caroline came along and that put joy back in her heart. Mine too." He sat down at the table, shoulders slumped.

Schwartz removed the coffee pot from the stove, poured two cups, and joined Elton. "Guess I need to tell you one more thing, and I don't know if it's going to help or hurt. After the shooting, I had to make a decision. I buried your wife and daughter, and I'm sorry you didn't get the chance to pay your respects. It seemed like the right thing to do, considering your wife…she needed to be buried."

"Hardly an appropriate way to memorialize her life. By tossing her body in a hole for all eternity."

Schwartz tapped his fingers together. "Maybe I should have taken them to Sturgis instead. Undertaker."

Elton's hand jerked and coffee spilled on the table. "No," he said after a moment. "Waiting around for two funerals won't get me any closer to the daughter I have left. You did the right thing. Can I ask where you buried them?"

"Prettiest place I could find, down by the creek, where the big rock is. Off to the side there's a little clearing, looks like flowers bloom there in the summer. I thought that'd be a pleasant resting place."

"When we saw that spot we knew the ridge would be our home. Amelia and I used to walk down to the creek often and sit on that boulder." He struggled with the words. "And Caroline used to 'frow' rocks there." He bowed his head.

Schwartz rose to tend the stock. That's a broken man, he thought. Yet when he neared the barn he heard the house door close. He turned to see Elton following him.

Elton said, "Let's get these animals fed."

As Schwartz opened the barn door an icy gust of wind blew down the valley and sunk its teeth into him.

CHAPTER 34

Marie awoke suddenly as dawn's feeble light crept over the wall of the canyon. The fire had burned to barely-glowing embers. The trees, scarcely more than an arm's length away, were mere shadows. She tried to make out where Russell and Earl had bedded down. After squinting through the low fog that shrouded the canyon floor her eyes grew accustomed to the sparse light and she could make out two lumps. They were still asleep.

She slipped from her blankets and stood.

The lumps didn't move.

Like a prisoner who realized the jail cell door was open, she momentarily froze. She glanced at the horses. They stood, silently dozing. She took a handful of tentative steps, and then turned around. Nothing.

Her heart pounded. She shuffled a few more steps, skirted a large pile of boulders, and then looked back at the horses. They remained still.

She stared, hoping to see a gun nearby. If she could get a gun, this would end. Quickly.

But she couldn't see anything except the blankets covering the men.

Should she ride out? She'd cover a lot more ground by riding, but she was afraid the horses might rustle around if she went to them. No. She'd walk, and try her best to hide her tracks. She pivoted away from the camp and walked squarely into Earl's large chest.

"Whaddaya doing, Marie?" he whispered. "Jeez o'mighty, Russell might wake up any time now!"

"I had to pee."

"No, you wasn't going to pee," Earl tenderly said. "I been watchin' you. You was sneakin' off. You was tryin' to escape."

Marie nodded, sick to her stomach.

Earl patted her head. "You can't run off. Russell would kill you. You don't want to get killed, do you?"

Marie snorted. "No, I'd rather be poked by nasty men."

Earl's head snapped back like he'd been slapped. He wiped his palms on his pants. "Marie, it weren't exactly like that."

"If it wasn't like that, what was it? Did I ask to go with you?"

He shook his head, eyes downcast.

"Did I ask Russell to rape me?"

He moaned.

"And, by the way, you watch me every time I lift my skirts to pee. Do you think I want that, too?"

Earl moaned again. He looked at her, tears forming in his eyes. "Marie, I'm sorry, I'm sorry. You know I ain't touched you. Well, except your hair after Russell was done with you."

"But you never stopped him from raping me, either."

"Well," Earl stammered, "he wanted to do that and he said he was gonna do that, and—"

"And I needed you to stop him, but you never did a thing to help me. That's just as bad." She slumped against the boulders, weeping softly.

When she finally dried her eyes and looked up, she saw that Earl had plopped down on a patch of snow and was crying as well. Aren't we a pair of ninnies, she thought, blubbering like babies. She reached into her dress pocket, found a handkerchief, and held it out for him.

Earl took it, gave his nose a fierce blow, and tried to stop crying. He looked at Marie, lips quivering, and mumbled, "I'm sorry. I am. I coulda stopped him. I shoulda stopped him." That started him crying again.

She watched him, head down, sobbing. She'd never seen a man cry before, and hoped she never would again.

When his tears began to taper she put a hand on his shoulder. "You didn't mean to kill my mother, but you did. You didn't attack me, but you let Russell do it. So I won't forgive you, not ever."

He shook his head and huge teardrops fell to the ground. "My mother always said I was bad. I know good and bad, but I always seem to do bad, not good."

"Still, there is good in you, Earl. I saw it when you gave me your extra blanket, though you were cold too. I saw it when you made your silly excuse about how you wanted to stretch your legs, and you let me ride your horse yesterday."

He tried to smile. "Well, you was this little girl whose horse died, and you was walkin' in the snow and there we was, two grown men ridin'. It didn't seem right, that's all."

"You and Russell kidnapped me, and that's not right, either. But you can still fix what you did by helping me get away. Russell is the bad one. Not you."

Earl sighed. "Ain't that easy, Marie. Russell got so mad at me one time when I done somethin' stupid he left me alone for like a week. I was so scared I thought I was gonna die without him, so I ain't gonna cross him again. And you, he'd pull out his gun and bam! Like your horse. You know bam, like your horse?"

"But I can't go on like this. If he shoots me, at least he won't do those horrible things anymore."

"You may not have so much time left anyway," Earl said.

Marie stared into his eyes. "What do you mean?"

"Nothin'." He looked down and swiped at the snow with the toe of this boot.

"You meant something. Tell me. Please."

"Oh, Russell gets to talkin' sometimes, and when he gets real mad he says things he don't really mean."

Marie's stomach tightened. "Like what?"

Earl sucked in a large breath. "Like maybe killin' you if you cause any more trouble. He figures the best way to make you disappear is to let the coyotes scatter your bones. So you may want to keep sayin' 'yessir' and droppin' your drawers till there's a better time to get away. Anyway, this ain't the place to run. 'Cause out here you got no place to run to."

Marie tightened her grip on his arm. "How will I know the place? How will I know?"

"My momma used to say, most things we don't know till they turn up. Important thing is to recognize them when they do."

Her heart sank. "I'm not sure I'll know when the right time is."

"You'll know," Earl said. "'Cause if I know I'll tell you."

"How are you going to know?" Marie snapped.

Earl set his jaw. "I'm not an idiot about everything, you know."

Marie saw the hurt in his eyes. "Of course you aren't," she said. "I'm sorry."

Earl said, "I can help you. You gotta trust me and wait for the right time."

Marie sucked in a quick breath. "You'll help?"

He gritted his teeth. "Can't promise nothin'. But I can try."

She forced a smile that she hoped looked sincere. "Thank you."

"Jeez o'mighty," Earl said, a rosy flush rising up from his neck. "C'mon, let's go back to the camp before Russell sees we're missin'."

They slowly crept around the boulders, then froze at the sight of Russell stirring the fire.

"You been gone a while, you two," Russell said, his voice flat. "Sightseein', I imagine."

"Peeing," Marie quickly interjected. "I had to pee."

Russell stared at Earl. "And you had to pee, too?"

Earl violently tossed his head from side to side. "Watchin' her is all."

Russell poured himself a cup of coffee, angrily eyeballing the two of them. "Well, you do like watching. Okay, watch this!" He sprinted a handful of steps and threw the cup of coffee in Marie's face.

She screamed as the lukewarm liquid stung her eyes.

"You got off easy this time, missy," Russell hissed. "Wander off again, you won't be so lucky. Now where's my goddamn breakfast?"

CHAPTER 35

Elton shook his head as he and Schwartz drank another cup of coffee. "I'm not exactly sure what I'm looking for, but whatever it is I'm not going to find it here." He finished the coffee and stood. "I'll ride by my house this morning and see what I can find. Then it's time to be on her trail."

Schwartz massaged his knee. "Just two guys talking, but what do you really think happened to her?"

"Who's to say? The ribbon, the rifle against the corral rail, and the tracks Ben saw, that's all I have to go on. Until I find something that tells me otherwise, I'm going to play a hunch those tracks on the ridge have something to do with Marie."

"Be nice to know for certain."

Elton gritted his teeth. "Lot of things I don't know. Why Amelia was killed. What Nix was doing. Why someone rode by the house.

Yes, it'd be nice to know the truth. For now, I don't know a damn thing except that I don't know where my daughter is. But trust me, I'm going to find out."

Elton rode Sparky toward Elk Creek, soon making out the tree line that marked the creek's edge. Then he could see individual trees. A particular section of trees caught his eye. He reined Sparky toward them. On the edge of a stand of aspen he saw the large boulder. Nearing it, he saw two piles of dirt under a few inches of snow.

One large.

One small.

He slid off the saddle and slowly walked forward.

He stood at the edge of the graves. Back at the Schwartz house it had been so important to see this, but now that he was here he didn't know what to do. He stared at the shapes. He'd seen many graves before and had dug more than his share, including the one for his infant son.

The loss of his son had hurt, but the boy had died two days after childbirth. The pain was in the loss. Not the loss of a person, but the loss of opportunity, the 'what if'? What if the boy had lived? Who would he have turned out to be? Elton had grieved over the 'what if' of his son's lost life, but it was never a fully developed pain. Not like the loss of Caroline.

Or his beloved wife.

One night many years ago while they lay in bed together he'd asked Amelia why, of all the men she'd known, she decided to marry him. "Don't think so hard about this," she said. "From the first second I saw you I believed you were the perfect fit for me. Appears, after all these years, I was right."

He'd thought about it long after she'd fallen asleep in his arms. And he realized she was the perfect fit for him too.

Amelia Beauregard Collins.

Of one thing he was certain. She'd made him a better man.

She'd made it easy for him to be a husband and a father.

And now he was barely either.

He dropped to a knee beside the large grave. "Melie." His eyes swam. He composed himself and tried again. "Melie, I'm so sorry. If I hadn't left…" Tears clouded his vision, and this time it took longer to control his emotions.

He finally stood and walked to the large boulder. He climbed up the side of it, struggling as his feet slipped on the slick surface, but he was determined to get to the top. He wiped the snow away and sat there overlooking the graves, the creek, and up the ridge toward their house.

He squinted against the sun, feeling its warmth as it rose higher in the sky. Remnants of flowers poked up through the snow near the graves. In the spring and summer they'd bloom again. They'd make this a beautiful resting place.

He closed his eyes and rocked back and forth. Amelia and Caroline were gone. Now that he'd seen their graves he couldn't ignore it, couldn't push it from his mind, couldn't hope beyond hope that maybe it wasn't true, maybe it was all a mistake.

No. They were truly, honest to God dead.

Gravesites don't lie.

He heard a rock splash in the creek. A child's laughter rang in his ear. He saw the sunlight bounce off blonde hair. The girl laughed again as another rock splashed. He closed his eyes tighter, trying to shut out the sound of her joy. She took another rock in her hand. "I'm gonna throw this one too, Daddy!"

"Make a big splash," he heard himself say, and then they both laughed as water slopped on her dress.

"Uh-oh, Momma's gonna be mad!"

"No she won't, Marie."

Marie.

His eyes shot open. Marie needed him. Not to sit on a boulder and feel sorry for himself, but to find her. He looked at the graves. He wasn't going to add another one here.

Not any time soon.

Ben had ridden to the Collins house soon after the gunfight and brought the cow and calf back to turn them out with the Schwartz's stock. Now, as Elton approached the house, he saw no life whatsoever. Just a stark, gray sky, bare hardwoods, dark evergreens and a fresh coat of white powder on the ground, unmarred except for two sets of rabbit tracks that laced across the yard.

Elton dismounted and walked to the house. He tried to prepare himself for what he'd see inside.

When he was ready, he swung the door open.

He looked at the floor where Nix had fallen and saw a small stain. Blood was hard to get off a floor once it had set. He walked around the table where he and Caroline had been shot. He searched, but could see no sign of blood. Someone had done a lot of scrubbing there. Ben.

He turned in a slow circle and took in the entire house. This, he thought, is where she died. It had always been a happy home, one filled with laughter and love.

What was it now?

An empty shell, perhaps, much like himself.

Waiting for life to begin again.

Trudy Schwartz had packed enough food to last him a couple of days. Elton gathered a bedroll, a slicker and a warm coat, a coffeepot, tin cup and a frying pan, which he quickly packed. The sun had already crept past noon, and he briefly thought about getting one more night's sleep in a bed before setting out. Another night to build up his strength. Chances were better than good he was going to need it.

Or maybe a fire, at least, to take the chill off before he set out.

He walked toward the fireplace and saw a charred stick lying on the stones. When Marie was younger, she had a favorite flat stone on the edge of the hearth near the wall where she would use half-burned sticks to practice her letters.

Elton walked closer, squinting at her stone. Once again, there were letters.

As he studied them a chill gripped his body.

2 MEN HELP ME

CHAPTER 36

This is not happening," Russell sputtered as he observed smoke curling from the chimney of their claim.

They'd been jumped.

Though he and Earl held the paper to the claim, this wasn't the time to see Sheriff Ballew and demand that the jumpers leave. For lately he was even more convinced that the sheriff was on the hunt.

For them.

No. He'd have to solve this problem himself.

Russell motioned Earl closer. "You see what I see?"

Earl said, "Someone's livin' in it. And that someone ain't us."

Russell hissed, "Of course it isn't us. Now get into those trees behind the claim and watch the back door so we can figure out the lay of the land." He took Marie's arm. "You're coming with me."

A few minutes after Russell and Marie left Earl the front door of the cabin swung open. Russell pulled her off her feet and they scrambled for cover. As they hunkered down behind a small stand of aspens, two men and a young boy exited the claim.

All carried firearms. And the men, especially the one who resembled a grizzly bear, looked like they knew how to use them. The big man's weapon was a Sharps buffalo gun. The other man carried a scatter gun. The boy wore a pistol that dangled to his knee and slapped against his thigh as he walked.

It appeared they planned on keeping the claim.

Russell cursed. To take the claim back would mean killing, and killing tended to leave a trail. Such as the trail Sheriff Ballew was now on.

Which led to them.

So what was another death or three? Because Russell damn sure wasn't going to walk away now, for a sizable chunk of the money he and Earl had earned was stashed inside the claim.

Even if they could do without the claim, they couldn't do without the money.

As Russell began to piece out what to do next, a rider entered the clearing about a hundred paces south of the claim shack. Russell couldn't make out the rider, but he knew the horse.

The snow white stallion Midnight. Therefore, Sheriff Courtney Ballew.

Which made an already bad day take a double turn for the worse.

Russell wrapped his arm around Marie's neck and clamped his hand over her mouth. "Want to live?"

Bug-eyed, she stared at him.

He pulled his arm tighter. "If you so much as let your belly growl I'll empty my six-shooter into your head. Then I'll reload and do the same to your sister. Got it?"

She nodded.

Russell pointed to a dry creek bed a few strides to their left. "You and I are going to drop into the bed and we're going to move like a whisper. Make believe you're sneaking out to see that feller of yours and you don't want your Daddy to catch you. Then be even quieter."

They crept into the creek bed and squatted low as they moved. By the time the rider made it to the men, Russell and Marie were no more than a stone's throw away, lying flat under some brush on the snow-covered sand.

"Hello boys," Sheriff Ballew said when he was in front of the men. He stayed on his horse.

"Hello yourself," the big man answered. "Who are you?"

"Sheriff Ballew from Hill City." When the men shared uneasy glances, Ballew pushed. "You boys have names? Or just handsome faces?"

The skinny one said, "I'm Zeke Abernathy. This here's my brother Otto. That boy you see skulking around like a dog that stole a bone is our nephew Caleb."

Ballew pulled a toothpick from his pocket and slipped it in his mouth. "Don't know any Abernathys from around here. You on the roam?"

Zeke said, "Doubt there's anyone from around here 'cept the Injuns, and they been run off mostly. So that means we all roamed from somewhere to get here. How 'bout you, Sheriff?"

"Topeka."

Otto said, "I rode through there once. I understand why you left."

Ballew chuckled. "Where you boys hail from, now that we know it's not here?"

The men glanced at each other again before Zeke offered, "Up-country a ways. Aberdeen."

Ballew worked the toothpick between his teeth. "Not that I'm one to pry, but you mind telling me what inspired you boys to leave God's country and end up here?"

Zeke shrugged. "We had enough of farmin'. Too much work for too little return. So when we heard there's gold in these hills, we headed out."

Otto rolled a small black stone away with his toe. "Can't prove the gold end of the story by me. Why anyone built a claim here in the first place is a mystery I can't unravel."

Ballew studied the stone Otto had kicked. "Sometimes it's hard to assess the value of things you don't fully understand."

Otto nodded like he understood what the sheriff was talking about. "You here for a reason, Sheriff?"

Ballew said, "Come by for coffee if you have some. Come by to visit if you don't."

"Got the best coffee you'll taste for miles around," Zeke said. "Mostly because we're the only living souls for miles around. Light and set."

Ballew glanced at the guns the men held, and then studied the cabin. "Today's a day to be under the good Lord's eyes." He looked at the boy. "Youngster, you wouldn't mind fetching me a cup of that fine coffee such as this gentleman offered, would you?"

Ballew's eyes followed Caleb as the boy walked to the claim shack. "Used to be I knew a couple of gents who occupied this place. You want to tell me how you came across it?"

Otto shrugged. "We rode up that same trail you did and straight to the doorstep. This place was as empty as church on a Friday night. Good place to lay our heads, but it ain't been worth much else."

Ballew scanned a hollowed-out place in the rocks where a sizable amount of digging had occurred. He doubted it had been from this crew. "Abandoned claim is an abandoned claim. No reason you can't inhabit it. But no mining luck, so far as you can tell? Not even over there, where someone else has dug?"

Zeke spat. "Not a God-blessed thing. Between pannin' and diggin' and sweatin' and prayin', we ain't found enough color to fill a small boy's tooth. Instead we been wrestlin' with this stuff here," he said, indicating a pile of grayish-black stone. "I'm so damn sick of this junk I'm about ready to pay someone a dollar a ton to clear it out of the way so we can get to the gold."

Ballew looked at the pile of rocks. "That stuff there?"

"That's it," the skinny man said. "Can't hardly move it out of the way, there's so much of it. Maybe that's why the others left the claim. You can't convince me it's worth a damn. But," he said, glancing toward the claim shack as the boy approached, "it's a place to live while the snow flies. Maybe that's as good as it'll get for us."

"Maybe it is," Ballew agreed. "You say you have no idea where the other fellers ran off to?" He studied the boy's square-toed boots as Caleb handed him a cup of scalding coffee. No way could they be confused for the small footprints he'd found at the campsite. "Obliged."

The big man shrugged. "Probably wasn't a reason for them to stay. I imagine they took to the wind and sailed off."

"Sailed off." Ballew looked again at the pile of stone and shook his head. "No, I don't think that's the case at all. If those boys went somewhere, they went for a reason." Although for the life of him, he couldn't think what the reason might be.

Zeke noisily cleared his throat. "All these questions, I'm startin' to suspect you didn't come by for our hospitality."

Ballew fingered the dodger inside his coat pocket. "It's my job to know who's in these hills. Also my job to kind of correlate who they've been and what they've done in the past. Helps to keep life harmonious that way."

He looked at Otto, who'd begun to fidget with the Sharps. An edgy man with a gun was never a good sign. Ballew eased his hand a bit closer to his pistol. "No offense, but you boys haven't been a bit sideways with the law recently, have you?"

"Not recent," Otto blurted, before he was shushed by Zeke.

Zeke earnestly looked at the sheriff. "What Otto means to say is, we ain't been sideways with the law."

"That's not what he said, though. You boys have a story to tell? Something that happened in the mines by Lead, maybe? An event that made you want to leave in the dead of night?"

Zeke stammered, "Don't know anything about up in the mines. This here's the first mine we've seen, and if they're all like this I hope we don't never see another. But we got cockeyed in Aberdeen a while back with one of them big land baron-type rancher's sons, and Otto busted the guy's nose. Since we worked for the man and he was howlin' about wantin' justice, that sped our departure, truth be told." He stared at the ground. "You ain't tracked us down for that though, have you? All the way from Aberdeen over a busted nose?"

Ballew gulped down the last of the coffee and handed the tin cup back to the boy. "I was a knucklebuster myself back in the day, and I've worked for some downright disagreeable folks who needed nothing so much as a busted nose. Best thing about working for someone like that is you can always leave and start over. By the looks of things here, it'll turn up roses for you before you know."

Zeke slapped Otto on the back. "Well, we sure do hope so, Sheriff. We could use a lucky break. Now if you don't mind, I'm about ready to dig up some of them roses you mentioned. Preferably gold ones."

"You may find that silver ones aren't half-bad either, should you find yourself so lucky," Ballew said. "Now you keep an eye out for a couple of travelers bearing a grudge. Look a bit like you two. Not quite so handsome, though."

"Few are," Zeke said.

Ballew chuckled. "They aren't quite as pleasant, either. One's big as an ox, one stick-skinny and looks like he swallowed the devil whole. Those boys ride in, you send young Caleb to get me. And you'll want to keep those firearms handy. They might be a mite insistent about taking their claim back."

After Ballew rode away, Russell dragged Marie into the woods where Earl waited. "Don't imagine you heard any of that," he said to the big man.

Earl shook his head.

Russell said, "The sheriff's looking for us on account of that miner you got into a fight with in Lead. Without that, we'd be home free. You're about the worst luck I've ever lugged around."

Earl grumbled, "You shot him."

"Because he pulled a gun on you after you hit him! If I didn't shoot I'd be standing here having this conversation with myself! Because you'd be dead!"

"But I ain't, 'cause you shot him."

Russell momentarily debated adding Earl to the tally. "Anyway," he said after he'd cooled down a bit, "I wanted to rush those boys and take our claim back. But now that the sheriff is hunting us for sure, we have to go. Now."

"Where we goin', Russell? To town?"

Russell closed his eyes and waited for his anger to pass. "With Sheriff Ballew looking for us, you think that'd be the best plan?"

Earl's face reddened. "Not Hill City. I was thinkin' about Sturgis. Then catch the stage to anywhere but here."

Anywhere but here. Which meant saying goodbye to the lucrative mine. To the claim shack tucked away from civilization. The claim shack that could have been their home until the mine played out. Until he'd acted like a damn fool by chasing the Collins women. Now, from the looks of it, that decision was going to cost them. Greatly. "Don't guess we have much choice."

"That's why I said go to town. Best place to get the stage, dontcha think?"

Russell had to agree with Earl again. But a trip to meet the stage jacked the risk up, for towns like Sturgis meant sheriffs, and sheriffs meant trouble. With Ballew on the hunt, catching the Hill City stage was impossible. As was the stage out of Lead, where he'd shot the miner.

If they chose to ride south instead, they were about twenty miles from the nearest stage depot, on the edge of Rapid City. With Marie walking, it'd take them nearly two days to reach the depot. But she could walk to Sturgis in half a day. And she could ride to Sturgis even faster.

Of course, he could shoot the girl and be done with her. And then he and Earl could travel a lot faster.

But she still served a purpose.

And as long as she did, she was safe.

Then he'd put a bullet in her head. Right after he put a bullet in her father.

Because Collins was a murderer.

And murderers didn't deserve to live.

"Listen," Russell said, "we have to move and we have to move quickly. We can't have the girl walking anymore." He glanced at the corral. "You think you can get one of those horses?"

Earl looked at Marie. "How about I stay here with her and you get one of the horses? You're quieter than I am."

"I could do that," Russell said. "But I want to make damn sure she doesn't wander off while I'm gone. Now why would I jump to a conclusion about her wandering off?"

Earl shrugged. "Jeez o' mighty, I got no idea."

"Well, to make sure you don't get any ideas like that, you get the horse. I've got to see a few gents about some money. Now skedaddle."

CHAPTER 37

After he left his house Elton rode south near the trail to Hill City. Less than an hour into his ride he cut across a set of tracks in the snow. It didn't take much studying to determine Sheriff Courtney Ballew had been in the area.

Elton followed the tracks for a quarter-mile or so, then turned west. Whatever Ballew was looking for, he didn't need Elton riding up on him and interrupting his work.

Wind continued to rattle the branches overhead, making the already cold day feel far colder. He flipped his collar up, pulled his coat tighter, and wondered what Marie was wearing.

And what she was doing.

And if she was still alive.

No. She was still alive.

She had to be.

Anything else was unbearable.

So she was alive.

He thought about the message she'd left. 2 MEN HELP ME

Two men. Likely the same tracks Marie and Ben had seen the afternoon she was taken. Just as likely the miners Shorty had seen riding over the ridge. The miners with a claim north of town.

He needed to find out where.

Soon he crossed Ballew's trail yet again. The tracks were headed toward Hill City.

This time Elton followed them.

He had a daughter to find.

And Hill City was the place to start.

CHAPTER 38

The wind began to blow harder, whipping the fresh flakes into a frenzy. Marie wrapped a blanket around her and watched the fire as the flames dipped and darted in the wind. This was the worst day they'd had on the trail. So far, she reminded herself. They were still on the move, and it appeared things would get worse before they got better.

She looked at the bony withers and gaunt frame of her new horse. When Earl had led it back to her, she'd been thrilled.

Until she'd gotten a better look.

The tired horse had stared at her with weary eyes that seemed to say 'Have you looked at yourself lately?' Her mother had a favorite saying: 'Don't look a gift horse in the mouth.' So she hadn't bothered asking if maybe there had been a better horse to ride. Instead she thanked Earl, then she thanked Russell.

And then she'd said a little prayer.

She had a feeling someone needed it.

Because after Earl had left to get the horse, Russell had gagged her, bound her hands and feet and then he'd slipped away. Soon after, she'd heard gunshots.

Two, then a pause.

Then two more.

She didn't bother asking about that, either.

Russell stared at the fire. He'd avoided the usual trail to Sturgis, but by doing that it had taken them far longer to get off the ridge. More than once they'd found themselves riding along rocky ledges choked with thick, nearly impenetrable brush, unable to find a way to the valley floor. And the ride down hadn't improved much once the snow started falling again.

At first it'd been a few meager flakes, the type of late fall snow that doesn't bother to stick to the ground when it lands.

But by the time they'd reached the bottom of the ridge he could hardly see the trees a half-mile away on the other side of the valley. The ground was covered with a deepening white sheet and the temperature had dropped significantly.

This snow would stay.

And they still had a couple hours' ride to Sturgis. Which would put them into town long after the stage had already left.

A night in a hotel, or another night holed up in the valley?

The wind howled and the trees across the valley disappeared in a soft whisper of deepening gray.

The sky darkened.

And the snow fell harder.

Russell stared past the fire at Earl. "You have any more bright ideas about this excursion?"

Earl brushed snow from his pants leg. "You want to know what I think? Really?"

Russell grumbled, "Yes, I want to know what you think. Really."

Earl looked pleased. "Best way to not miss the stage tomorrow is to get there tonight. Get us a hotel room. Eat. Sleep in a bed. That's what I think."

Russell stiffly rose, tossed a bit of brush on the fire and watched it burn. He wasn't afraid of being found by Collins. That had been the plan all along.

They'd meet, so to speak. With Russell's gun aimed at Collins' back. Then a bullet. That's how this would end.

So Collins wasn't the problem. It was the law. That was the problem with going to town.

Because while he didn't have anything to say to the law, he figured the law had a hell of a lot of things to say to him.

His stomach burbled. This was nowhere near the plan he'd laid out when he'd first decided to visit the Collins women.

Rape them.

Humiliate them.

That would be enough.

But then Earl had killed the mother. Then he'd mentioned Loretta, and that had opened up a whole new line of thinking. It was no longer enough to violate the Collins women.

Not after the way Loretta had died.

Russell wanted Collins to see Marie, broken and disintegrated. So ruined that she was no longer a person at all.

But still alive.

For the full effect, she had to remain alive.

So going to town was a risk worth taking. Board the stage tomorrow. Go someplace warm for the winter.

Then return the girl, fat and pregnant, to Collins in the spring.

That would be the best feeling of all.

Until he watched Collins die.

That would be better still.

Earl said, "Guess we'll have to figure out how to do the sleepin' though. Look pretty funny if we all get one room."

Russell jabbed a finger into Marie's chest. "Don't you move. You take one step away from that fire and it'll be the last step you ever take. You hear?"

"Yes, sir."

"Yes, sir?" Russell spat. "Now you find your manners? Christ." He looked at Earl, and jerked his head sideways. "Over there."

They walked until they were away from Marie's earshot. Russell kept a sharp eye on her while he spoke. "This can still go wrong faster than your heart beats. We make a mistake in town and we end up dangling from a rope. You want to dangle from a rope?"

Earl's eyes grew wide. "Not if I got a choice."

"Then you do what I tell you. You and your 'daughter' ride in a few minutes in front of me. You take her to the Rosewood and you don't let her out of your sight. I'll come in behind you and get another room, since I can't trust either one of you as far as I can throw you."

Earl said, "I always wanted to be a father."

"Well now's your chance, papa. And so help me, if you turn your back on her for a second, I'll slit her throat just to stay in practice. You got it?"

"I got it. Me and my daughter at the Rosewood."

Russell turned to Marie and whistled. "Get your ass over here."

Marie walked toward him. When she came close, his hand flew up from his hip and slapped her on the left side of her face.

Her head snapped back. She silently dropped to her knees, glaring at him.

Earl shoved Russell's arm. "Whattaya gotta do that for?"

Russell lurked over her. "I don't like the way she looked at me." His toe thudded into her thigh. "Now you wipe that look off your face or I'll smack it off for you."

Marie felt around in the snow with her hands and came up with two fist-sized rocks. She cocked one arm back. "Try it, you bastard."

Russell's gut burned. "Why you little..."

He lunged forward and shoved Marie. One of her hands still held a rock. He stepped on her fingers, grinding them into the rock until she begged him to stop.

When he did she threw the rock at him, hitting him in the chest.

"You bitch," he hissed. That's going to earn you a black eye."

He pulled back his fist to slug her. As he did, Earl dove into him and knocked him over.

"What the hell are you doing," Russell bellowed after he untangled himself from Earl.

Earl yelled, "You got no call for that, crushing her fingers. Sayin' you'll hit her!" He seized Russell's coat and pulled him close. "You got no call for that."

Russell swatted his hand away. "Oh, so it's like this now?" He spun and yanked himself from the big man's grasp. "You remember this. She opens her mouth, you hang."

"You raped her! That was you!"

Russell slowly drew his pistol and pointed it toward Earl. "Push comes to shove, I wonder who they're going to believe. The idiot, or me? I'm banking on me. Of course, you also killed her momma. Don't forget that little misdeed." He waved the gun's barrel in a tight spiral, but it never left the big man's chest.

Earl looked at Marie, who was running her hands around in the snow, searching for more rocks. "They'll believe you," he grumbled. "But you don't gotta hit her. Let's get to Sturgis and then get on the stage, okay? And go to wherever."

Russell kept his eyes on Earl while he spoke. "Girl, you pick up another rock and you'll never leave the valley." He kicked her in the ribs.

She scrambled behind Earl and glared at Russell. She screamed, "Why are you doing this to me? Why do you hate me so?"

Russell tugged on the brim of his hat. "May want to ask your daddy about Loretta Marsh."

CHAPTER 39

Elton knew the conversation would probably extend the limits of his patience, so before he went to the livery he reminded himself to slow down. He was far behind Marie. What difference would another few minutes make?

He rode to the livery, dismounted, and walked inside. "Shorty, you around?"

A voice echoed from the back room. "Hold onto your 'spenders, I'm comin'!" A moment later, Shorty came charging around the corner. "Elton Collins! First I ain't seen you in years, now I can't get rid of you." Shorty looked at the bandage under Elton's hat. "Someone try to scalp you?"

Elton shook his head. "Victim of a bad haircut. Have you seen the sheriff?"

"He blew into town a couple of hours ago, before this little bitty snow hit. But he kept right on a goin'."

So Elton would hunt the men alone. "Those two miners who rode over the ridge toward my place, have you seen them recently?"

"Naah," Shorty said. "Them birds are as gone as gone can be. Ain't seen a load of ore from 'em since before you come through the first time. Since you're askin', I don't suspect you ever fetched up with the rascals."

Elton grimaced. "The solo rider you told me about, I saw him again. But a description of the other boys would be useful. They're the ones I have to find."

Shorty slowly rolled a cigarette, offered the makings to Elton, and then continued. "Skinny now, you don't have to see him to know he's near. Him you can smell 'fore he rounds the corner, and you ain't smellin' lilacs. Looks meaner'n a bag a rattlers, too. The big one, talkin' to him's like waitin' for molasses to run in wintertime. Slow, that feller is, no way around it."

Elton fought a smile. Talking to Shorty had its own molasses quality. "Anyone ridden out to their claim to see if they've left the area?"

"Jimmy Loomis, a feller I bend an elbow with when he's buyin', he rid by their claim a while ago. He said there was neither man nor beast in sight. Could be they rode off to winter someplace. 'Course you know, around here when the winter wind gets to blowin' the ground gets hard and the women get harder. Got to be a better place to rest my weary bones. Sad to say I ain't found it yet."

"Before you find that better place, how about you tell me where their claim is, and what they ride?"

Shorty stubbed out his cigarette. "All these questions, you sound pretty serious about findin' these boys."

"You have no idea."

—

Ben had been tracking all morning and had yet to find anything significant. He rode on, poking into draws, riding on top of small crests, kicking along ice-rimmed streams, but he saw nothing that gave him hope.

Near noon, he spied a set of tracks heading south. With nothing better to do, he followed them. They never wavered, and then he realized they were going to Hill City. And they were probably tracks made by Mister Collins. Nice job, he thought. You found Marie's father. Resigned, he hung his head and continued to town.

The street was a muddy, snowy mess. Snow continued to fall, making further tracking impossible. He debated searching the town to see if Mister Collins was there.

You're not looking for him. You're looking for Marie.

He tucked his chin, pulled his hat lower, and rode out of town toward Lead.

As the snow continued, Elton nudged Sparky into an easy lope. A few inches of fresh powder dusted the landscape, and it puffed from Sparky's flashing hoofs with each stride.

They eased toward Alkali Creek. Elton had only seen it flow after a hard rain, when water frothed and boiled down the ridge and raced across the flat prairie to join the larger Elk Creek. Today, like most days, it was dry.

He swung Sparky toward a small copse of trees where the bed flattened out, making a crossing easier. As Sparky walked forward to step down the gravel banking, Elton heard a metallic click. Close by. His pistol flashed into his hand.

A wide-eyed boy of no more than fourteen stepped from the trees and pointed an old Colt Paterson revolver in Elton's vicinity.

The boy's eyes locked onto Elton's pistol. His voice shook as he said, "Mister, you ain't planning to shoot me, are you?"

"Depends. Are you planning to shoot me?"

The boy dropped the pistol to his hip. "No sir, I ain't gonna shoot you."

"Then we're even. Mind if I get down from my horse?"

The boy shook his head and holstered his pistol. "No, sir."

Elton noticed that tears had carved streaks down the boy's filthy, pale face. His clothing was little more than rags, and both his boots were split open along the sole. He'd wrapped a rag around one of them to keep the snow out. Apparently he'd run out of rags, for through the hole in the other one Elton saw a bare, sockless foot.

"What's your name, son?"

"I'm Caleb Forrester."

"Elton Collins." When the boy showed no recognition of the name he reholstered his pistol, dismounted and looked up the trail. Through the falling snow he could see the claim a little ways up the trail. "Caleb, why aren't you there instead of here?"

The boy's face tightened. "My uncles are there. But they're shot dead."

Elton's heart raced. "Is a girl there?" He shook Caleb by the shoulders. "Is my daughter there? Is she dead too?"

"There's no girl, there's no girl!" Caleb twisted away from Elton. "There's no girl, mister. Only my uncles."

"Are your uncles a couple of miners? A big one and a skinny one with black hair?"

Caleb wiped his runny nose with the back of his hand. "Uh-huh." His breath hitched. "They're dead."

Elton shook Caleb again. "Where's the girl? Damn it boy, where's my daughter?"

Caleb started to cry. "There ain't no girl, mister. It's only me. Please, it's only me here."

Elton steadied the boy. "A big man and a skinny man with black hair kidnapped my daughter a little more than a week ago."

Caleb ran the palms of his hands over his face, smearing away the tears. "Just past a week ago me and my uncles were riding here from Aberdeen. I ain't seen no girl, honest. I ain't seen your daughter."

Elton clutched Caleb's shoulder again. "You weren't here? This isn't your claim?"

"We found it empty so we moved in. I cleaned it up some. It was close as I had to home in a long time. Till a while ago."

"What happened?"

Caleb closed his eyes for a few seconds and swayed. "Well first, a man on a white horse rode up to talk to Uncle Zeke and Uncle Otto. Said he was the sheriff, and he told us to look out for the men who used to live here. But my uncles said they had guns and they didn't have to worry about nothing."

Caleb swiped his patched boot through the snow. "They did though, 'cause when I went out to use the outhouse I heard someone yell. Then I heard gunshots. I peeked out through the boards in the door and saw a man leave the house. Tall and skinny."

"Did he have someone with him?" Elton asked. "A girl?"

Caleb sighed. "Mister, my two uncles got shot dead. I figured I was next, so I weren't looking for no girl. I was looking to live."

"Sorry, son."

"My uncles, they was all I had for family." A tear tumbled down Caleb's cheek.

Elton rested his hand on Caleb's shoulder. "Listen Caleb, I have to go up there and look around a bit. You want to go with me?"

Caleb firmly shook his head. "I ain't going in there. Never again."

Elton could see two snow-covered horses in the corral. "Why aren't there three?"

"The man who shot my uncles took my horse, too. I heard them ride off. I seen the tracks."

"How many were there, son? How many riders?"

"Three."

Elton looked at the white, unbroken blanket that stretched in all directions. His spirits fell as fast as the drifting snow. "Any guess as to which direction they went?"

"Yes sir." The boy dutifully walked to the trees and pointed north.

Elton knew a trail close by that wound its way to the valley below. It led directly to Sturgis.

The most logical place to go during a snowstorm.

"Saddle the horse you like, Caleb. We have some riding to do."

CHAPTER 40

Rosewood Hotel desk clerk Sherwin Smithson knew his job. Welcome the customers, make each of them feel as if they were the most important people who would ever walk into the hotel, and attend to their every need.

With grace and dignity.

Still, at the sight of the bedraggled pair walking toward him, Smithson fought to keep his mouth from hanging agape. While the huge, ungainly man was a mess, the girl accompanying him looked far worse. People of their type never stayed in a hotel of the Rosewood's quality. However, with the snow falling as hard as it was and looking like it wouldn't stop until spring, the Rosewood would take all the business it could get.

Despite the way they smelled.

Then a tall, skinny man stepped through the door behind them and leaned against the wall. When Smithson got a good look at him his blood iced over. The man's eyes glittered with a fury Smithson had never seen before.

Death, he thought. I'm looking at Death.

Smithson nervously watched him. The last time trouble had walked in the door a desk clerk had been shot. While this had provided Smithson a welcome job opening, he was in no mood to provide another employee with the same opportunity.

The big man who'd accompanied the girl glanced at the man leaning against the wall, then stepped to the hotel counter and said, "Jeez o'mighty, we had a time of it on the ride here."

Smithson eyed the girl who stood, eyes downcast, beside the man. Her hair was a matted mess and her soaked dress was stained. A filthy blanket was draped over her shoulders. He'd never seen a woman look like this. Or smell like this. He wasn't sure he could keep his face neutral.

As he wrestled with a lip that wanted to curl he realized that, without prodding, the man was likely to stand there all night and not say anything else. Smithson quickly said, "Of course, sir. But you're here now. What may we offer you?"

"My daughter and I would like two rooms. With tubs," the man added, nodding toward the girl.

"Certainly, sir." Smithson saw the girl's eyes light up at the mention of a bath. "Do you have a bag we can carry upstairs for you?"

The man shook his head, spraying the ledger with a shower of melting snow. "Only the shirts on our backs." He looked at Marie. "And dress. My shirt. Her dress. On our backs."

"Of course, sir. You'll find your rooms at the top of the stairs. First and second door on the left."

Smithson studied them a bit longer. "*After* you bathe, the dining room will still be open. And if you'd like," he went on, studying the dark stain on the front of Marie's dress, "we can arrange to clean your daughter's things."

The girl pulled the blanket tighter around her shoulders. "I'm fine."

The man who'd been leaning against the wall now stepped toward the desk. "You won't want to be letting this girl in the dining room. Something wrong with her, healthwise. I followed her up the valley and she never did stop coughing. 'Course," he said, "you might not mind her passing this on to your other customers. Don't know for sure. But if it was me in your shoes…"

The man shrugged and slowly moved back against the wall. "Just saying, is all."

Smithson's breathing quickened. If it wasn't for desk clerks getting shot, it was for letting the wrong customers into the hotel. And maybe he already had.

But three rooms were three rooms. "What I can do, folks," he said, "is have dinner sent directly to her room. That'd be fine, wouldn't it, miss, to eat in your room?"

The big man glanced at the man leaning against the wall, then returned his gaze to Smithson. "My daughter would enjoy that."

The girl dropped her head, turned, and walked to the stairs with her father close behind.

"Some kind of hotel you run here," the tall man muttered as he reached for his key. "Possibly you should be a bit more selective with your clientele."

After he walked away, Smithson dropped onto a nearby stool, pulled out a handkerchief and mopped his perspiring face. A bit more selective? He couldn't agree more.

CHAPTER 41

Marie felt a wave of disappointment when she saw the tub.
It was empty.

She sat on the bed and twisted her soiled blanket in her hands, fighting back tears she couldn't fully understand.

A light knock at the door caused her to jump.

Tentatively she eased across the floor.

She reached for the knob, then dropped her hand. What if it was Russell?

If it was Russell he'd have knocked the door down and he'd be on top of you. Open the door.

A stooped, elderly Oriental woman stood before her with water to fill the tub.

Tell her!

As she started to speak Russell stepped into the hallway behind the woman. He ran his index finger across his throat in a slashing motion.

Marie sullenly motioned the woman in. When she tried to close the door Russell caught it with his hand and held it open. "Hotel as classy as this, I want to make sure you get everything you deserve," he said. "The considerate thing to do." His hateful eyes contrasted his words.

When the woman finished filling the tub and left, Russell quickly stepped into the room. "Another chance like that comes up, don't get any stupid ideas," he growled. "Stupid ideas are how people get dead. You have other family depending on you to be smarter than normal."

She nodded.

Russell twisted her chin and forced her to look in his eyes. "Dead."

He turned on his heel, walked out and closed the door.

As his footsteps drifted to silence down the hallway, Marie jammed a straight-backed chair under the door knob. "Bastard," she hissed.

Minutes slipped by as she stared at the door. When she was absolutely, positively sure he wasn't coming back she took off her torn, dirty clothes, rinsed them in the bath water, hung them to dry and then slipped into the tub.

She worked the soap with a brush, trying to rid herself of the filth that had accumulated since she'd been kidnapped. She scoured her hands, scrubbing them as clean as she could, and then she washed her hair.

The hair that Earl stroked every night. She shivered. She never wanted her hair touched again.

The tick of boot heels approached her door.

They slowed.

Stopped.

She stared at the door.

At the doorknob.

A moment later she heard click, click, click as the boots moved on.

Only then did she allow herself to breathe.

The warm water gently embraced her and washed her guard away. No longer would she have to convince herself that nothing had happened.

Of course, nothing would have happened if you'd shot Earl.

She slammed her hands down into the water, throwing a wave on the floor. "I know. I know," she moaned, her chin dropping to her chest. "It's all my fault."

Her mother's death. Likely, her sister's death. Russell's repeated rapes. Her fault.

And what would happen when her father came home? Would something happen to him too?

Then you'll have killed the entire Cole family.

Not the Cole family. The Collins family.

Cole. Collins.

Was her name even Marie?

The tears flowed unabated.

After she felt she couldn't cry another tear she quelled her sobs, washed her face, and forced herself to think. There had to be a way to escape. To save her sister.

Save her father.

And, maybe, save herself. She looked at the chair by the window, where her mother's package sat. She'd promised herself that when she was safe she'd open it.

She looked around the small, tidy room. She might be alone for now. But she was nowhere near safe.

She closed her eyes and tried to recall the town's layout. The Double Eagle saloon on one side of the street, the general store on the other. Three houses on the right, two more on the left. Then on the right, the Sheriff's office.

She was so close to the Sheriff's office.

One chance to make it there.

That's all she'd get.

She stepped from tub, wrapped a towel around herself, unlocked the window, lifted the sash, and looked at the now-dark Sheriff's office. Swirling snow blew in around her. Teeth chattering, she slammed the window shut. But she'd noticed the sloping porch roof outside her window.

Conveniently located to help her sneak out and escape.

If you dare.

If.

Marie walked to the mirror and dropped her towel. Her gaunt appearance shocked her. She'd lost so much weight she was able to see each of her ribs. She hadn't looked at a mirror since before she'd been kidnapped, and while she didn't know what to expect, she hadn't expected this.

She checked her entire body. She had a bruise on her jaw where she'd been punched by Russell. She had a dark bruise on her ribcage, and multiple bruises on her arms and legs. Just bruises, she told herself. You're none the worse for wear. Except for what Russell had done to her.

You'll carry that forever.

She looked closer at her reflection. At her eyes.

She'd never seen those haunted eyes before. It was like she was looking at a stranger. A person no one would ever want to see.

Like Ben. Even if she escaped, he'd take one look at her and disappear. For good.

And she couldn't say that she blamed him. After what Russell had done, no man would want her again.

Eyes downcast, she picked up her towel, wrapped it around herself, stared at the wallpaper and thought about Ben while she waited for her clothes to dry.

When they were still slightly damp she pulled on her torn underwear and then her dress. She glanced toward the window. A wall of whirling snow met her gaze. She slid the armchair next to the window, pocketed her mother's package, and watched the snow pile up, flake by flake, on the windowsill.

A hammering knock on the door made her jump away from the chair, sending it clattering across the floor.

Marie stared at the chair wedged under the doorknob.

It could stay there until Hell froze over.

The door knob twisted. Back and forth.

Back and forth.

The door opened a bit.

She'd forgotten to lock it.

And then the chair held it in place.

She heard a soft curse. Then, "It's me, Marie." Earl. "I got your food."

"Is Russell out there?"

"Russell? Naw, I think he's at the bar drinkin' his dinner. It's me."

Her father always told her 'Never pass up a meal. You don't know when you'll eat again.' And she was hungry.

Ravenously hungry.

She pushed the door closed, slid the chair out, and allowed Earl to enter.

He'd combed his hair, had shaved for the first time since she'd met him, and wore a clean shirt and pants. Even his boots looked clean. The clothes appeared to be new, and he seemed mighty proud of himself.

"General store was open," he said, "and I swang by." He handed her a black shawl. "It ain't much," he said as he glanced at her dress, "but maybe it'll be helpful."

Marie wrapped it around her shoulders and the fringed edge hung low enough to cover the stain.

Low enough to hide what they'd done to her. She glanced one more time at the mirror. Would others see the truth that she saw when she looked at her reflection?

She feared it would take far more than a shawl to cover that.

CHAPTER 42

Sheriff Courtney Ballew stood his horse on a knoll near the mouth of Piedmont valley, watched the snow drift over the pines beside him, and admitted that he was no Donovan McCready. He'd been riding steady for four days and, other than the claim jumpers, he hadn't seen anyone else.

If McCready had been on the job he'd have already corralled the two men Ballew futilely hunted. Hell, McCready would have probably also rounded up half the other folks on Ballew's dodgers and still been home in time for dinner.

Alas, the citizens of Hill City were saddled with Courtney Ballew instead. Who, from the looks of things, couldn't even catch a cold.

To top it off, he was now on the far side of the ridge. In good weather, it was a full day's ride back to Hill City.

And it wasn't good weather. Not in the least. The snow was at least six inches deep along the valley floor, and Ballew had already encountered drifts up to Midnight's knees.

Ballew faced northwest and peered into the gray mass of driving snow. In an hour it'd be black as a kettle bottom.

But with luck, by then he could also be in Sturgis. He nudged Midnight's flank and they set off into the teeth of the storm.

She was young. She was blonde. Even in the dim hallway lighting she was beautiful. And Major Robert Tinsdale plowed into her with all the grace of a runaway bull elephant as she exited her hotel room door with a tray in her hand as he walked his mother down the hall.

Her tray crashed to the floor and food remains splattered against the wall. She stumbled awkwardly, slipped on a scrap of food, and ended up on her knees.

A huge man barged from her room, but Tinsdale quickly stepped in front of him and offered his hand to the young lady.

She looked at him, shook her head slightly, then tentatively held out her hand.

Joyously, he helped her to her feet.

Then he observed his mother's bemused stare.

"What, mother? This woman required my assistance."

"Of course she did, Major Tinsdale. I'm sure her father, the man whom you elbowed out of the way, couldn't have aided her any better than you did."

"Mother," Major Tinsdale wailed. "Please. These people...this fine young lady..." He fiercely rubbed his hands together. "The father...yes, the father. He's a prominent businessman. I must pay my respects."

Tinsdale stepped toward the father and stepped on the edge of the metal tray. The other side of the tray flipped upward and hit the girl in the shin. "Sorry!" he blurted.

She winced. "It's okay, sir."

Tinsdale thrust his hand to the man, who hesitated before finally taking it. "Major Robert Tinsdale, commander, Fort Meade," he rapidly said, as if the words couldn't escape fast enough.

The man extended his hand. "Pleasure."

Tinsdale turned to the beautiful woman. "Miss, may I be so bold as to ask your name?"

She squinted, bit her lip, and rocked in place for a moment before she spoke. "This is my father, Earl..." She hesitated, then in a rush finished, "Pearl?"

Earl glanced at her, then said, "And she is my daughter Marie. We met before, you know. One time you stopped us out in the valley. Me and Russell. Could be you don't recollect, but I sure do."

Marie reached for Tinsdale's arm. "Sir, I need your—"

"You don't need a thing from him," a voice behind Tinsdale said.

Tinsdale flinched, then turned.

A man stood there.

His eyes, buried deep into his eye sockets, burned coal-black.

His scarred face rippled like a mask as he rolled his tongue around in his mouth.

Tinsdale's knees buckled. He reached for the wall and struggled to remain standing.

The man looked at the young woman and spoke. "Miss, I expect your room is the safest place for you." He pointed toward the door. "And keep it locked. Because you don't ever know who may want to get in."

"But there's no need, sir," Tinsdale said. "My mother and I were—"

"Talking. I heard you. But a young lady talking to a man old enough to be her father is highly improper. I'm surprised your mother didn't intercede on the young lady's behalf. Regardless, I'm sure you agree the best place for her is inside."

Marie glanced at Tinsdale, who leaned hard against the wall, then toward Earl. She took one last look at the black-eyed man, then dropped her head and walked into her room.

The door closed, then the lock clicked. Tinsdale heard a chair slide across the floor, then a thud as it was jammed under the doorknob.

The dark man looked at the closed door, then to the people in the hallway. "Lock and chair? Apparently she does want to keep you out. Guess I'll mosey." He looked at Tinsdale's mother and touched the brim of his hat. "Nice son you raised, Ma'am."

She turned in a huff, entered her room and closed the door.

Without another word the dark man went to the stairs. His spurs jangled lightly as he descended.

CHAPTER 43

According to the plan, Earl was supposed to wait until Russell came back to talk to him. But after the way things had gone in the hotel hallway, he knew he couldn't wait. As soon as Tinsdale left, Earl clumped down the stairs.

A new clerk manned the reception desk. Breathless, Earl stepped to the counter, impatiently waving the clerk over. "Russell Belfour, I gotta see Russell Belfour. But I don't know what room he's in."

The clerk thumbed through the register, then solemnly closed it. "We have no Russell Belfour registered here."

"'Course you do." Earl reached for the register, but the clerk snatched it away and held it close to his chest.

"Sir, I have reviewed the register, and we do not have a guest named Russell Belfour." He peered at Earl over his glasses. "Perhaps you have another name?"

Earl shook his head. "No, no, his name is Russell Belfour. Tall, black eyes. Mark on the side of his face. If you'd seen him, you'd remember."

"Ah yes," the clerk said. "We have a Herman Smith who fits that description."

Slowly it dawned on Earl. "That's who I'm lookin' for, Herman Smith. What was I thinkin', callin' him Russell Belfour? Where's Herman Smith at?"

The clerk said, "He walked out a moment ago. I believe he's at the Double Eagle bar next door."

"Why aren't you watching her?" Russell shouted as Earl pulled out a chair and sat. When no guns came out, the patrons relaxed slightly and went back to drinking.

Earl said, "She's fine. She's safe behind the door. That Army guy seemed some taken with Marie. Like he'd never seen a pretty girl before. Jeez o'mighty, ain't he kind of old for her? After he knocked her over he talked to me like we was best of friends."

Russell stared at him. "What would he say to a dumb no-account like you?"

"He called me a businessman. Which I don't know how he knew about our minin' business, 'cause he didn't even remember when he met us."

The hairs on the back of Russell's neck stood up. "How do you know he didn't remember?"

Earl said, "I had to remind him."

"Ahh, Christ! You reminded him of when he inspected our ore? Are you a complete fool?"

"But Russell, it's true. I thought—"

224

"No. You didn't. Jesus, just when I believe I've seen the dumbest thing you'll ever do, you top it."

"Well, jeez." The big man's brow crumpled. "Sorry."

"Did you tell him your name, too? Certainly you didn't do that, Mister Businessman." Russell winced, fearing the answer.

"Well, Marie did the 'how you doin's', and said my name was Earl."

"Tell me you didn't use her name."

Earl smiled. "Well, of course. It's her name."

Russell downed his drink, flipped the bartender a coin and said, "First thing we're going to do is go back to the hotel so she doesn't slip out and see the sheriff. Now."

After he'd verified that Marie was still in her room, Russell leaned against the wall outside her door and angrily stared at Earl. "So we planned to come into town separate and not see each other until we got on the stage. Then I leave you alone for an hour so I can get a meal and you let the man in charge of all those Army soldiers know about us, and you used our real names to boot. Then you left Marie alone, you came charging into the bar like your hair was on fire, and blurted out your story loud enough so everyone could hear it."

Russell pursed his lips. "I want you to think about this. Really get it straight in your head. What will happen if she tells someone about us?"

Earl said, "I guess they'd know what we did."

"And then they will arrest us. And then they will hang us. So do you understand why it's important to keep her quiet?"

Earl nodded. "I understand why it's important."

"So keep her quiet."

Earl nodded.

Russell expelled a heavy breath. "Good thing you found me so we could sort that out. But wait. How did you find me?"

"The clerk told me where to find you."

Russell slapped the wall with his palm. "This gets more funny, every word. Because I didn't use my name when I signed in, now did I?"

Earl beamed with pride. "That was the hard part. They don't have a room for Russell Belfour."

"No, they don't have a room for Russell Belfour, because while I'm here I'm not Russell Belfour. I'm Herman Smith."

"And that's what that clerk feller told me. We ain't got a Russell Belfour, but we got a Herman Smith who fits Mr. Belfour to a T. Right down to the face. That's how we knew it was you. I told him I wasn't lookin' for Russell Belfour, I was lookin' for Herman Smith. And here you are. Mr. Herman Smith." Earl stuck out his hand. "Pleased to meetcha."

Russell slapped it away. "Why I'm not dead yet, I have no idea. You are as stupid as the day is long. So this is what you're going to do. Until the stage comes, you're going make sure no one sees Marie, not even for a second. You're going to keep your dumb ass in this hotel until I come for you. Don't leave it to eat, don't leave it to piss, don't leave it to take long walks and watch pretty sunsets. When I want to see you, I'll find a way to see you. Otherwise, you don't do so much as fart without my say so, you got it?"

Earl winced. "I got it."

CHAPTER 44

Marie awoke with a start, then slowly became aware of her surroundings in the dark room. She was in a bed. And not just any bed. This one was soft with a real mattress, not like the straw tick she slept on at home. And certainly not like the hard ground that had been her bed for many nights.

Content, she could feel the stress slipping from her. This was heavenly. For the first time in weeks, she was clean. Her body. Her hair. The room around her. She inhaled deeply. It smelled like...

Oh God.

It smelled like Russell.

She threw herself to the side of the bed, up against the wall. Russell was here. She scanned the room. Where he was he?

"You remembered the door, but you also have to be careful about windows when you live in town," he said, his voice piercing the darkness. "Never know who might slip in."

He was in the chair. She heard him strike a match and the flare illuminated his face. His eyes were hidden deep within their sockets, shadowy, undefined. The scar seemed to dance on his face. Finally the match burned out.

Silence, like the darkness, closed around her.

Too dark.

Too quiet.

What was he waiting for? Panicked, she finally found the nerve to speak. "What do you want?"

"I want you to follow a few more rules. Since you like wandering around the hallway and meeting people, rule one is don't do it again or I'll introduce you to a new kind of hell. Got it?" He struck another match and held it up.

Marie mumbled, "Yes," her panic choking her.

"You like your sister?"

"Y-y-yes," she stammered.

"You like her alive?"

She squeezed her eyes shut and gasped a quick yes.

"Then you stay away from the sheriff and his fool deputy. That's Rule Two. Think you can remember those rules?" His match burned out.

Darkness.

"Yes."

"Now, one last thing. There enough room in that bed for me? You on bottom, me on top?"

"No," she moaned. Not again.

"Well, you see how easy it is for me to get to you. You want to keep me from between your legs, you remember those rules. One thing I can promise you is this. Earl and I are getting on the stage tomorrow. Now you know what it takes for you to be on it too. Follow the damn rules."

She heard him stand. Footsteps creaked closer and closer to the bed. She strained to see him, but the room was pitch black.

And then his hand clamped hard over her mouth. "Not a goddamn peep, you hear?"

She struggled against his hand to nod.

"Good," he said. "And since we're getting along so well, how about you open up those legs after all? I think I want one more taste of your honey."

CHAPTER 45

Marie awoke to sunshine.

Without moving a muscle, she sampled the air. She tried to sense his presence.

He was gone.

But he did it again.

He'll do it until you stop him.

I know, Marie thought. But I couldn't stop him when I had a gun. How can I stop him now?

She got up and locked the window. The floor felt like ice. She scurried back to bed and buried herself under the blankets.

You could give up.

You could.

I could.

Or you could save yourself.

She threw the blankets off again and rapidly dressed. She pulled a chair over to the window, sat, and studied Russell's fresh bootprints in the snow on the roof.

If he can, then I can. Let the town help me escape.

Town. Something she'd only seen while riding in the back of the family wagon before, and then it'd seemed to be no more than a cluster of houses and buildings. Now she saw it in a different way. She saw it as a means of survival.

She cast an eye at the Sheriff's office across the street. Smoke billowed from the chimney.

She furtively glanced up and down the street.

Russell wasn't in sight.

Her heart hammered in her chest. It was now.

Or never.

She quickly rose from the chair and walked to the door.

Two raps sounded. Heavy-fisted. Earl.

She opened the door.

He stood there, his arms full of clothes, his eyes scanning both ways down the hallway. "Lemme in," he blurted. "We ain't got much time."

She slid out of the way as he barreled into the room. "What is it?"

"I been to the dress store," he said.

"Well, I'm not sure I need a dress," Marie said, eyeing the clothes he carried. "But thanks."

He rushed to the bed and spread them out. "Look," he said. "I didn't buy a dress. I got you a coat and some wool socks and some mittens and a hood."

"Why did you buy me a coat?"

"'Cause it's gonna snow again today. And when it does, you're gonna be in it."

She squinted her eyes closed for a moment, her stomach turning. "Aren't we leaving on the stage?"

"No," he said. "You're leavin' before the snow hits this afternoon. That's when you're gettin' away."

A sense of helplessness washed over her. "Till you came I was headed for the Sheriff's office. I was going to make a run for it."

"You weren't never gonna make it," he said. "Come here. See that feller?" He pointed out the window at a fat man sitting on a bench outside the Alhambra Hotel, adjacent to the Sheriff's office. "Russell hired him. He has one job. Shoot you if he sees you."

"My God," she gasped. "He hired someone to kill me?"

Earl said, "Russell says if you try to come out before the stage arrives you ain't never gonna make it."

Marie dropped to the bed. "So this is it? I have no chance?"

"Who said you got no chance? I come around back of the hotel with these clothes and that feller didn't see me at all. You're gonna leave the same way."

"You don't get it! We're in the middle of nothing! I have nowhere to go."

"Yes you do," Earl said. "Remember that Army guy? The fort with all them soldiers is a safe place for a woman. So that's it. You're goin' to the fort. You'll travel while it's snowin'."

Marie dropped onto the bed and stared at the floor. "I don't even know where the fort is, Earl. I can't—"

"You're sayin' a lot of things you can't do. You ain't even tried one yet. You wanna live?" He reached out and raised her chin. "You wanna live?"

She slowly nodded.

"Say it."

Marie took a deep breath. "I want to live."

"Don't forget that. So when Russell is doin' other stuff, you go. You walk to the edge of town. When you get to the creek you turn right and the storm will blow you all the way to the fort. No matter what, don't you stop. Don't never stop."

CHAPTER 46

Whaddaya mean, the stage isn't here?" Russell bellowed. "It's supposed to be here, and it damn well better get here."

The round, walrus-mustached stage agent patiently said, "Sir, it's been my experience that a yelling customer never makes the stage appear any faster."

"Oh, did I hurt your feelings? Well, cram it up your ass and see how that feels! Now where's that stage?"

The agent pulled out a silver pocket watch and studied the hands. "My guess, and it's no more than a guess sir, although somewhat educated, is that the stage is between here and Deadwood."

"And why would you say that?"

"Because the stage runs between here and Deadwood, sir."

Russell sputtered, "Then why did you look at your watch?"

"I was uncertain of the time."

Russell dug both hands into the counter as if he were on a rolling ship. "Hazard a guess as to why the stage isn't here?"

"Look outside, sir."

Russell spat on the floor. "That snow is hardly anything. Half a foot, no more."

"Half a foot here. But Deadwood sits way back in a canyon. When the wind howls through there drifts get waist-high in a hurry. That would be the guess I'd hazard. Drifts. Big ones. Waist-high."

"Please tell me there is another way to get out of town today."

"Certainly, sir. I can think of two. You can walk, or you can ride a horse. But another storm is brewing and it's going to hit soon. I wouldn't want to be stuck out on the prairie when it does. Walking or riding."

Russell looked out the window at the blackening sky, then plucked a pencil from the agent's pocket. He scribbled a name on a scrap of paper and shoved it across the counter. "That stage shows up, you break your neck getting to the Rosewood to let me know."

"Of course, sir," the agent said. "It will be my pleasure to see you go."

CHAPTER 47

Elton ignored the sputtering private at the front desk. He told Caleb to take a chair and wait, and then strode to Major Tinsdale's door and threw it open.

Tinsdale squawked in surprise. "Cole? What are you doing here?" He steadied himself and regained a bit of composure. "How was your trip?"

"My name isn't Cole, it's Elton Collins, and I'm not here to talk," Elton said. "I'm here to punch you in the mouth."

Tinsdale scuttled away from Elton and kept his desk between them. "Whatever your name is, this isn't the time for savagery. We're all gentlemen here."

Elton spit on the floor. "You might think the world is full of gentlemen, but it's not. You're about to learn that the hard way." He walked around the desk to Tinsdale, grabbed his shoulders and spun him toward the window. "You see that ridge?"

"Of course I see the ridge. It's hardly more than a mile away."

Elton shoved Tinsdale and the major had to stutter-step to keep from falling. "Hardly more than a mile. Yet you refused to ride to it to check on my family."

Tinsdale smoothed the front of his uniform and walked around the desk once again. "As it turned out, my mother was quite fatigued when she arrived in Hill City. Out of concern for the frailty of her condition my men and I returned directly here."

"Out of concern for her condition." Elton's words crackled. "Yet we had an agreement that you would ride by my house and check on my family. To check on their condition."

Tinsdale dismissively waved his hand. "Well, I was forced to reconsider." He rubbed his hands together. "But where are my manners? I trust your family is well?"

Elton fought the wave of anger that threatened to envelop him. "My wife and youngest daughter are buried on the banks of Elk Creek. Feel free to pay your respects the next time you ride down the valley. My oldest daughter was kidnapped around the time you went to Hill City to get your mother."

Tinsdale leaned against the wall near the door, his face bathed in crimson. "You cannot be serious."

"My family is destroyed. All I have left is my oldest daughter. And I have no idea where she is."

Tinsdale slowly approached Elton. "This is a tragedy I can barely comprehend. Your poor family. I am so..." Tinsdale shook his head and dropped into his chair.

Elton felt some of his anger ebb. It was replaced by heartbreak. "Yes. They're nearly all gone now. With no family...what do we have left without family?"

Unanswerable questions continued to rattle around in Elton's head, ones that had haunted him since he'd returned. Why was Nix at his house? Why was his wife killed? And mostly importantly, where was Marie? He no more knew the answers to those questions than he knew if Tinsdale held any responsibility for his wife and daughter's deaths. And maybe the time for blame was past, for no amount of blame could bring his wife and daughter back.

Drained, Elton walked to a chair and sat. "So, my wife and daughter are dead. I don't know if you could have done anything to stop it. If I hadn't left it likely would never have happened, so no matter how I slice this pie there's blame for everyone."

Tinsdale fingered an ink well on his desk. "It appears you have decided not to punch me in the mouth."

Elton shook his head. "It won't help me find my daughter."

Tinsdale rose and walked to him. "I'm not a husband and I'm not a father and I'm not the best listener. But you came to see me. What can I offer you?"

Elton pointed toward the window. "You have a fort full of troops. They may be the last hope to find my daughter. If she leaves this valley I may never see her again."

Tinsdale jerked his head up. "Tell me what happened and then we will discuss our options."

"As I arrived home I was shot, and I killed the man who shot me. When I came around, I was told that my daughter didn't return from seeing a boy."

"Where is he?"

"He's riding the hills, looking for her too."

"So the boy's not a suspect. Do you have any idea where your daughter might have gone?"

Elton spread his hands. "I've been trying to finish a puzzle and I don't have all of the pieces I need. But what the picture looks like, best as I can tell, is that my daughter came back from a walk one afternoon and was kidnapped by two men."

"I thought you didn't have much information."

"I don't have much in the way of fact, but I have a lot of information. Soon after I left, two men were seen riding up the trail toward my house. A neighbor saw their tracks and also found my daughter's rifle, along with one of her hair ribbons. And the two men who were riding the trail? They'd been near Hill City for months working a productive mine, but haven't been back since then."

"A lot of information, very little fact, as you said," noted the major. "Not a lot to act on."

"I can't say for certain the miners had something to do with my daughter's disappearance. But two men vanished about the same time as my daughter. One last thing that's keeping me going, and it means I'll never stop. My daughter scratched a note on the hearth. 2 MEN HELP ME. Those two miners, from what I can tell, are on the move. I think they're in this valley, and I think my daughter is with them."

Major Tinsdale paced the room, stopping for a moment to watch his men drill on a small patch of cleared ground. When he turned he said, "After the next storm passes I can send patrols north and south along the valley floor. If you're right, my men will sew this valley up so no one can move without us seeing them. Would you describe the men you're after?"

"They tell me there's one big fellow, rides a fleabit gray with a roman nose. The other fellow is rail thin and rides a buckskin."

"A fair description. And your daughter?"

"Looks for all the world like her mother did at seventeen. Blue eyes, long blonde hair, petite. Would make a man proud to walk the streets with her. Do you know what I mean?"

"I do. I met a young lady similar to that last night. Daughter of a local businessman by the name of Earl Pearl. We'll keep an eye out for your daughter. Collins, you said?"

"Our name is Collins."

"Well, if your daughter is anything like the Pearl girl, it won't take long for word to get around. Could I ask her Christian name?"

"Marie."

Tinsdale flinched. "Ahh. The girl I met last night, her name was Marie as well. Interesting coincidence."

Elton jumped to his feet. "I don't believe in coincidences. Where did you see her?"

CHAPTER 48

Russell barged into Earl's room. "What are you idiots doing?"

"Eating," Earl said. He shoveled another bite of chicken in his mouth.

"I can see that! But what is she doing outside her room? I told you she wasn't to leave there for any reason. Last damn time she left her room she got to know an Army major a little too well." He lunged forward, snagged Earl's string tie and jerked him forward. "That's the problem with you. You don't... ever...listen."

Earl held up a finger while he swallowed another bite of chicken. "Okay, but we had to eat. I didn't figure one room was different than the other. When's the stage comin', anyway?"

"Stage isn't coming," Russell fumed. "Not for a while. Too much snow last night, and another storm on the way this afternoon."

241

Earl's face lit up. "You don't say?" He turned to Marie. "Guess we're stayin' in town some more, like regular folk!"

Marie coughed lightly. "Regular folk. Except one of you is a rapist and the other is a murderer."

Russell stared at Marie. "Keep runnin' your mouth, girl, and you'll see what happens." He looked at Earl. "Get her back to her room. As soon as the next stage rolls into town, we're on it."

Earl said, "One thing I been wondering about. What are we gonna do with the horses? If we leave 'em at the livery it won't be hard to figure what we done next. We took the stage."

"Shit!" Russell grumbled. "Shit."

"You're pretty busy, doin' the thinkin' for all of us," Earl said. "How about I take 'em to the Army and sell them? 'Cause ain't they always lookin' for horses?"

Russell said, "Last thing we need is for you to see the Army major and try to sell the horses. You do that and before we know it we'll end up owing him money."

Earl's face sagged. "So you're gonna take 'em to the Army instead?"

"Hell, no. I'm going to take those horses on the prairie and put bullets in their heads. Out there no one but buzzards will find them."

"Okay," Earl shrugged. "If you think that's best."

CHAPTER 49

Marie slipped on the coat. "You think it'll do?"

Earl said, "Don't really matter at this point. It's all you got."

She picked up the blanket she'd worn to the hotel. "I'll take this, too." She glanced at the closed hotel room door. "How much time do I have?"

Earl gazed at the ceiling. "Russell will take the horses far enough away so no one will hear the gunshots, then he'll have to walk back, so you got maybe an hour to get outta the hotel and on your way. When you're ready to go I'll start an argument with the feller waitin' the shoot you. You hear him yellin' at me, that's your time to sneak out the back door."

Marie stepped to him and gave him a brief hug. "Russell will know you helped me."

Earl said, "Now ain't the time for talkin'. Now's the time for walkin'."

"But—"

"But nothin'. Time for you to go. There won't be another chance."

She said, "I can't thank you enough for this."

Earl fidgeted with the edge of the blanket. "You'd a done the same for me. Now I'm gonna punch that feller in the chin and he ain't gonna be happy. You make for the bushes along the creek. 'Bout the time you get there the snow's gonna be flyin'. You wrap the blanket around you and let the wind push you where you're goin'. Anything else you need?"

Marie said, "A little luck would be nice."

Earl grimaced. "Gonna take more than a little."

Sheriff Courtney Ballew saw two riders leave Fort Meade and angle toward Sturgis. He urged his stallion into a jog, passed through a narrow tongue of trees that paralleled the creek, and came out of a draw not more than twenty paces from the riders. They reined their mounts and waited as he approached.

As Ballew neared, he recognized one rider. "Long way from home, Henry," he said.

"Sheriff," Elton said. "You are too. And since I've told everyone else in the Dakotas, I might as well tell you too. I'm Elton Collins."

Ballew's eyes widened. He began to speak, but Elton cut him off. "Looks like we're headed in the same direction. We can talk about anything you want, but I'd like to ride while we do."

"Fair enough," Ballew said. He looked at the boy. "Who's your partner?"

"Caleb Forrester. Got hitched up with him north of Hill City."

Ballew stared. "You're the boy who gave me coffee yesterday. Where are your uncles?"

Caleb looked at his horse's neck. "Those men came back. They wanted their claim like you said."

Ballew started to ask, then stopped when he saw Elton shake his head. "But you made it out okay," he lamely said.

"I did."

Ballew leaned closer to Elton. "Any chance those boys are still in that vicinity?"

"Doubtful. They rode off. Toward Sturgis."

"You looked around town yet?"

Elton shook his head. "We rode to the fort first. I had a little business with the commander. He agreed to send his men out to block the valley south and north of here once the storm blows through, but I can't wait that long. I'm heading to town now. If the men are there, I'll find them."

"I'm riding that way myself. Wait," Ballew said. "Why are you looking for these men?"

"My daughter is missing and I think these men are involved. We trailed them until nightfall, then lost them in the snow. Now there's another storm about to blow in, so my guess is these boys are laying low in town. And I think I know where."

CHAPTER 50

Russell rushed past the front desk and up the stairs to Earl's room. He pounded on the locked door. In a moment he heard feet hit the floor and walk to the door.

Earl opened it, yawned, and gave him a half-smile. "Hey, Russell. Come sit down and we can talk like the old days."

"No, I'm not sitting down." He looked at the bruise on Earl's cheek. "What the hell?"

Earl shrugged. "That feller you hired, he took a poke at me. Guess I was runnin' my mouth too much. You know how I am."

"Yes I do," Russell said. "How about you stop being so stupid for a bit and maybe you won't get your face hit."

"I am pretty stupid, that's a fact," Earl agreed. "I looked outside and I seen some snowflakes flyin'. Glad we won't be out in any more storms."

"Change of plans. When I was at the livery I saw the Hill City sheriff nearing town. You can see that white horse of his from a mile away. Plus, he's riding with two others. Chances are they aren't coming for coffee so we're going back to the claim. That's the last place he'd look for us. Good thing I didn't kill our horses. I'll get them. You get the girl. Let's go."

Earl pulled the curtain back and looked out the window. "This storm, though. We should wait it out."

"That sheriff is sniffing after us. Two hotels in town, he knows we're in one of them. How long do you think it'll take before he finds us?"

"Jeez o'mighty, if he's riding in he'll head straight for the livery. If we go there, won't he see us?"

"Hard to get a trick past you. So get the girl now and we'll be gone before he gets there."

Earl shook his head. "She's probably sleepin'."

Russell looked at Earl. He was dragging this out.

For a reason.

Russell ran out the door and down the hall.

Earl followed, close at his heels, saying, "No, don't wake her. Don't wake—"

Russell got to Marie's door. It was locked.

He rammed it with his shoulder and the door flew open.

He charged into an empty room.

Russell spun around and stood inches from Earl's face, spraying spit as he yelled. "Where is she? Where is she?"

"Whoa, whoa Russell, I dunno! I didn't do nothin' but fall asleep after we ate."

Russell caught a handful of Earl's shirt and pulled him close. "You better hope we find her before she tells someone what we've done. If we don't, you just put us in the grave."

247

CHAPTER 51

A wall of snow slammed into Elton, Ballew and Caleb as they reached Sturgis.

"Let's put these horses up," Elton shouted over the howling wind. He motioned to the livery stable at the end of Main Street.

Elton took Ballew's horse inside, along with Sparky.

Ballew stood at the door as sheets of blinding snow whipped past. "You ready to go, Caleb?"

The boy shook his head. "I'll wait for Mister Collins."

Ballew turned to Elton. "Meet us at the Sheriff's office before you go to the hotel. Sheriff Thomas is a mite particular about folks taking the law into their own hands. Especially—"

"Especially gunmen. I know." Elton stared through the snow, trying to see the Rosewood. Marie could be that close.

He took a deep breath, then exhaled. "I've waited this long. I can wait ten more minutes. Tell the sheriff I'm right behind you. When I get there, we get Marie."

Ballew tucked his shoulder against the wind and made for the Sheriff's office.

"What'll it cost to put these horses up?" Elton asked the hostler.

The one-eyed hostler said, "Four bits per horse per day and I'll treat 'em like they was my own." He shrugged. "It's that or the snowbank."

Elton said, "The white horse belongs to the Hill City sheriff."

"He ain't the sheriff here, though. Four bits for him, too."

Caleb tugged on Elton's sleeve. "Hey mister."

"What's on your mind, Caleb?"

"My horse."

"Don't worry son, I'll cover the four bits."

"No," Caleb said. "Not that horse. *My* horse. The one that was stolen. He's in one of the back stalls."

Elton's chest tightened. "Show me."

Caleb led Elton to the last stall in the barn, where a scrawny paint stood. He nickered when he saw the boy, who gave him a firm scratching behind the ears.

Elton said, "You sure this is your horse?"

"Hard to mistake him, sir."

Elton yelled for the hostler, who ambled to the back of the barn. "Can I do you for?"

"The man who brought you this horse, did he ride a fleabit gray?"

"Him and a girl rode in together last night," the old man said. "Man rode the gray back out a bit ago."

"But the girl didn't leave with him?"

The hostler looked at the paint. "With her horse still here, don't appear so."

Elton felt like he was talking to Shorty. "When did he leave?"

The hostler scratched his beard. "'He took off not ten minutes ago, moments before this blizzard come roarin' in."

"You see which way he left?"

The hostler squawked, "You're crazy if you're goin' out in this! Batten down the hatches and ride 'er out, that's what I say. This storm's gonna blow a while."

Elton said, "The man who took the gray didn't batten down the hatches."

The old hostler plucked a piece of straw from the floor, stuck it in his mouth, and began to chew on it. "You lookin' for the other feller too?"

Elton said, "Tell me about him."

"Tall and skinny. Looked like this wind would blow him straight to Nebraska without hardly tryin'."

Elton shook his head. "You see which way they went when they left?"

"One went thisaway, and one went thataway."

In a blink, Elton's pistol rested under the hostler's nose. "You want to be a little more specific than thisaway and thataway?"

The hostler leaned away from the pistol, but his eyes never left it. "Skinny feller left me the godly sum of a twenty-cent piece so I wouldn't say a peep. Twenty cent piece," he scoffed. "Can't even rent me an ugly woman for that. So here's the truth as I seen it. The skinny feller turned left out of the barn and headed north like he was on a mission. God knows why, 'cause they ain't nothin' but nothin' out there. And the big man rode down the street you presently can't see before you due to the blindin' snow. Right through town."

—

Elton rode Sparky and Caleb followed on Midnight. They tied the horses to the hitching rail in front of the Sheriff's office. As Elton pushed the office door open the wind caught it. It banged against the wall as a whirlwind of snow blew in.

Elton quickly closed it and looked around the neat office.

A rotund gray-haired man wearing a star on his pocket looked up from the dime novel he was reading. "How you doing, boys?"

Elton stepped to the desk, stuck out his hand and said, "Elton Collins."

The sheriff said, "John Thomas. I ran across you once in Amarillo, long time ago. You were just a youngster, but already half the folks west of the Mississippi knew about you." He glanced at the pistol Elton carried. "You're officially back in the gunfighting business."

"Not by choice."

Thomas nodded to Ballew. "Young sheriff here told me a bit about your story. Caleb's, too. Sorry, son."

Caleb said, "Me too, sir."

Elton said, "So you know I'm on the trail of two men who took my daughter. She may have been at the Rosewood last night."

"Father trying to find his daughter is as close to honorable as a gunfighter can get," Thomas said. "But honorable or no, I can't have you blasting away at folks who you think have her. The people of Sturgis pay me to keep the gunplay to a minimum."

Elton pulled himself a little taller. "Are you planning to take my guns?"

Thomas said, "Depends on what you're going to do with them."

"That depends on what those men do when I find them. If my daughter walks away they will too. The hostler said the men are on the move, but he didn't see a girl with them. Skinny feller headed north, and the big one rode right through town."

Ballew said, "I'm of a mind to go after the skinny one."

"Figured you would," Elton said. "Midnight's at the rail."

Ballew took his coat from a hook by the door and rapidly put it on. "Keep a cell ready," he called to Sheriff Thomas. "That, or the undertaker." Ballew charged outside and slammed the door shut.

"Undertaker's more likely, but for which one of those damn fools?" Thomas muttered.

Collins drummed his fingers on the sheriff's desk.

Thomas said, "Okay, tell me about the boys you're looking for. Maybe I've seen them myself."

After Elton gave a basic description the sheriff said, "We've got all types in town, but I can't match the pair you describe. Nor the girl."

"Major Tinsdale said he'd met a girl at the Rosewood last night named Marie Pearl. Matches the description of my daughter."

"Don't recognize that name. New in town, I imagine."

"Tinsdale said her father was a local businessman."

Thomas scoffed. "Tinsdale says a lot of things he can't back with fact." He walked to a jail cell and beat on the bars. "Wake up, Yankton."

A few moments later a young, bleary-eyed man stumbled from the cell. "A little nap is all," he said. "No harm?"

"No harm. Yankton Blake, I'd like you to meet Elton Collins."

Blake gasped. "You ain't dead?"

Elton tersely said, "Not yet."

Blake stammered, "My daddy used to tell me all about you. Fastest gun he ever saw. Then nobody heard nothin' anymore."

Elton shrugged. "I'm sorry it changed."

Blake leaned forward and excitedly said, "How many you shoot? A hundred? Then a hundred more?"

Thomas shushed his deputy. "Yankton, this is no time to be foolish. Mister Collins is looking for his daughter."

Elton said, "She's a pretty blonde with blue eyes. Rode into town last night."

Yankton grunted. "I seen one of them not an hour ago when I was out back taking a leak."

"Girl you know?" Thomas asked.

"Never seen her before. She was in some helluva rush, all bundled up like she'd be hiking awhile in this cursed storm. Wrapped up in a blanket, too. I tried to stop her, but she put her head down and off she went toward the creek like she was heading for salvation."

Elton jammed his hat firmly on his head. "You check the Rosewood for Marie. Toward the creek is where I'm headed."

Thomas said, "What if that isn't her? You'll be out chasing shadows in this blizzard."

"You asked the wrong question, Sheriff. I ask myself, what if it is?" Elton hurried to the door, pulled it open, and dashed out.

CHAPTER 52

As Ben headed up the valley toward Sturgis the howling wind tore his hat from his head. It fluttered and spun as it bounced along the snow. And then it was gone.

Ducking his head against his horse's back, they trudged toward town. As the sky turned darker the landmarks familiar to Ben became no more than gray, undefined shapes. Nothing looked the same. He squinted ahead, hoping for a glimmer of light that would tell him they were close.

Snow was all he could see.

Ben traced the route in his mind. The valley narrowed near Sturgis, but in this weather a rider who got off track a bit might ride by town and miss it entirely.

And he would never even know.

He would keep riding and riding and riding and riding until he could ride no more. And they would find him in the spring.

Suddenly the wind shifted, not in his face anymore, but whipping hard from the side.

His horse slowed and then stopped.

Ben urged him on.

The horse stood.

"Come on boy, we'll freeze out here. We've got to keep going." He cracked the end of the reins on his horse's rump.

The horse remained still.

Ben slithered from his back, found the horse's bridle, and tried to pull him forward. As he leaned, his shoulder hit something hard.

A wall.

A blessed, wonderful wall.

Ben felt along the wall with his hand, pulling his horse behind him.

It was the bank building. Ben turned to the west. The livery was at the end of the street. All he had to do was stay between the buildings on each side of Main Street as he walked, and he'd find it.

If he could stay between the buildings.

How far was it? He closed his eyes. No more than a hundred steps.

He made a quick decision. If they didn't reach the livery by the time he counted a hundred and twenty, he'd turn. Walk a different direction.

And start counting again.

They set off.

At step number ninety-three the two-story livery appeared as a vague shadow in front of him. Stomping snow from his boots, Ben quickly led his horse inside and away from the howling storm.

Two days of stabling his horse and he'd be broke, but with a storm like this he had little choice. Nor did he have much choice about where he'd sleep. The livery's loft was free.

After rubbing his horse down he followed his rapidly-filling footsteps past the bank, and continued to fight through the wind and drifting snow until he reached the Alhambra. The waitress soon came over to his table and filled his coffee cup.

"Thank you, ma'am. I do believe I'm frozen right to the bone. But how much is the coffee? I only have a few coins left."

"Honey, you go ahead and keep drinking. Afterward, I have a plate of food in the back, and it has your name on it."

He looked at her, confused. "Ma'am, I don't have but a bit more than a dollar, and they charge me fifty cents a day to keep my horse at the livery. This coffee will do fine, and I have some grub in my saddlebags."

"Don't you worry about a thing, Ben. You go ahead and eat to your heart's content."

He nearly dropped the coffee cup. "How do you know my name?"

"Your father came here two days ago. Said you were on a ride, and he expected you'd come through town sooner or later. He described you right down to that scar on your chin."

Ben tapped the scar. "Got bucked off when I was eight, and went face first onto a rock. That scar will never go away."

"And that's how I knew it was you. Now, are you ready for some food?"

CHAPTER 53

Marie was no more than a mile out of town when the storm's wind drove her to her knees. Breathless, she scrambled up and fought through the drifts she encountered, working toward the trees along the creekbed.

As she stepped over a fallen log another gust of wind hammered her, knocking her down. She rose to her feet and hugged her arms around her. Even though she had a proper coat and mittens, too much time spent in a blizzard and it wouldn't matter. She would freeze to death long before she made it to the fort. She pulled the blanket tight around her shoulders.

Suddenly hoofbeats thundered up behind her. Panicked, she dove behind a tree.

Russell.

He'd found her.

Michael Shepherd

She peered from behind the tree, but all she saw was swirling snow.
She staggered to her feet.
Head down, she started walking again.
The wind. It was the wind.
She prayed it was only the wind.

CHAPTER 54

Ben finished his meal and coffee. The waitress approached him and gave him a warm smile. "Makes me happy to see a man enjoy a meal. Your father also left enough money for a room and tonight you'll need it. Go on upstairs and get some rest, sweetie."

Maybe.

But first he was going to see the sheriff. He pulled on his coat and hurried past the front desk, then stepped off the porch.

The wind roared down the street as he neared the Sheriff's office.

He dashed the last few steps jumped onto the porch and opened the door.

The office was empty.

Cursing, he spun on his heel to return to the hotel.

He'd walked a half-dozen steps when he collided with an older man with his hat pulled low.

"I'm Sheriff Thomas," he said. "Come with me." Thomas pulled him back across the street and into the office.

They'd shaken the snow off their coats and stomped it off their boots when the door slammed open and another man covered in snow hurried in. "Now that's a blizzard!" he exclaimed. "Hate to be out in it for more than a minute!"

"Yankton, you see anything?" Sheriff Thomas asked the man.

"Lot of snow. That's about it." He walked over to Ben. "Deputy Blake," he said, offering his hand.

Ben took it, and then turned to the sheriff. "Sir, I'm Ben Schwartz. The way it's snowing they'll still be telling stories about this storm when I'm an old man."

Sheriff Thomas offered Ben a chair. "Your father came into town saying you'd run off after a girl. No luck yet?"

"No, sir. I've ridden along Piedmont ridge over to Deadwood, and finally up the valley to here. To tell the truth, I've seen a whole lot of nothing so far."

Thomas said, "I talked to Elton Collins a few minutes ago. He hasn't had much luck either."

Ben looked around. "Is he still here?"

"No. We believe the men who took Marie are on the ride, and we think she's on foot. She was at the Rosewood earlier today, but we checked both hotels in town and there's no sign of any of them. Deputy Blake saw a girl fitting her description walking toward the creek before the storm hit. She was bundled up like she planned on being out a while."

Ben started for the door, but Sheriff Thomas stopped him. "Where are you going, son?"

"If Marie is out there, that's where I'll be."

Thomas shook his head. "Too many people in this blizzard already. Marie. Her father and Sheriff Ballew. Right now the chances of any of them surviving this blizzard is pretty small. Letting you go, that's one more person we might lose. I don't want to risk it."

Ben's eyes narrowed. "She's my girl."

Thomas placed a hand on Ben's arm. "I guarantee the last thing your father wants is to lose his son."

Ben pulled away. "I'm not going to stop until I find her. So unless I've broken the law, I'm going."

Thomas stepped from the door. "I can't stop you. But think about what you're doing, son."

"I'm thinking about Marie. You say she was heading out of town, so that's where I'll go." He pulled the door open, fought against the blowing snow, and headed for his horse.

CHAPTER 55

The drifts. Marie hadn't counted on the size of the drifts. In the near-dark she couldn't see more than a few strides in front of her, and nearly every drift she hit tripped her.

She struggled to stand.

She took five steps.

Another one pulled her down.

This one held her a bit longer.

Marie lay on her side, buried in snow.

A moment's rest, and then she'd continue.

Just a moment longer.

She fought to breathe in the howling wind. Her body was bathed in sweat.

Her father's voice came to her. *Move or die.* She'd heard about travelers who'd been stranded outside when blizzards hit.

Eventually they stopped moving.

Then they died.

She rolled onto her knees, thrust her arms into the snow, pushed herself up, and began walking.

She patted her mother's package in her pocket. Today was not her day to die.

As she trudged along she reached to her shoulder to pull the blanket tighter.

There was no blanket.

Didn't she have a blanket when she started?

She wasn't sure anymore.

She took a step.

Another.

And went down again.

After Russell left Sturgis he'd done a quick sweep north of town. Not a track coming or going. He'd then turned east and worked his way toward the creek. When he got there, he found Earl waiting for him. "We gotta find her, Russell," Earl yelled.

"Yeah, no shit. Wonder why you let her go, *dad.*"

Earl squinted at Russell. "She slipped away while you was tryin' to get rid of the horses, is all. Jeez o'mighty, if we don't find her she's gonna die."

Russell looked at it differently. They were going to find her, *then* she was going to die. But that wasn't worth clarifying. He needed Earl's full attention on finding the girl. "I'll take the far side of the creek and you stay on this side. You see anything—anything—you shoot and I'll come running. You understand?"

Earl wiped tears from his cheeks. "I'm gonna find her. And save her." He turned his horse and started following the creek.

After Russell crossed the creek he stared toward the brush, trying to see Earl on the other side.

Swirling sheets of snow pounded him. He could see nothing else.

He hollered to Earl, but all he heard in return was the howling wind.

He studied the snow on his side of the creek but could see no footprints. Of course her tracks might have already filled in.

Or Earl could have lied about where she was going.

He recalled the look on Earl's face as he'd spoken about Marie. The big dummy had been devastated, like he'd betrayed her.

He'd begged Russell to help him find her.

Which exactly matched Russell's plan.

He leaned forward in the saddle.

He'd find her.

Oh, he'd find her.

CHAPTER 56

Marie went down in another drift.

Panting for breath, she lay there.

Rest.

The snow that piled around her felt like an embrace.

Even the wind that had been furiously whipping up her skirts while she'd been walking seemed to ease. Instead of biting her face as it had been, now it brushed softly against her skin.

Like a caress.

Then it began to call her name.

Marie.

She nestled further into the snow's warmth and listened to the wind's gentle song.

It begged her to stay.

Marie.

Marie.

MARIE!

The earth shook violently.

No, her brain moaned. I belong here.

It pulled harder.

Lifting her up.

Away.

Marie.

Marie!

You gotta wake up.

Her eyes fluttered open.

Earl held her in his arms.

The wind ripped against her face, screaming in betrayal.

"No, Marie! You gotta wake up." He shook her hard. "You gotta keep movin'."

He carried her to his horse and placed her foot in the stirrup. "Push yourself up."

Her leg muscles quivered but refused to work.

He pushed her up until her belly was on the saddle.

"Now hold the horn and flip around," Earl encouraged.

She extended a club-like arm but her frozen fingers refused to grasp the saddle horn. "I can't," she groaned.

Earl eased her leg over the horse's rump.

Marie's dress hooked on the saddle's cantle. Losing her balance, she teetered toward the ground.

Earl caught her before she fell. "Saddles don't work so well with you wearin' that dress. Once we get you up there you might hike it up a bit. I found your blanket back there in the snow. You can spread it over your legs."

"Might as well hike up my dress," she mumbled, her fuzzy brain struggling to form the words. "You've already seen everything I have."

"Jeez o'mighty," Earl said. He lifted her higher, hooked his hand under her right leg, and pushed it over the saddle.

He cupped her hands in his and massaged them until she began to feel a painful tingling. That's good, she told herself. That means they're not frozen.

Yet.

She flexed her clawed fingers until they could bend. "I can hold on now." Earl wrapped the blanket around her and draped it over her stockinged legs. When he was done she held the horn with one hand.

The other briefly brushed against Earl's cheek.

"Okay," he said. "Them aspens is halfway to the fort, and you passed 'em before I come onto you." Earl took his horse's reins and led it along the creek. "Now, you hold on and stay awake. Awake means alive."

She nodded again, too cold to speak.

CHAPTER 57

Elton dismounted from the saddle and studied the tracks in the deepening snow. One horse. No footprints. Although the drifting snow had wiped nearly everything clean, here and there he'd found a place where a drift had been broken. He could no longer tell if it was the same horse he'd trailed from Sturgis or, given the direction the horse was moving, it could be no more than a soldier returning to Fort Meade.

He closed his eyes in frustration. Nothing in his life was certain anymore. When Amelia had been alive, he had certainty. She was the rock upon which they'd built a life. Now his wife lay in a cold grave across Elk Creek from the home they had built together.

Across the creek.

He tried to picture the route the thin man would have taken. North out of town. Follow the Custer wagon train route east a half-mile or so.

Where there was a shallow, gravel-bottomed crossing that the freight teams used when hauling supplies to Fort Meade.

The men were on each side of the creek.

And if he couldn't find Marie's tracks on this side…

He nudged Sparky to the edge of the creek bed. The bank here was steep, a six-foot drop to the water. Impossible to go down.

He figured he'd ridden at least three miles since he left town. It'd be a three-mile ride back to the creek crossing.

But if Sheriff Ballew had been able to stay on the tracks of the man headed north, he'd seen where he forded the creek.

So he'd already be on the other side.

And he'd be headed to Fort Meade, too. Where Elton was now certain Marie was headed. Smart girl.

He climbed into the saddle.

And pointed Sparky toward the fort.

Ballew hadn't seen a track in a while. An hour at least. Or maybe it'd been ten minutes. In the storm, with snow assaulting his face and freezing his eyelids nearly closed, time ceased to be relevant. Time was not the enemy. Distance was. The distance between him and the man he sought.

He slapped Midnight's neck and drove the horse onward. All that mattered was the next step they took. Because that could be the step that put them back on the killer's trail.

Marie and Earl made their way toward the fort as the wind tore through the trees along the creek bed, ripping heavy limbs away. The sound of splintered crashes as the boughs plummeted down seemed never-ending. A volley. Another. Another.

Like war, she thought. Like I'm in a battle for my life.

Gust after gust of wind attacked them. Whirls of snow spun around them. Marie lifted her mittened hand and wiped her face.

Most of it was frozen over with snow. Matter-of-fact she thought, *and frostbite is next.* Once she'd seen a man who'd lost the end of his nose to frostbite. She tried to picture what her nose would look like, blackened with frostbite, something the children would point at and then scream…

Earl slapped her leg. "Hey, stay awake! Awake is alive, so you stay awake, you hear?"

Marie sat, nearly immobile. She'd been a fool to leave during a blizzard. At the time it'd made a lot of sense. While everyone else was hunkered down for the storm she'd slip away unnoticed. The storm would wipe out her tracks and she'd be safe. But now, Earl had found her, and…

She panicked. "Earl, why are you here? You were supposed to stay back in town."

"I was gonna keep our secret, but then Russell seen a sheriff and he decided it was time for us to leave and so he looked for you…and you was gone."

A wave of despair smashed her. "Russell knows where we're going?"

"Said he'd kill you if I didn't tell. We're gonna rescue you."

Marie spun to look behind her, but could see nothing but darkness and a wall of snow. Still, she could almost feel Russell. He was hunting her. And he was getting closer.

Earl patted her leg again. "Marie, I can get to the fort. We just gotta keep tryin'."

"Get me there before Russell finds us. The last thing he wants is for me to live."

CHAPTER 58

Ben slapped the saddle's pommel in disgust. Usually when he followed a trail he would build a story from the clues he found. Why did the horse stop here? How big or small was the rider? Did he double back if he thought someone was on his trail?

But none of these questions mattered when tracking in a blizzard. After a while he'd given up hope of figuring out what was going on ahead of him. He decided to keep the creek on his right side, for he could see the trees hugging the creekbed.

That, and a set of horse tracks that were almost indecipherable.

He drummed his hands on the saddle, trying to get blood flowing in his fingers. They'd become so numb it was impossible to hold the reins. After dropping them many times he decided to tie them together. Not that he needed to use them anyway. His horse wanted to keep his tail to the storm.

Ben didn't know where they were going, but as long as he followed the trail of the horse in front of him, he'd end up somewhere. Anywhere was better than here.

He rapped his heel against his horse's flank and drove him forward.

Earl led Marie out of a small draw and toward a knoll. He stopped the horse and walked back to her. "Now, you're gonna notice a big change in the wind," he said. "It ain't gonna be behind you anymore. More like on the side. You ready?"

"Y-y-yes," she mumbled through chattering teeth. But they'd taken no more than ten steps when a gust threatened to knock her from the saddle. She fumbled for the saddle horn.

Earl struggled forward, staring into the dark, pushing his way through the waist-high drifts. Many times he went down.

He won't make it to his feet, she thought, every time he fell. But time after time he rose.

Head down, he trudged onward.

Through the billowing snow, once or twice Marie thought she saw pinpricks of light.

But she wouldn't say a thing.

Not till she was sure.

Because if it wasn't the lights from the fort after all, if it was another trick her mind was playing on her, she didn't think she would have the heart to continue.

Sheriff Courtney Ballew was on the ground beside Midnight, who lay nearly motionless in the snow. Below the rim of the creek bed wall that had collapsed under the great horse's weight the wind was less severe. Snow continued to fall around them but now, without the brutal wind, the storm seemed almost benign. Ballew leaned against the creek wall. It was as good a place as any to die.

He rested his hand on Midnight's neck. All he could see moving were the horse's sides as he tore one breath after another from the frigid air. Even now, when Ballew suspected Midnight had fatal injuries, the horse continued to fight. But now he was in a fight to live.

"You gave all you could, boy," Ballew said as he patted the horse's neck. "One thing about you I appreciated. You always gave me all you could." He ran his hand along Midnight's mane, watching it drift from his hand like the blizzard around them. "I hope I met you halfway."

Ballew looked at his own broken leg. "Because I don't think I have anything left to offer you."

He reached for his handgun. "Except for peace."

CHAPTER 59

Then Marie was certain. "Lights, Earl! The fort!"

"I see 'em. Almost there." He continued to plow forward.

A rider suddenly appeared from the dark. He angled toward them from their left side, cutting them off. His pistol was aimed at Earl. "Hold it, mister."

Earl looked at him and then stopped.

"Ben!" Marie gasped when he rode closer. "How did you get here?"

Ben dismounted from his horse and motioned Earl to move. "Step away from Marie."

Earl shook his head. "I promised I'd get her to the fort, and we ain't there yet. My job ain't done."

"I'm telling you your job is done now."

Another rider appeared through the wall of snow. "Looks like you got the drop on him, Ben," Elton said. "But why don't you put the gun away? I think we can talk our way through this."

Russell watched it unfold from behind a nearby, brushy blowdown. Moments before, the kid had galloped close by him in his rush to get to Earl. Pistol drawn, Russell had settled behind him, ready to shoot him in the back. Then he heard another horse approach from his right.

He considered himself lucky that he'd found cover before the rider saw him, for this rider was far more deadly than a runny-nosed kid.

The rider was Elton Collins.

When he thought it was the kid he was up against, those were odds he liked. Shoot the kid in the back, shoot the girl in the face, and he and Earl would ride far and fast and forget the Dakotas forever.

But now that Collins had arrived it was two against two. He flexed his fingers, trying to get some feeling into them, but they were so cold he doubted he'd be able to shoot accurately.

He'd only get one chance with Collins.

He flexed his fingers again. Was this it?

Russell stared through the snow, for one of the few times in his life unsure of his next move.

Elton dismounted from Sparky. "Easy, Ben. It won't take a gun to solve this. Put it away."

"No sir," Ben said. He spoke to Earl. "You get away from Marie. And you do it now." His hand shook slightly as he pointed the pistol at the man's chest.

Earl shook his head. "I ain't leavin' her. I promised her we'd get to the fort, and we're gonna."

Marie leaned forward to explain. "You were going to protect me from Russell. I'm safe now. My father and Ben are here."

"Jeez o'mighty, you ain't safe yet. Russell could kill them easy, but he won't hurt me so he won't hurt you. You gotta trust me, Marie." He started walking.

"Stop!" Ben commanded, agitation shaking his voice. "I said stop right now!"

Elton could see this was getting out of hand. Fine. Let the man take Marie to the fort. Right now, it was the boy he was worried about. "Ben, put the gun away and we'll take her there together."

Russell stared down the barrel of his pistol and fought to hold it steady. All he could see was the girl, the horse she rode, and Earl.

Earl was blocking Collins.

Russell slowly moved away from the blowdown. Crept a bit more to the right.

He was out in the open. But he could almost see enough of Collins to take a shot.

A little more. He stepped again. Then the thumbed back the hammer and crossed his left arm under his right to steady his aim.

Ben skirted around the side of Earl and blocked him from continuing. He jammed his pistol against Earl's chest. "I said stop!"

"And I said Marie ain't safe." Earl lowered his shoulder into Ben, causing him to stumble.

The shot rang out so suddenly that Marie fell off the horse in surprise. Lying in the snow, she looked over at Earl, who continued to plod forward.

He took another determined step.

Another.

Slower.

Then he hit a drift. He struggled to pick his feet up but this time his legs wouldn't listen.

Earl collapsed.

CHAPTER 60

No, no, no! Russell's mind screamed as he saw Loretta's brother fall to the snow.

Earl.

His last link to her.

As he stared at the man's huge bulk in the snow he felt Loretta slowly, gently, finally slip away.

Grief battled with furor. *Bastard shot Earl. I will kill him.*

From no more than a dozen paces away he studied the boy, who looked at Earl like he couldn't comprehend what he'd done.

You won't have long to worry about it, Russell thought. *Maybe three seconds.*

Collins, who had been kneeling over his daughter, suddenly turned toward Ben. "Get down, son," he barked. "The man you shot had a partner. He may be close."

The boy dropped to a knee behind the horse and swept his eyes across the whirling mass of snow.

Now Russell was the one in trouble. He fell to the ground and crawled behind the blowdown where his horse stood.

Quietly stepping into the stirrup and swinging into the saddle he walked to the creekbed and then rode his horse along the line of trees away from the fort, muttering curses on Elton Collins' soul.

Elton scooped Marie into his arms. Ben uneasily stood nearby as Elton rocked his daughter.

"It's okay now," he said, gently holding her. "It's over."

Marie pulled away from Elton's chest, shot a wild glance at Earl, and then buried her head against her father again. "It's not over," she moaned. "It's not over. It'll never be over."

Elton whispered, "We need to get you inside the fort. Then you'll be safe."

"It's not going to matter," she said. "I'll never escape from him."

He wrapped his arms tighter around her. "We'll get through this together."

Marie sniffed back tears. "Some things can't be fixed." After a moment she stood on shaky feet. Elton began to help her onto Earl's horse, but she pleaded, "No Daddy. On Sparky."

He helped her onto Sparky's saddle. Without a word, she rode toward the fort.

Elton looked at Ben, and then toward Marie. Ben walked back to his horse, mounted, and trailed her.

Elton looked at the big man lying in the snow. "If you never leave the prairie, that's still a better burial than you deserve."

CHAPTER 61

Marie, let's talk a bit," the fort's doctor, Elijah Garretson, said after he'd examined her. "Are you ready?"

Marie sniffed back tears. "I'll try."

The doctor slid a chair next to her bed. "They raped you…" He watched her face tighten and her eyes squint shut.

"He raped me," she said. "Russell."

"As you know, there is the chance you may be pregnant."

She inhaled deeply, eyes still closed.

Garretson said, "At this time, I cannot determine if you are pregnant. In fact, you will know before anyone else."

She opened her eyes and looked into his. "I cannot carry his child," she said, and then sobbed, "I can't!"

He patted her hand. "I am truly sorry, but that is the good Lord's decision, not yours."

—

Elton stood as the doctor entered the front room. "Tell me."

Garretson said, "Your daughter was beaten, but those bruises will go away in time." He lingered, shifting his weight from foot to foot, searching Elton's face.

Elton dreaded discussing this, but he had to know. "I imagine they weren't gentlemen with her."

Garretson solemnly shook his head. "They weren't."

"Is it too early to tell if she is pregnant?"

"I can hope..." Garretson placed a hand on Elton's shoulder. "I'm glad you have your daughter back."

Garretson bade him goodnight and assured him he would return in the morning.

Elton opened the bedroom door and glanced at his sleeping daughter. "My sweet girl," he whispered. He wanted to rush to her, to pull her into his arms, to tell her she was going to be okay.

Instead he walked to the chair, quietly sat, and watched her sleep.

An hour later Elton and Ben walked to Major Tinsdale's quarters, where Elton rapped on the door. Soon Tinsdale appeared, dressed in pants, untucked shirt and socks. "Good news, I hope?"

Elton said, "We found Marie. She's alive and she's here."

"We?"

"This is Ben Schwartz, the rancher's son from the valley north of my place. He is the one who found her."

Tinsdale motioned to two stiff-backed chairs in the front room. He dropped into an age-weary leather one. "I expect it wasn't quite as simple as that. Since the men here learned your name, I heard stories about you from the past. Gunman."

"True," Elton said, "but father and husband is what I prefer. These are things I cultivated, not something that was cultivated for me. Even though I changed my name, it seems I can't shake what I was. And this time it came back with a vengeance."

Tinsdale frowned. "Getting your daughter, did that situation call for using a gun?"

"Marie was being held by one of the men we were looking for, and he would not give her up. When he drew a weapon, I shot him."

Major Tinsdale glanced at Ben. "You all right, son? You look pretty pale."

"Yes, sir," Ben stammered. "Never saw a man shot before."

"Well," Tinsdale said as he hoisted himself out of his chair, "here's hoping you never see another." He walked over to the door and opened it. "Sheriff Taylor must be notified. As soon as this storm ends I'll send one of my men into town with a message."

He clapped Elton on the back as he walked out the door. "Glad you found her."

"Why'd you say that?" Ben hissed as they neared Marie's room. "You didn't shoot him, I did!"

"Easy, son," Elton said. "This is a tricky problem."

"But it's *my* problem! I did it!"

"No. Let it stay with me."

"Oh I get it," Ben said. "I'm still a kid who needs to be protected."

Elton placed a hand on Ben's shoulder. "That's not it at all. But it's for the best if it plays out this way. Trust me."

Ben's face flickered from anger to confusion. "Why?" he finally asked.

"Because once you shoot a man stories are told, and the stories grow, and pretty soon people know you as a gunfighter. And once you're known as a gunfighter, someone will always be chasing you. You don't want to start running now."

"So you'll run instead?"

Elton sighed. "I won't run. But I'll never live in the shadows again, either."

CHAPTER 62

The rough hand clamped over Marie's mouth. Before she could jump out of bed a body climbed on top of her, forcing the air from her lungs. She fought to get away, but he held her so tight she could hardly move.

She didn't need to see who it was. She recognized his smell.

Russell.

She tried to scream, but could not. She bit his hand instead. She could taste his blood.

His hand never moved. It was pressed so tightly over her nose and mouth she couldn't breathe.

If he didn't move his hand, she'd suffocate. When he shifted his weight her leg swung free and she kicked out, trying to free herself, but he wouldn't relent.

He fumbled between her legs, tearing away her clothes, and

then he was in…

Marie woke, bathed in sweat. Panicked, her eyes darted around the dark room.

Other than her father asleep in the chair next to her bed, no one was there.

But Russell had been there, had been on top of her, *had* been tearing at her underclothes. She reached down. Nothing was torn. But she had smelled him.

She had felt him.

He was here.

He was here.

She inhaled deeply.

He was here.

Sunlight gleamed into the eastern window as Marie awoke. A bugle call echoed in the courtyard outside her window.

She was at Fort Meade.

Earl was dead.

And Russell had come visiting in the night.

She shook her head. It was only a dream.

Was it?

Perhaps she was safe now, surrounded by a hundred or more soldiers. Her eyes wandered around the room. On the side wall two crossed swords were mounted over a small fireplace, which crackled as flames lapped the wood. Beside the fireplace was a closed door. She imagined it must lead out to the front room, but she was too tired to move.

Instead, she thought about yesterday.

Earl was dead.

And Russell was only a dream.

No.

A nightmare.

When she opened her eyes again, Elton sat in the chair next to her. "Dad!"

He reached out to touch her face.

But he was Earl, stroking her hair after Russell had done his business. Repulsed, she recoiled.

Elton jerked his hand away.

She saw hurt flash across his face. She should tell him why she'd done that. She should tell him how Earl used to lay with her, how he used to fondle her hair like she was a doll. And how Russell used to clutch a handful of her hair, force her to her knees and hold her in place, and how she'd never felt more humiliated...

She burst into tears.

Elton sat there, reached out to place his hand on her leg, and then let his hand hover over the quilt. After a moment he dropped it to his side and watched his daughter cry.

Marie's tears began to slow at last. She looked at her father.

Please do something.

Elton lifted his hand, slowly so she could see it, and brought it toward her. He placed it softly on top of hers.

"Daddy," she choked out the words, "I was there when he killed Momma. Right beside her."

She saw her father flinch. "Why did Mr. Nix do that?"

"He didn't. But he saw me in the woods when I was with them and he...didn't...help...me." Tears tumbled down her cheeks.

Elton gently wiped them away.

When Marie's tears slowed he said, "It wasn't Nix? It was them?"

She shook her head. "They were in this together. Mister Nix worked for them. They made up the story about the telegram to take you away so they could get to us." More tears threatened, but she fought to control them. "I came back from seeing Ben, and Earl found me by the corral."

Elton cupped his daughter's hand. "That's where they found a hair ribbon. And the rifle. But you don't have to talk about it. I don't need to know."

Her voice quivered. "I...held...a...*rifle*...in my hands. If I had shot Earl, none of this would have happened." Rivulets of tears ran down her cheeks. "It was my fault." Sobs racked her body.

"Shhh," Elton said. "It's not easy shooting a man. Did you know what was going on when you saw him?"

"N...n...no," she said. "I was with Ben before. I came back and Earl was there. Before..." Marie shook her head and angrily wiped her eyes. "Before I knew what was happening, he had the gun."

"Yet look at you. You are still alive.

"Look at me?" Marie asked. "*Look* at me? Do you know what they did to me? I'm..." She bit her lip and shuddered. "I'm ruined, Daddy."

She fell forward into his arms.

He held her until long after her sobs abated.

She mumbled against his shoulder, "Earl made me put the rifle down, then he dragged me into the house with Momma."

"You don't have to tell me this," Elton said. "You don't have to say—"

"And Earl threw me on the bed and he held me down and he... he...and then Momma tried to protect me—"

"Marie, please. Don't."

"And Earl threw himself backwards against the wall and she was behind him and…she hit the wall…and…the sound—"

"Stop. Stop! I can't hear this!"

"Listen to me!" Marie yelled, holding his face with both hands. "You have to listen to me! If I don't say it I may never get it out of my head. Do you understand? I have to say it, and I need you to listen. Can you listen to me?"

He pulled her tighter. "Oh my girl."

Over and over she moaned, "Momma," as Elton rocked with her.

CHAPTER 63

Elton was sitting with Marie when Major Tinsdale stopped by before lunch to let him know that two soldiers had dug the dead man from a snowbank and had taken him into town. Sheriff Taylor planned to be at the fort that afternoon.

When Elton saw Taylor ride in he made his way to a sitting room outside Tinsdale's office. Soon Taylor entered and headed straight for the coffee pot. "I trust your daughter is okay," he said after he'd filled a cup and settled himself in an armchair.

"She's had a rough go. I don't know the whole story, but from what I know and what I suspect, it adds up to nothing but bad."

"I'm sorry to hear that. On the other hand, I can think of nothing better than to have her reunited with you."

Elton said, "I'd have fought an Army to save her. As it turned out, I only fought one man. Tell me, did Sheriff Ballew get back to town? He didn't show up here."

Taylor shook his head. "Likely on his way to Hill City as we speak. Those folks have helluva sheriff over there. Damn shame they aren't aware of it yet."

"Good man."

"That he is." Taylor finished his cup, refilled it, and topped Elton's cup. He sat back down and gazed at Elton. "Ben Schwartz strikes me as one, too."

"He was determined to find Marie. He did."

"Major Tinsdale told me Ben left at first light today. Headed home, I imagine."

"I didn't notice. I was too preoccupied with Marie."

"Of course you were," Taylor said. "After all, a father's first priority is protecting his children. It's an admirable trait, protecting a child."

"Marie is all I have left."

Taylor sipped his coffee. "Yes. We were talking about Marie."

"I was," Elton said. "Who are you talking about?"

Taylor said, "Don't mind me. Just an old man's rambling thoughts. Here I am talking about children, and we should be discussing the shooting last night. Paint me a picture, would you?"

"Gladly. Two lowlifes kidnapped and raped my daughter. The first one ate my bullet. I don't know where the other one is, but when I find him he'll get worse."

Taylor's laugh held no humor. "I'm aware of that part of the story. But the part where the man was shot, can you walk me through that?"

Elton took a deep breath. "As you know, it was snowing so hard I could hardly see the hand in front of my face. A sheet of white.

You thought it was bad in town, you should have been on the prairie with us."

"I can imagine," Taylor said.

"I rode forever and didn't see a thing. Figured they'd eluded me. Then as I approached the fort I saw a shadow cut across the lights. Turns out it was Ben talking to the man who had Marie. Earl."

"And this talking that Ben and Earl were doing, how did it turn into a shooting?"

"When Earl drew on Ben, I feared for the boy's life."

Taylor said, "That's when you shot Earl."

Elton finished his coffee. When he set the cup down, it clanked against the table top. "A man does what he has to do."

Taylor grunted. "Simple as that?"

"Simple as that."

Sheriff Taylor stared out the window before he spoke. "Nothing's simple though, is it? When the soldiers brought Earl into town his coat was still buttoned. Hard to draw iron when a man's coat is buttoned, that's the first thing I thought. I asked the soldiers and they said that's the way they found him. Now, I wasn't out there in the storm, was I? And in the end, the right man died."

Elton shifted in his chair. "End of the story as I see it."

"It's my belief that no one will begrudge a father who kills a man while protecting his daughter. No need to dig deeper. Because digging deeper might turn up additional details, like Earl's coat being burned by the gunpowder when the pistol was fired. Something a gunfighter would never do, getting that close to another man."

"An unfortunate detail, if it were ever to surface," Elton said.

"Yes. I thought about that on the ride out here today. How unfortunate details may cloud the judgment of those who have never looked down the wrong end of a gun."

"Meaning?"

Sheriff Thomas shrugged. "The unfortunate details will remain unsaid."

"Because sometimes words serve to complicate things."

"Therefore we will not preoccupy ourselves with who else might have been involved. On this shooting, we will let the results speak for themselves."

"The results that say an old gunfighter did what he had to do to save his daughter."

Taylor stood up and offered his hand. "I hope the gunfighter remembers that the dead man had a partner. He may not be too happy that you made him a solo act."

CHAPTER 64

Ben kicked at a cat that ran by him in the barn. It yowled as it spun away from his foot. He leaned on his pitchfork, hoping the cat would run by again. He wouldn't miss this time.

Little had gone right since he arrived home. Initially his parents had seemed happy to see him and his mother had fussed over him at the table, giving him an extra piece of pie after dinner. He thought he could detect a proud look on his father's face as he told him about the ride through the hills, how he got to Sturgis, and eventually how he and Elton had rescued Marie.

"So that's it, then," his father said, after Ben had finished the story.

"That's what, sir?"

"You saved the girl, spent the night at the fort, and then came home?"

Ben thought he had clearly laid it out. "Yes, sir."

"And the girl is home with her father?"

"I don't know. They were still at the fort when I left."

"And you weren't worried about her? You didn't wait to see if she was okay?"

Ben squirmed in his chair. "I guess...I guess I was thinking about coming home—"

His father snorted. "You left here without telling us you were leaving. You chased criminals high and low, fought a blizzard, and shot a man in order to save a girl. And when you rescued her from this great tragedy she endured, when she would have looked to you for comfort and understanding, you chose then to come home?"

He rose from his chair and limped toward the front door. "I won't expect grandchildren any time soon."

Ben's mother stood over him and stroked his hair after his father left. "Your father was worried sick when you were gone. Now that you're home, he doesn't know how to tell you he's happy you're back."

Ben shook his head. "I'd tell people I'm happy they're back."

His mother laughed. "So would I, but that's not his way. I know this is a confusing time right now. A lot of things have happened to you. But remember, a lot more things have happened to Marie. And as bad as you may feel, she feels worse." She kissed his forehead as she left the table. "You'll find the right time to go see her."

But now, as he watched the cat stalking a mouse, he wondered if there ever would be a right time. He loved Marie. With all his heart he loved her, but two men had kidnapped her. If they'd done anything to her...if...if...

But of course they had.

So what was he supposed to do? Forget everything? Say it was fine, and then he and Marie could go on with their lives as if nothing had happened?

He remembered the last time they were together, when he'd thought that nothing could ever be more perfect.

Now, how could things ever be the same?

CHAPTER 65

Caroline slid into Marie's lap and cuddled up to her, thumb jammed into her mouth. "Marie," she said, talking around her thumb, "when's Momma coming back?"

Marie hugged her, then stroked her hair. "Momma's not coming back, honey. Those men took her away from us."

"Why?" Caroline asked, whimpering.

"They were bad."

Caroline nuzzled deeper into Marie's chest. "Did they kill her?"

"Yes."

"Like you killed me?"

Marie jumped out of bed, blinking at the mid-afternoon sun. "Daddy!" she yelled. "Daddy!"

The bedroom door crashed open and Elton burst in. "I'm here, Marie."

Trembling, she sat on the bed. "I need you to tell me about Caroline. I know...I know..." She rapidly clenched and then unclenched her fists in time with her breathing. "Tell me."

Elton sat next to her and drew a deep breath. "When I arrived from Uncle Andrew's place I met Ben. He was coming to see you. We rode to the house together, and then Mr. Nix shot him."

Marie gasped. "Shot? But he was here. He was here with Earl."

"Even wounded, he hunted day and night to find you."

Marie murmured, "Oh my," and ducked her head.

Elton tilted her chin up. "Because Ben was shot, he stayed outside while I went to the back of the house to try to get Nix. But Caroline saw me, and ran to me...she jumped toward me and—" Elton shuddered.

"It's okay," she said. "It's okay to say it." She reached to his cheek and brushed a tear away.

Elton stared at the bookcase in the corner. "Nix shot her."

"And she's—"

"It's only you and me now."

CHAPTER 66

The sun shone through the south-facing window again this morning, lighting the small room that Marie had begun to think of as home. Daily, soldiers snuck had her food and small gifts when they weren't drilling in the large yard outside. Their marching, like the ticking of a clock, had become expected. Welcome. Something to rely on.

But, in the end, it wasn't home.

Home was outside the fort's fence.

It was a wagon ride down the valley toward Piedmont.

It was walking into the house where she'd grown up.

Where her mother and sister had died.

Doctor Garretson had reassured her father that, after a week at the fort, now was as good a time as any for them to return home.

She wished she were as certain, for in her mind it could never truly be her home again until she felt safe.

Still, when her father questioned her, she packed her few belongings and waited by the door for him to bring the wagon around.

He walked in moments later. "Let's go home. You ready?" His words sounded bright. Happy. Optimistic.

"Almost." Dread enveloped her. "There's one thing I want to show you." She handed the small package to her father.

"What's this? Another gift from a soldier?"

"No," she whispered. "It's Momma's. Open it."

He slid his finger under the wrapper and pushed it away. "Dear God," he murmured.

"I found it after they killed her. I read it yesterday."

Her father delicately re-wrapped the book and handed it to her. Marie said, "Dad, this is really you?"

"She knew. All this time she knew, and she never said a thing." Elton backed slowly away from Marie and reached his hand out until he found a corner chair. He sat in it, leaned forward, and waited.

"It's true, then? The things in this book are true?"

He drew in a slow breath, then nodded. "This is who I was before I met your mother. A life I didn't want, a story I didn't want to live. Then I met her and I fell in love and suddenly I had a family. You offered me a chance to escape who I once was. Or so I thought."

She sought her father's face. "You told me one time, 'What we must do does not define who we are.' You wore a gun. You used it. Men died. But that doesn't make you a bad man. You're a good man. You're my father."

He grimaced. "Others don't see me in as kind a light, Marie. A man dies and that is one man lost. But that man had friends, and he had a family. One death creates many enemies."

Death creates enemies.

Enemies create hate.

Hate creates the desire for revenge.

Revenge.

Marie closed her eyes. "Who is Loretta Marsh?"

Elton flinched. "Where did you hear that name?"

"Who is she, Daddy?"

For the longest time, all Marie heard was her own breathing. Her heartbeat thumped in her chest.

"Now this makes sense," he said. "The man who kidnapped you...his name was Russell?"

She nodded.

"Some things you can never escape," Elton said. "Loretta Marsh is one of those."

"Tell me about her," Marie said, opening her eyes and looking at her father.

This time he was silent longer. "A gunfight," he said, "isn't as simple as you may think. You read a book like that trash and you think it is between two people. But bullets sometimes find other targets."

Marie gasped. "Did you shoot her?"

Elton shook his head. "Why don't you sit? This will take a moment to tell."

Marie backed to the bed.

Elton said, "This story starts in a little town in Texas, a place you'd forget as soon as you left it. I was drifting, as I often did before I met your mother. That day I drifted in the wrong direction. What happened is what always seemed to happen in those days. When I rode into town someone recognized me. That person told someone, and that someone told someone. In this case, that someone told a farmer. And, half-crazed over the loss of his sons, that farmer came to find me."

"What happened?"

"He stood in the middle of the street bellowing my name, saying he wanted to shoot me. Said I killed his boys."

"Did you?"

He pointed at the book. "This farmer's sons thought they were gunfighters."

"Yes," she said. "The author made you sound like a hero."

Elton snorted. "There is never heroism in killing a man. But the farmer had lost his sons. These were tragic deaths of men who didn't need to die, yet it was at my hand that they perished. He had to do something. He was honor-bound, he said. So there he was, a heartbroken man who could hardly stand, holding a pistol he'd probably forgotten how to fire, but he was determined to do this."

"Did you...you didn't—"

"I talked. I told him I was sorry that I'd taken their lives and I hoped he would find solace in his memories. He seemed to listen. If it had been the two of us on the street possibly it would have ended there. But a gunfight draws observers. And those observers want to see someone die."

Marie felt like a wide-eyed girl at her father's knee. "What did they do?"

"The crowd became restless. I could hear their frustration growing. One man bellowed 'He murdered your boys, Frank.' I hear that to this day. 'He murdered your boys.' And then Frank's hands started shaking. I tried to talk to him again, but he was done listening to me. He was listening to the fools in the crowd.

"Frank waved the pistol around, yelling that he'd kill me. My eyes were on him and I wasn't aware that a wagon had rounded the corner behind me and was approaching the crowd. A simple farmer and his wife, on the wrong street of the wrong town at the wrong time. I don't think the man driving knew what was happening. Just a throng of people yelling. A wild, foolish throng urging us to shoot. One of us did. Frank."

Elton walked to Marie and took her hand. "Frank was no gunfighter, he was a father who didn't know how to deal with the death of his sons. His bullet missed me. His bullet missed everyone in the crowd. But he didn't miss the pregnant woman riding in the wagon. Loretta Marsh."

Marie sucked in a sharp breath. "When I asked Russell why he hated me, he told me to ask you about Loretta Marsh."

Elton's words were clipped. "I knelt in the dirt with him as his wife died. I didn't shoot her, but it happened because I was a gunfighter. When she took her last breath, he told me that I destroyed his family. If he ever got the chance, he would destroy mine."

CHAPTER 67

Marie knew early on that she was with child. Before the snow disappeared completely her stomach had stretched and grown, slowly at first, hardly noticeable, and then in a great rush as spring arrived and buds showed on the trees. With each day that passed she became more and more convinced that she was carrying a monster. A horrible black-eyed demon, like the black-eyed demon that had impregnated her.

And who still haunted her nightmares.

You deserve this demon child.

I know, she thought. I know.

Day by day the child grew in her womb. It was Russell's child, she was certain. Almost never...almost never, ever did she let herself hope it may be Ben's child. Because what was the use? Although she and Ben had spent one sunny, warm afternoon together, life didn't work out that way. Life wasn't about falling in love.

It wasn't about hope.

It was about heartache.

One April evening as she rested in the rocker, the baby kicked her. Hard.

Like it was angry.

It continued to grow.

CHAPTER 68

Elton put the axe down, wiped his brow, and looked at the growing pile of split wood. Though it was only June he was determined not to get caught short on firewood this winter.

He glanced at the path that led down the ridge to the creek. Marie hadn't come back yet, but he supposed it was a good thing. When they'd first returned home she wouldn't be out of his sight for more than five minutes. She had become his shadow again.

She was still fighting her memories. Many times he'd woken to her screams, only to find her wrapped in a blanket, sitting in the rocker, staring into the fire.

And they'd stayed up the rest of the night and she'd talked about Russell.

But as minutes and hours became days, as days turned into weeks and months and Russell didn't return, she'd started gathering eggs in the morning.

One day she took a walk to the rocky outcropping higher up on the ridge.

He'd followed close behind.

Today, on Amelia's birthday, she'd asked to visit her mother's grave. Alone.

Marie reached down to pick daisies and black-eyed Susans that grew near the creek bed. She snapped off some purple blooms to add more color to the bouquet. Arms full, she placed the arrangement of flowers on the grave and then whispered, "Happy Birthday." After wiping a tear from her cheek she stepped back to admire her work. She slowly stretched, trying to work the crick out of her back.

A warm breeze blew lightly from the north. She gazed out at the rippling prairie grass.

Her world, which for many months had extended no further than the distance where she could still see her father, today had grown.

She was determined to take back what Russell had stolen from her, because what was the value of a life if you were afraid to live it?

When she'd returned from the fort there were times when she'd wondered if she could go on. If she could have the baby. If she could live a life that seemed in any way normal.

And then she'd thought, what is a normal life anyway?

Her parents had lost a son at childbirth. They'd still found a way to live their lives.

Her father carried the burden of dozens of gunfights won, and now he carried the additional pain of the loss of his wife and youngest daughter.

And he still met Marie with a smile every morning. Today, that smile was what pushed her out the door.

Alone. And unafraid.

So, in the end, maybe 'normal' wasn't what happened to you in life, it was what you chose to do about it.

She picked a few more flowers and placed them on Caroline's grave. When she was done she glanced again at the prairie.

Then her eyes noticed the slightest movement in the brush along the creek. A deer maybe. Or a coyote.

Something.

She looked back at the prairie, yet watched the brush from the corner of her eye.

She could see it, but whatever it was had no idea that she could see it.

Intrigued, she continued to watch.

It moved again.

Closer to her.

She kept facing the prairie, but saw slow, steady movement. It wasn't the wind.

It wasn't a deer. Or a coyote.

Now she was sure it was a person creeping toward her.

It could only be one man.

This time it wasn't fear she felt.

It was relief.

Because she was tired of cowering from his memory.

And she would stop today.

She removed her bonnet, stretched her arms open wide as the sun caressed her, and then turned.

She tightly tossed her bonnet toward the boulder.

It hit the top, and then tumbled over the far side.

Marie cursed lightly, then eased behind the stone to pick it up.

As she squatted down she glanced at the brush.

The man had crept closer.

Now she could see him clearly.

It was Russell.

She lifted the rifle that had been leaning behind the boulder, jammed it against her shoulder, aimed at his chest, pulled the hammer back, and fired.

A rifle! Jesus, the girl had a rifle! Russell dove to the ground as the bullet sailed past him.

On his hands and knees, he frantically searched for cover.

There wasn't enough to avoid dying.

He flattened to the ground and tried to wrestle his pistol from its holster.

Marie shoved the lever forward to eject the spend cartridge.

It jammed.

And wouldn't move.

Until she could remove the cartridge the rifle was no better than a club.

A stick…a knife…something. She frantically searched the area around her.

She found a stick. As she worked it around the side of the cartridge, it splintered.

The cartridge was stuck.

She looked at Russell.

He knew.

He slowly rose.

And smiled.

CHAPTER 69

Hearing the gunshot, Elton raced down the path.
As he crossed the creek the first thing he saw was Marie, crouched behind the boulder.

She screamed, "Get down, Daddy! It's Russell!"

"How about "Don't move, Daddy," a voice said from behind him. "Well, well. If it isn't the great Elton Collins."

"Russell," Elton said. "How about I turn around so we can talk, face-to-face?"

"How about I put a bullet in the back of your head instead? Now, toss your gunbelt over there or I shoot Marie. Not much she can do to stop me with that jammed rifle."

Elton glanced at Marie's panicked face. "We're okay," he said.

He unbuckled the belt and tossed it near Amelia's grave.

Elton could hear Russell move closer to him. "How's it feel to be unarmed, Collins?"

"Not my favorite way to be."

"Imagine how my wife felt. Imagine how I felt as I watched her die."

"I do," Elton said. "Every day."

"I'll bet…you don't," Russell said. "And speaking of watching someone die, your daughter is going to experience that in a moment. Before she does though, I have to know something. How do you feel about me being the father of your grandchild?"

"You aren't my first choice," Elton said.

Russell snorted. "And Marie wasn't mine. It was your wife that I wanted." Russell sighed. "But being as we killed her instead, I was a little short on options."

Options.

Elton glanced at his gun. With it on his hip, he'd have a chance. On the ground, none. Even if he could reach it, he was facing away from Russell. There was no way he could turn and fire before Russell killed him. Then Russell would shoot an unarmed Marie.

There had to be a way out of this.

Elton could only think of one.

Marie continued to dig at the cartridge with the stick. He gazed into her determined eyes, so similar to Amelia's. He studied every detail of her face.

The wind flickered a bit of her hair.

He tried to picture what she would look like holding the baby.

She would be beautiful.

Elton chuckled. "You're going to die, Russell." He edged slightly toward the gunbelt.

"Hardly," Russell barked, stepping closer. "I'll fill you with lead before you so much as touch that pistol."

"You can try," Elton said.

"Daddy?" Marie called, fear fraying her voice. "What are you doing?"

"I've always been partial to the name Amelia," Elton said. He glanced at the nearby gravesites, then at his daughter. He heard Russell take another step forward.

"Shut up, Collins," Russell said. "That baby will never see the light of day."

"Don't leave me," Marie said, her voice wavering. "I can't do this alone."

"You know what I loved most about your mother? No matter how hard things were, she never gave up. You're exactly like her. You can do anything you put your mind to."

Marie bit her lip.

"She never put her mind to stopping me," Russell said. "Of course, maybe she liked it."

Elton smiled at Marie. "I love you."

"I love you too, Daddy." She gulped, her eyes brimming with tears. "But why this?"

His eyes shifted from Marie to the gunbelt, then back to Marie. "Put the rifle down, dear. How do you feel about Amelia Caroline?"

She dropped the rifle, and then backhanded the tears from her cheeks. "Could be an Elton, you know."

He nodded. "Of course. Could be an Elton."

Russell growled, "There isn't going to be a goddamned baby! I'm going to kill you all!"

Elton winked. "Smile for me, would you, Marie?"

She did her best.

It was good enough. "You can do this," he said. He edged toward the gun.

"That's enough," Russell snapped. "You move again and I'll pepper you."

"Deal," Elton said. He dove for the gunbelt, grabbed it, and threw it toward Marie.

Russell opened fire.

Marie snatched the gunbelt and ripped the pistol from its holster.

She aimed at Russell.

His face was euphoric as he watched Elton Collins crumple to the ground.

Then full comprehension hit him as he looked toward her.

Marie thumbed the hammer back and fired until the pistol was empty.

CHAPTER 70

She turned the earth.

She felt the shovel handle tear the skin from her hands.

She sweated.

She cursed.

Most of all, she cried.

But Marie, and no other, would prepare her father's final resting place.

The funeral was sparsely attended. She saw the sheriff from Hill City. Major Tinsdale and a small troop of soldiers arrived as the minister began to speak. A couple of people whom she didn't recognize stood off to the side, heads bowed, hats in hand.

The Schwartz family stood closest to her.

When the funeral ended the mourners slowly filed past. Each person said something to console her.

Few words stayed with her.

But she thanked the attendees for their thoughtfulness.

When they drifted away, she glanced once more at her father's grave. Now, if it was finally over, she could grieve.

She stood alone, eyes closed, and thought about him.

And then Ben was at her elbow. "I should have come to see you before now."

"Yes," she nodded, opening her eyes and looking at him. "You should have."

"My father told me the same thing."

Anger rose within her. "So, are you talking to me now because your father wants you to, or because you want to? It's important that you know." She sucked in a quick breath. "It's important that I know, Ben."

"I'm here because I want to be."

She shook her head. "Yet it took you seven months to decide this?"

Ben gulped. "All winter I thought about you. When I imagined what they did to you I felt—"

She snapped, "It must have been awful having to *imagine* what it was like, so let me make it easy. Every night Russell raped me. Every night, Benjamin. Then Earl would lie next to me and stroke my hair. I'm not sure who he was trying to comfort, himself or me. If it was supposed to be me, he failed."

She shook with furor. "Do you understand…what happened…to *me?*"

He stared at the ground and nodded.

She tossed her head, causing her hair to fly around her face. "Then forgive me if I seem a little less concerned about how it makes you feel."

She spun away from him and fought to compose herself. Inadvertently, her eyes wandered to the rocky ledge where they used to sit.

314

And dream.

Once upon a time, they dreamed.

When she turned back she tried to smile. "That was unfair. Sometimes I don't know what to do with these feelings inside me. They come like a flood and I can't seem to control them. If my mother...or my father...maybe if they were here to help me understand—"

She wouldn't let him see a tear. She couldn't. Because one tear might lead to a million.

Ben took her hand. "I don't know how to help you with this. The only thing I know is that I want to be here, every day, and try."

"Some nights I still wake up screaming."

"And I'll wake up with you."

A small smile slipped out. "My father used to do that. When I needed him, he was always there. Now—"

Ben said, "He'll always be close by, Marie. He'll never leave your heart."

Marie sighed so hard she quivered. "None of them will." She looked at the three gravesites. "It's so sad when I think about it. My father sacrificed himself so that I could live. How can I ever repay him for that?"

Ben placed his hand on her swollen belly. "By living a good life. By raising a family, Marie. Our family." He tilted her chin so their eyes met. "If you'll have me."

And like the ice melting enough to allow a tiny trickle of water to flow in a creek, something inside her let loose.

Not a lot.

Only a little.

But it was enough to inspire hope.

CHAPTER 71

The wedding was rushed, only a week after the funeral, but Ben was insistent. They would be husband and wife before their baby came.

They stood in the exact spot where her father's funeral had taken place. It was silly, Marie thought, as the minister droned on, to think that her parents would know that she and Ben were married.

But when Ben had asked where she would like to hold the ceremony, she didn't hesitate. She looked into his eyes and said, "With my family." He'd smiled and said, "They will like that."

The sincerity with which he'd said it meant more to her than she could try to explain. Instead, she'd whispered a thank you, hugged him tightly, and hoped that said enough.

After the ceremony ended Ben carried his wife across Elk Creek. They climbed the familiar path up the ridge.

Heart fluttering, she stopped as they entered the clearing.

They silently stood and looked upon the Collins house.

When Marie was ready, she took Ben's hand and started walking.

"Let's go home," she said.

Less than a month later, Marie gave birth to Amelia Caroline.

A little girl with green, gold-flecked eyes.

Just like Ben's.

ACKNOWLEDGEMENTS

I want to thank my wonderful critique group—Ron Cree, Barb Nickless, Kirk Farber and Bob Spiller—for their enthusiastic feedback about how to best present the story of Elton Collins. Working with them is a treat, for not only are they wonderful writers, but they're also great friends.

I want to thank my wife for understanding that writing is what makes each breath that I take feel that much sweeter every day.

I want to thank Pikes Peak Writers for continuing to provide a warm, enthusiastic, welcoming environment for writers to flourish.

I want to thank Dave Fymbo for the cover artwork, and DeAnna Knippling for the layout.

I want to thank my friends and family for their continued encouragement as I travel along this road.

And to anyone who chooses to read Hell With A Gun, thank you. I hope you enjoy it.

ALSO BY THIS AUTHOR

Just when you think you've got it made... Hard-headed, quick-fisted and sometimes as funny as he thinks he is, small-town Maine private detective Paul Doyle is equally adept at throwing haymakers and one-liners. But when his go-for-broke style fails to produce missing stripper Cherry Delight, Doyle realizes it'll take more than a string of snappy quotes to save her. He'll have to think his way through this case, and thinking has never been his strong suit. As the bullets fly and a trail of bodies appear to be linked to Cherry's disappearance, Doyle believes he's getting close to the truth. And he knows he may be the next one in the killer's crosshairs.

ABOUT THE AUTHOR

orn in Massachusetts and raised in New Hampshire and finally Maine, Michael Shepherd stopped moving north when he ran out of country. An unabashed Red Sox fan, he recently retired from the Air Force after a 29-year career. He lives in Colorado, continues to work for the government and tries to carve out stolen moments to write in between business trips and baseball games.

Made in the USA
Lexington, KY
14 June 2014